Som M000306611

'A darkly twisted crime novel… Fantastically imaginative and gripping.' Angela Clarke, *Sunday Times* best-selling author of *The Social Media Murder Series*

★★★★★ 'An exciting psychological thriller with few characters, and plenty of "who did it". The ending was just stunning! What a great author Jem Tugwell is.' —Emmabbooks

★★★★★ 'OMG. I know it's fiction but it can and does happen. Twists and turns, ups and downs. Wow! One that left me reeling.' —Nickisbookblog

★★★★★ 'Intense, interesting and insanely well written. A highly recommended read. The shock factor is 100 percent and beyond!' —MamaMummyMum

★★★★★ 'utterly captivating…a psychological thriller that feels fresh' —HookedFromPageOne

★★★★★ 'brilliantly written fast paced story…hooking you from the beginning to the end' —JackiesReadingCorner

★★★★★ 'compelling, entertaining and incredibly addictive…had me turning the pages with intense edge of the seat trepidation' —A Mother's Musings

Some praise for Jem Tugwell

'An ingenious and highly plausible' Claire McGowan, bestselling author of *What You Did*

'Very topical, terrifying, superb concept for a crime novel.' Stav Sherez, Award winning author of *The Intrusions*

'An immersive, entertaining high-octane … Well-written, thought-provoking escapism.' Adam Hamdy, *Sunday Times* bestselling author of *Black 13*

Jem Tugwell is a crime fiction author with a Crime Writing MA from City University. In a past life, Jem had a successful career in IT and investment management. He lives in Surrey with his wife and has two great children. Outside of his family and writing, Jem's loves are snowboarding, old cars and bikes.

Jem is inspired by the law of unintended consequences, the fascinating possibilities of technology and all the things that might happen.

For more information on Jem and his books, please visit his website – www.jemtugwell.com or join the discussion on Twitter @JemTugwell, Facebook @JemTugwellAuthor, Goodreads and BookBub.

Also by Jem Tugwell

Proximity
No Signal

Dishonoured

Jem Tugwell

SERPENTINE

BOOKS

First published in Great Britain by Serpentine Books
This edition published in 2021 by
Serpentine Books Limited

www.serpentinebooks.com
info@serpentinebooks.com

Copyright © Jem Tugwell 2020

A CIP catalogue record for this book is available from the British Library.

ISBN (paperback) 978 1 913874 04 9

In Loving Memory of

My dear Uncle Peter…

…About to open the batting for the Heaven XI Cricket Club.

Peter Ayrton
12 August 1934 – 18 July 2020

Molly

16 years young

the best Giant Schnauzer

well-travelled and always happy

04 August 2004 – 20 August 2020

Chapter 1

Numb was easy.

I'd had twenty-three years of practice.

More than half of my life. Every day of Paul's.

I had nearly exploded with pride, a smile splitting my face in two, wiping a tear from Kat's exhausted face as she clutched the little bundle we named Paul. He'd been impatient to get into the world and arrived two days early.

The shake in my hand almost made me drop the phone. 'Mum, Dad. He's here.'

'Brilliant,' Mum shouted. 'We'll be there as soon as we can.' Then a softer aside to Dad, 'The baby's here.'

The journey should have taken my parents an hour, but my increasingly frantic 'where are you' calls went unanswered. After three hours, it was the police and not my parents who pushed open the door to the side room in the hospital and told me that their ecstatic race to see their first grandchild ended crushed under the wheels of a jack-knifed lorry.

'I'm sorry,' the police officer said.

After that I couldn't hear, I couldn't see. I couldn't feel.

I couldn't cope.

All I could do was cry and hold Kat and Paul. I shut everything else down, but the nagging questions remained: How could the best day of my life also be the worst? How could a god that gifted us Paul, snatch my parents away on the same day?

I learnt that the price of joy was pain, and that I couldn't function if I acknowledged my grief. The only way I could stagger through each day was to keep numb. To keep every emotion inside, compressed and packed away. Definitely not acknowledged or given any space to ambush me.

If I didn't remember it, then it never happened.

A few months later, Paul's happy gurgling dragged the first glimmer of joy from me. Over the next four years, his smile thawed my edges and I thought there might be a way back.

Then an accident took Kat from me, and God reminded me why numb was better than the roller-coaster of highs and lows, joy and pain.

I built a dam, pushed my memories and emotions behind it and prayed the wall of numbness held.

I needed to keep it all in.

Chapter 2

I thought Jerry would be in one of two places. Mornings usually saw him tucked into the little stone right-angle that formed the corner of London's Cheapside and Wood Street, trying his luck with the bankers and lawyers heading to their offices. Most scurried by, their hands full of phones and expensive coffee in single-use cups. Their eyes invariably tracked away from Jerry as they got within a few paces of him. Somehow, the opposite side of the road to where he sat was the most riveting sight in London.

Maybe his black bin-bag wardrobe offended them. Maybe it was his crudely scrawled sign propped against his knee: *I lost my leg serving the country so you can be served a latte.*

Every time I told him that swapping the sign for something less confrontational might be more effective in getting donations, he'd lean forward and say, 'I'm sure you're right, Dan. But my sign tells the fucking truth.'

On most shops, the point of the building's corner poked out towards the road and maximised the interior space. For some reason, this building's architects had designed it so that the point was inverted and faced in towards the shop. It cut a small, sheltered pavement refuge out of the shop that Jerry called home. It hid him from the worst of the weather and the contempt of the staff and customers of the men's clothing store.

This morning the corner was empty, so Jerry would be further along Wood Street at what he called his second home, his country residence. The small garden of St Peter Cheap was the site of a former church that burned down during the Great Fire in 1666. The greenery of the tiny garden punctuated the sterile line of glass and grey office buildings that surrounded and dominated it.

Perched on his favourite bench with his eyes closed, Jerry was positioned to bask in the small patch of warming sunshine.

My hand was getting clammy from the heat of the all-day breakfast baguette I'd got from the locally owned bakers across the road. 'Breakfast is served,' I said, sitting on the bench and waving the baguette like a nutritious relay baton.

Jerry took the baton, peeled away the top of its paper wrapper and took a mouthful. He concentrated on chewing and savouring the flavours. 'Thanks, Dan. Excellent as always, all the food groups,' he said.

Another couple of mouthfuls later, he said, 'Ahh. Meal fit for a king.'

He turned to look at me. 'Today the day?' he asked.

I nodded.

'Well, good luck, mate. You deserve it.'

***

Shop windows provide a perfect cover for thinking.

If you stand on any pavement and stare into space, eyes locked on the distance, churning whatever troubles you, people think you're mad. Or drunk. But pretend to stare at a display of consumer gadgets that you'll throw away in a few months and you're in tune with the world. You're one of them.

But I never had been one of them, or even one of anybody.

I focused on my reflection in the shop's glass front. My skin, my hair, my nose. I was the obvious product of the agreement my parents' genes had hatched in the womb. With a dark-haired, olive-skinned Spanish father and a pale, ginger English mother, my skin had ended in the middle of them both. My hair was pure Mum and my nose was Dad's – flatter and wider than mum's. If I was lazy and didn't shave for a few days, then my beard blossomed into a medley of Dad's black hair flecked through Mum's ginger.

When I was young, Dad would sit with his arm wrapped around my shoulder, fussing and nursing my cuts and bruises. And tears. 'Be proud, son. Be strong. You're the best of both worlds. It's boring to be like everyone else.'

But I wanted to be boring. I was dark enough to stand out amongst all the pale-skinned locals, too pale and ginger to fit in with Dad's extended family. All I wanted was to belong – to be one or the other, but I fell in between.

It was the same now. I was 'too City' to fit back in at home – my car and clothes were 'too flash' for rural Northamptonshire. At the same time, I was 'too country' to be a real City boy – the twang in my voice was north of Watford rather than public-school plummy or ducking and diving Essex.

Years ago, on my first day in the City, I didn't know about the unspoken grey or blue suit and black shoes rule. I wore my only formal clothes, and my brown shoes and green suit had evoked stares and laughter. 'Here's the poor Country Mouse come to stay in the big city.' More laughter and like oil on a white cloth, the stain of humiliation couldn't be budged.

Another of Dad's sayings – 'use their words against them.' Country Mouse had started as an insult, but I grabbed it, embraced it and made it my own. Now, it was my brand and people used it with respect.

As Jerry had said, today was the day. The day at the end of years of hard work, of sacrifice and setbacks, of finding the inner strength to keep going – all the things my parents had given me as armour against the world.

Uprooting my feet, I walked a few paces along Cheapside and into the offices of Salamander Capital.

Chapter 3

Colin nodded and smiled at me as the revolving door deposited me inside the spacious, high-ceilinged reception area.

'Alright, Col,' I said.

He'd been the security guard at the entrance of Salamander Capital for as long as I could remember, but he still felt obliged to wave me towards the barriers. As always, I followed Colin's directions, and when I reached the barrier and touched my staff pass on the scanner, I waved at Maddie. Her reception desk was so high, it looked like she was nothing but a pair of bright eyes and glossy, dark hair.

Like every day, I'd been up at five. My body was used to it and I didn't need an alarm clock. Tiptoeing out of the bedroom so I didn't disturb Felicity, past the kids' rooms and into my study, I settled to see what had happened since I had logged out after midnight. I waded through the stream of messages, research notes and gossip and was done in time for a family breakfast.

Now, on office autopilot, I followed my habitual routine: lift, corridor, water station, waved hellos, glass door to my office, desk. Shaking the mouse, I woke my computer and its bank of six screens. They flashed and displayed emails, the scrolling stock price and news feeds from around the world. I studied each in turn, happy that the financial markets were where I expected them. Then again, I'd only left them long enough to complete my commute from home, and my morning delivery and chat with Jerry.

I never got into banking for the money. Of course it was great that it piled up, but it was never my driving factor. I had to admit that I loved the challenge of knowing that old hands and talented youngsters were trying to outperform and outsmart me.

But it had only ever been for my family – Paul, Felicity, my second wife, eight-year-old Hugo and six-year-old Victoria. The kids' names were a bit formal for my taste, but Felicity had chosen them and the simple names I suggested weren't strong enough to convince her.

A calendar alert popped up on a screen. The one-hour reminder for the event I had slogged so hard to make happen: *Signing, Boardroom.*

I was certain that the others would be smiling, their heart rates rising in anticipation of the signing, but I blocked it.

Sure, I could remember 'excited' and 'happy', but those emotions were distant, like I was a stranger shivering outside in the cold, staring through a window, watching a joyous Christmas family lunch. I didn't deserve happiness. Without my phone call, my parents wouldn't have been on the road when the lorry lost control. I was the siren who had lured them to their deaths.

I straightened and tried to shake the self-loathing loose, but like a dog coming out of a dirty river, shaking only got rid of surface water. The damp and the smell remained.

***

Salamander Capital's boardroom projected the modern, forward-looking vision that investors liked with its large glass table, chrome and black leather chairs, floor-to-ceiling glass windows and drop-down screen at one end. We couldn't preach that we were the firm for the twenty-first century if our boardroom was full of wood and looked like a stuffy Victorian gentleman's club. Yet it was identical to so many boardrooms I had been in. Even though every firm tried to differentiate themselves, we all chose the same generic look from the same designers. Salamander's furniture might be the same, but our people were different and we hoped that our message was clear:

Dishonoured

We're progressive, Salamander can change with the shifting markets, but we're not mavericks who are careless with your money.

As the managing partners of Salamander, Julian, Ezra, Rupert and I sat two on either side of the glass table. In our usual seats, no one at the head of the table as we were a team of 'equals'. They had been essential in bringing in the money and the contacts to Salamander. I had taken the money and made it grow. And growth was always in demand. The Mouse would always be needed.

The four of us had quit our jobs, borrowed big and risked everything going it alone ten years ago. We would be the owners for the next ten minutes.

I pushed a fake smile onto my lips, projecting what I didn't allow myself to feel in response to the glittering eyes and beaming smiles of the others.

Our lawyer, Vardah, had chosen a seat facing the door. She sat, her hands in her lap, with a stack of binders in front of her. The sale contract had been argued and negotiated over for the last nine months. We wanted all the money upfront, but KapGroup wanted us locked to them for at least a year. Each link in the chains that now bound us to KapGroup were only words. But each word had a purpose, its meaning considered, loopholes explored, trade-offs discussed and compromises agreed.

Yas pushed the door open and came into the boardroom, followed by her lawyers. Three lawyers to one. As good a way as any to measure the relative financial clout of Yas' firm, KapGroup, to us. We were pleased. She had been one of our top targets when we started looking for a buyer.

Yas looked at the table. Like everything she did, it was considered and deliberate. She took the seat at the head – a clear message to us. She was the boss now.

This was our last chance to back out, but I didn't want to. After my life's stuttering start, I'd finally got the security I'd craved for my family.

The act of signing was a strangely low-key, quiet, logistical exercise. The lawyers passed us multiple sets of folders which we opened and then put our initials against the key financial terms: £100m each – £2m to each partner on signing, followed by a further £98m to each eligible partner. The negotiation had split the £98m into two parts, but we'd refused to compromise on the immediate payouts to all of our employees.

The first was £40m in cash to be paid after three months. This was to ensure that we stayed working during the integration of Salamander into KapGroup.

The second part were 'put options' on special shares in KapGroup. The shares had a face value of £0.000001 each. On their own, they were worthless because KapGroup didn't want us to sell the shares immediately after we received them. They wanted us motivated and to have 'skin in the game'. So the put options gave us the right to sell our valueless shares back to KapGroup at a minimum price of £58m in one year's time. If KapGroup's value grew over the year, the price we could sell our shares at would grow too. We had significant upside to staying and working with Yas, and she wanted to ensure she got maximum value out of us and Salamander.

When we'd signed every page of every copy, we had sold our company into Yas' more than capable hands.

The sound of the last signature faded and the room fell silent for a second, only a police siren in the distance reached us this high up, then the spell broke.

Yas and the lawyers smiled indulgently as the four of us rose, headed to the far end of the table and locked into a four-way hug.

Chapter 4

One week earlier

If Leia called the room her boardroom, she would have oversold it. With bare brick walls, a long battered wooden table flanked by six old chairs, and a low-tech flipchart, she had spent the minimum on it.

The hard, cold light from the laptop screen spilt across the desk, and as Leia thought, she doodle-outlined the edge of a dent in the wood with a pen. The numbers didn't lie.

The payment for the latest batch of prosthetics was due and she couldn't keep taking the trauma consultants generosity for granted.

Her charity helped rebuild the lives of shattered soldiers whose sacrifice was taken so nonchalantly by the masses who complained about *their* mental health. So much stress and anguish caused by what? Modern life?

Try living through incoming hostile fire or half of what she and so many others had. They'd lived through hell. Literally. She'd felt the blood spurting out of a friend soak her face, held a trembling hand in their last seconds on earth. It lived with you.

It lived *in* you.

'The consultancy is overstaffed and you can't rebuild everyone,' Madhuk said.

He's right, Leia thought, but her frown remained. 'We can try,' she said.

Madhuk raised his hands in mock surrender and flashed a lopsided half-smile. The same grin he had given her the first time they met.

Leia had been special forces, Madhuk from the Gurkha Rifles and he'd scrambled into the desert dugout she was in, bullets flying overhead, pulling a broken soldier in after him. They had fought, hands red and slippery where his leg should have been, but he'd bled out before reinforcements arrived.

'The bank keeps calling. I can't ignore them much longer.' He looked hard into Leia's eyes. 'It's like the old days. Sometimes you have to sacrifice one to save the many.'

Leia held his gaze for a second and then nodded. He was right. 'I'll push all the new patients back a couple of weeks. Can you talk the bank into restructuring the debt again?'

'I can try.'

***

The client had seemed normal enough. Perhaps the meeting place had made Leia relax her guard. Her friend Fay raved about the Dukes Bar, St James in London which was said to have inspired Ian Fleming for James Bond's signature martini. Leia's gin was spectacular, and the cosseting, old-school charm, along with the theatre of how her drinks had been served all matched Fay's enthusiasm.

The client spoke and Leia clamped her hand over her mouth to avoid spraying her gin across the table. Her eyes wide in shock, she controlled her impulse, released her hand and swallowed the gin. She felt the burn of it slide down her throat. 'That will destroy him,' she said.

Hard, glittering eyes and a nod were her reply.

The request festered in the air and the savagery of her client's tone clashed with the genteel ambience of the bar.

Leia's consultancy's typical work was clinically corporate: executive protection, kidnap prevention consultancy, or a bit of clandestine pre-launch acquisition of a competitor's new product. This request was off-the-scale brutal and very personal. It wasn't right.

Leia looked across the little table at the client and started to say no.

But she needed the money and a chunk of cash would help Madhuk with the bank.

A number came into Leia's mind as she thought through the logistics. She could work it like a honey-trap, and men were so simple. She'd drop her hair down, touch her tongue to her lips shimmering with lip gloss and add a little smile. It worked every time, especially when her skin carried a vibrant tan from winter sun and contrasted with all her assets packaged invitingly into a tight, white shirt. But this wasn't a fidelity test, this would rip the man's life apart and scatter him to the wind.

Leila doubled the price.

How many ex-forces did she have to save to justify sacrificing this civilian?

Leila doubled the price again. A quarter for her consultancy and the rest for her charity.

The client baulked at the number. Not a verbal outburst to offend the bar's other patrons, but Leia saw eyes widen in surprise. Eyebrows knotted as mental calculations ran, and resulted in a bland, 'That's a lot more than I thought.'

Leia shrugged. 'You've given me a single date next week. One opportunity to get it done. It's rushed and given what you want, I should be asking for much more.'

She took another sip of the gin and rolled it around, savouring its perfection. She glanced down at her glass, not wanting to look straight at the client and make the price seem like a challenge. She'd give them the space to decide.

The client nodded.

'OK, do it.'

Chapter 5

Walking back down Cheapside, I knew that the signing in the boardroom had sent a hairline crack snaking down the dam that held my emotions back. As hard as I fought, a drop of pride leaked through, then a couple of beads of happiness mixed with a lot of relief. Work had stolen so much of the time that I could have shared with Felicity and the kids. All those lost evenings and the school plays and events I would never get back. The dads' races I had been a no-show at. Worse were the shrugs of Hugo and Victoria when I finally got home and said 'sorry'.

I tried to block out a memory of Victoria busy with a colouring book at the kitchen table, her legs jigging backwards and forward, still too small to reach more than halfway to the floor.

'How was the concert, Vick-ster?' I asked, hugging her. 'Something came up at work and I couldn't get away.'

She didn't look up, just carried on with her colouring. 'I know, Daddy.' The sadness in her bland acceptance cut me. Her next words went deeper and found bone. 'I didn't think you'd come.'

I was teaching her that the world would disappoint her. Worse, that I would disappoint her. *Don't believe Daddy's promise. He won't come.* I could see my numbness seeping into my kids.

From the outside, people only saw the money – 'Rich bastard', 'What works in the City and rhymes with banker? You'. A million other casual insults. I had money, therefore I was privileged, like the money had simply appeared in a gold carriage as a gift. They didn't think about the sweat-inducing risks, the unrelenting hours, or the memories I would never have.

I pulled my phone out and called Felicity.

'Did it go OK?' she asked. I could hear the smile in her voice.

'Yep, simple. Off to the party now.'

'Be careful, you know what happens.'

'Of course,' I said, trying to get my determination to travel over the airways and convince her. I screwed my eyes tight shut, trying to block out an image. Felicity and I didn't mention it. Her parents certainly didn't. New Year's Eve hadn't happened.

'I'm not saying don't drink anything,' she said. 'It's your big day today and you need to celebrate, but limit it to one.'

'I promise,' I said and hung up.

Alcohol gave me a different type of numb. A buzzy, happy escape from the past and my memories, but it loved me too much. While others could drink and drink, I went from sober to pissed in a flash and the coursing alcohol took over.

I tried to call Paul, but he didn't answer. So I relied on a message saying *Deal done* to Paul, then added the same messages to the in-laws. Messages plural as I had two sets: Babs and Monty, Felicity's parents and Rosalyn, Kat's mum.

Now you can finally look after our daughter properly was Babs' reply. They still thought of themselves as 'old money', better than me. I wasn't good enough, but my *new* money was good enough to pay for their share of every family holiday and event, while their old money stayed behind in the bank.

Rosalyn was kinder: *Congrats. I'm sure you'll look after me ;-)*

I reached the bottom of Cheapside, looked up and shielded my eyes as the sun peeked out from behind the only cloud in the sky. No. 1 Poultry always looked like a submarine conning tower or maybe the bow of the ship.

I checked my phone when it buzzed. A message from Paul. *Brilliant, Dad. In a meeting, call later.*

A second message arrived from Paul and I smiled. *I'm sure your day will be special. Xxx.*

Paul and I always had practical conversations. Occasionally I tried to show him the genuine, spontaneous love I'd got from my dad, but I was always stiff and awkward. It came across forced. So we avoided topics like happiness, feelings and love, and stuck to sport. It was only three little Xs on a phone screen, but this was the first time since before his rebellious teenage years that he had shown any overt sign of loving me. It was enough to force the crack in my dam wider apart. Waves of suppressed feelings flooded me and I pressed myself against a brick wall to hold myself up and hide my first tears since Kat died.

After some long minutes, the waves subsided.

Are there pivotal moments in your life? Was this one?

It felt like it.

Now the deal was done and I could give my family a future, I had a choice: rebuild the dam and try and push all my emotions back behind it, or let them free. Watch my life slip by or live it to the full and embrace all that it had to give?

It wasn't that simple. How do you go forward, when you're anchored in the past?

I started work on the repairs to the dam, but promised myself that I would work less and spend more time at home. Try and make it up to the kids.

Chapter 6

On the roof garden of Coq d'Argent at the top of No 1 Poultry, I set off across the lush green lawn. When I reached the end and stood at its 'bow', I stretched my arms out wide to let the sunshine warm me. It might have looked like I was re-enacting the scene from *Titanic*, but I was embracing the City of London with the Bank of England and Royal Exchange buildings that were almost in touching distance. *Did I finally belong?*

I turned back to where Yas, my partners and the lawyers waited. 'Let's get the party started,' I called.

They all held champagne flutes already, raised them and smiled. White teeth flashed, showing the result of much time and money spent at the dentists, and serious dedication to their tooth whitening regimes.

Yas' lawyers' smiles weren't wide enough to reveal any teeth. Vardah's smile was hidden by her champagne glass, but her eyes sparkled like they did when she was happy.

We all formed a circle. Despite now being part of the KapGroup team, our instincts hadn't caught up and the circle split along old, territorial allegiances.

A silver tray appeared at my side with a solitary glass on it. 'For you, sir,' the waitress said in her uniform of white shirt and black trousers. She lifted her eyes from the tray to catch mine and smiled.

***

I'd kept my one drink promise to Felicity, so couldn't believe the surging storm of alcohol fizzing in my skull.

Clumsy fingers wrestled with the top button of my shirt and pulled at my tie. My reflection in the long mirror above the toilet's basins blurred. I put my hand out to steady myself and disturbed the pile of crisp linen flannels – no cheap paper towels here.

I dampened a flannel under the tap and wiped the beads of sweat from my face. The fizz in my skull grew louder, sounding like I'd kicked over a nest of angry wasps, but the running of the water into the sink triggered a more pressing concern. As I got to the urinal and unzipped, the floor tilted and I stumbled.

Need to drink some water, I thought. Can't spoil today.

I made it back outside and forced my eyes to focus. The same waitress appeared at my side.

'Another drink, sir?' she said. Her tray held another single champagne flute and the sunshine made the delicate yellow liquid glow.

Instinct took over and my hand moved towards the glass, but I summoned enough control to pull it back. 'Got any water?'

A frown flashed across her brow as she stepped away. After a short pause, she returned with the same tray but the champagne replaced by a glass of water with some bubbles clinging to a floating slice of lemon. She moved the tray closer, a definite smile on her face and both eyebrows raised, inviting. Encouraging.

'Thanks…' I started but my phone buzzed in my pocket. 'Sorry, one sec. We're celebrating a deal and that should be my bank.'

Her head dropped to one side; the smile now more fixed than genuine as if she were upset that I was making her wait.

I glanced at the phone and saw the message from the bank confirming that the signing bonus of £2m had been deposited.

Yes, yes.

Looking back at her, I could see that she was staring at my phone. I smiled, confirming my good news, and her head straightened again.

I took the water from the tray and she hesitated like she wanted to see me drink. After a couple of large gulps, she left.

'Mouse, you old bugger,' Rupert called. My partners barrelled across the grass towards me. They all had their phones out, presumably all their banks had given them the same good news. Rupert reached me first, knocking the water glass out of my hand with an embrace that was half hug, half tackle. Then Julian and Ezra arrived, turning the embrace into a rolling rugby maul.

'We did it,' Ezra shouted.

'We sure did,' Julian screamed and the maul morphed into a tight circle, each of us facing in, linked arms across each other's shoulders. One of them started jumping and then we were all doing it. A tight, jumping scrum of shouting and swearing. Our exuberance, fuelled by booze, erupting in noise and action. When we finally stopped, we walked in a line, arms still across each other's shoulders, towards a table and the disapproving frowns and tight-lipped annoyance of some of the other guests.

'I need some more water,' I said and glanced around for the waitress but I couldn't see her.

'Water! We need champagne,' Rupert shouted.

This time their drinks and my water were brought by a burly waiter with a pencil-thin moustache.

'Where's that waitress? She's a cracker,' Ezra moaned.

The waiter gave a dismissive shrug. 'We 'ave some agency staff,' he said in a French accent. 'I don't know.' He shrugged again, implying a silent 'and I don't care'.

***

The haze in my head didn't clear despite lots of water and two double espressos. Somehow the one glass of champagne was still winning.

Only Rupert and I were left now in the late afternoon quiet, before the after-work drinkers arrived. I wasn't much company. It was hard enough to keep my head straight, let alone chat.

'I'm off, mate,' Rupert said. 'I'll sort the bill. See you tomorrow.'

I decided to go as well, standing a little unsteadily and aiming for the exit. My hand braced against the wall of the lift for support as it headed down, then held on tight as the escalators dropped me into Bank Station, joining the commuters heading home.

I'd planned to see Jerry and give him some cash, but I didn't feel well enough. There was always tomorrow.

Through multiple stumbles and stops to hold on to the wall, I got to the Northern Line platform and saw that the first train was to High Barnet. My Edgware train was one minute later.

The arriving train pushed a wave of air along the tunnel and platform, and as the train rushed into the station, my hair flapped around and I felt a hand on my arm. I staggered, worried that I was going to be pushed into the path of the oncoming train, but instead, I heard a soft voice behind me.

'Hello again,' the waitress said.

I turned and let out an, 'Oh, hi,' full of relief and surprise. Her work uniform peeked out from below a blue puffer jacket, and her hair was up in a ponytail and poking through the back of a plain black baseball cap.

We both took a step back as the High Barnet train disgorged some of its passengers, their flow blocked by the impatient press of the people waiting to get on. I leant against the wall, and said, 'After you left we had to suffer that grumpy waiter.'

'I'm agency staff and I had to do something else.' She looked at me, 'Are you OK?'

'I'm feeling a bit…' I paused, waiting for the noise of the departing train to subside, 'a lot… dizzy.'

She slipped her arm through mine to help keep me upright. 'I'm going to Camden Town. Which train do you need?'

'Edgware.'

Looking up at the scrolling information screen, she said, 'Next train.'

The zing-zing sound of the rails and the breeze coming along the platform signalled the arrival of my train. Even after all the people got off, the train was busy so she took my hand to help me on.

I let her guide me towards the train. Pace after pace.

I couldn't hear the cracking ground under my feet. I couldn't see the crevasse.

I should have run, got a bus, a cab – anything but get on the Tube with her.

But I didn't.

***

We stood at the end of the carriage and shared the short hop to Moorgate in the silence of two strangers in a confined space. Not that I had much to say – the swaying of the train was destroying my balance.

When the passengers started to move and get off at Moorgate, she twisted and directed me into a corner by the closed door. 'Lean here. It'll be easier,' she said.

We were both now facing into the carriage, with her standing in front of me. As the train moved, the jolt of the carriage made her fall against me, her upper body twisted and she pressed her breast against my arm. I felt its softness compress and tried to pull away, but she didn't seem to notice.

I kept my eyes shut all the way to the next stop at Old Street and concentrated on fighting the swaying of the train.

More people got on and the carriage filled up as it always did when the train got closer to King's Cross. More still pushed on at Angel and the movement of a man wearing a large backpack made the waitress take half a step backwards against me. She made no effort to move away. I eased myself back away from her and into the door as far as I could, trying to give her space, but the swaying of the train pushed the man's backpack towards her and she pressed her body into mine. I had nowhere left to go but she still didn't react. There were so many people on the train, too little room between the tired commuters for anyone to have space, except somehow most had manoeuvred their mobile phones into a tiny gap so that they could still see them.

Sweat broke out on my brow as the heat of the carriage rose. A wave of nausea hit me and I gulped it down. When it passed, the fog in my head rolled back in, as dense as an old London pea-souper. I pulled my eyes shut and rested my head back against the door. I concentrated on breathing and not being sick.

I could make out the train slowing and stopping at King's Cross. The press of bodies eased as people prepared to get off, lots of little shuffling movements around me as they tensed for the sprint to their next trains. The doors opened and it sounded like the passengers moved, all trying to get through the door at once. I sensed space around us, but the waitress didn't move away from me. Instead, she created a small gap between us and used her right hand to snake down my leg. What must have been her left elbow jabbed hard into my side. The shock and force of it drove the air out of me and my upper body pivoted forward.

My brain was having a hard enough time with the fog to cope without the overload of complaints from my side.

Her hand was on the zip of my trousers, dragging it down and I started to move my hand to block her but she repeated the jab with her elbow and pushed her hand inside my trousers. I could feel her nails climbing up to the top of my pants. 'No,' I said, but she landed a third blow to my side.

Her fingers hooked into the waistband and down inside.

I jolted as she pulled my dick out of my trousers and into the air. It snapped my head clear like someone had thrown the switch on some huge floodlights.

My eyes flashed open in panic. The carriage was half-empty and... and...

She was a pace ahead of me, turning. Her eyes full of revulsion.

Her hand pointed at me and she screamed.

'Pervert!'

Chapter 7

The carriage's remaining passengers pivoted around and stared.

No, no, no. I was on a train with my dick out.

I dropped my hand to try and hide the truth, but it made things worse.

'He's wanking on the train,' the waitress shouted.

The remaining passengers turned now, a mixture of angry, revolted faces and those smirking and using the video camera on their phones. She turned her shoulder as the angry passengers moved half a step towards me, letting them step past her.

I needed to get off the train and run, but I was blocked by the doors behind me and the angry faces ahead. My head snapped left and right as desperation kicked in and I looked for an escape. Nowhere to go.

What's happening? Why me?

She was getting off the train but looking back at me. I stared at her and she mouthed a single word. 'Sorry.'

Then she dipped her head to hide her face behind the peak of her cap and was gone.

I blinked. My brain and body shut down. The shock made me a statue.

A woman in the doorway of the carriage was waving and calling along the platform, 'Quick! Over here.'

She stepped to one side to let two unsmiling transport police officers clamber onto the train.

'I didn't... It wasn't...' I stammered.

What could I say that would convince them it was all a mistake? *It wasn't me?*

They shoved their way through the crowd as I tried to stuff myself back in my trousers and zip-up.

They could see what I was doing and anyway, the videos from all the phones would tell them all they wanted to know.

The videos would already be posted on social media and telling the world.

And Felicity.

And my kids.

***

What happened? Why me? Why now? The same questions kept crashing around in my head, like demented dodgem cars, tails sparking and jolting my senses every time they crashed into each other. *How can I explain this to Felicity?*

Any pretence at calm, rational thought was still waiting for the train at Bank Station.

The image of the waitress' face filled my mind. I tried to remember if I had ever seen her before, but couldn't. Not an ex-colleague or friend of a friend. If I had ever met her before today, my memory had redacted all trace of her. So why had she done it?

A crushing wave of fear hit me and I swayed on my feet despite the train still being stationary. My head turned.

One police officer held my elbow and her fingers dug into my arm. The other officer was collecting names from the people on the train. Most held their phones out, pinching and swiping as they paraded whatever they had recorded.

They'd dine out on it for months: 'Tell us again about that guy with his knob out on the train.' 'Well, let me show you…'

I was already tried and convicted. I'd be the 'banker wanker', 'pervert', 'knob on a train', 'scum', 'filth', 'depraved'. Held up as a pariah. The smartphone was the ultimate witness to my shame. And my destruction.

A guy with long, lank hair in a black t-shirt with the words 'What's it to you?!' scrawled across the front, waited at the edge of the witnesses. He dropped one hand to his crotch and mimed masturbating while he held his other hand high. Pinkie and index fingers raised in the *sign of the horns* hand gesture. 'Rock on,' he mouthed.

I closed my eyes to him and to the revulsion in the eyes of the others. I wanted to wake up from this nightmare, find myself tucked up safely in bed and laugh with relief.

What had I done to her that would make her do this to me?

Where was the flash of enlightenment? The logic, the magic answer?

Nowhere to be seen. Instead, it was like I was peering down a deep black well, with the word 'Why?' bouncing and echoing as it tumbled down and down.

She had seemed normal, no more than that: nice, sincere, genuine. I couldn't even write her off as deranged.

Grinding her fingers into my arm, the officer said, 'Come on, Casanova.' Her other hand in my back sent me staggering forward, towards the train doors and onto the platform. More hostile eyes from the rammed platform full of commuters anxious to get home, intolerant of any delay to their train. Some of them would have happily lynched me for making them late. Some were enthralled by their phones.

I dropped my head, trying to be as small as one of the little mice that run around on the Tube tracks, wishing I had Harry Potter's cloak of invisibility.

'Wanker.'

'Pervert.'

Shoulders banged into me. Deliberate accidents, some aided by a shove from the officer guiding me out.

Dishonoured

Eyes closed now, walking blind, I hid from the people and the platform. I wanted to be somewhere else, anywhere else. I couldn't acknowledge my new reality.

Finally, something appeared from the empty darkness of the well of my ideas. A question gradually formed and rose.

Why did the waitress say sorry?

Chapter 8

Bouncing in the back of the police van, I sat in silence, my eyes avoiding anything other than the deep shine of my shoes.

All my years of practice at keeping a lid on my emotions leapt to my defence. I shut everything down and tried to keep my brain still, like my skull was a dark, empty cave. Nothing to see, nothing allowed in.

It never happened.

But the cave leaked. Some crack in its roof betrayed me and ushered in drips of reality. When each drip fell and hit the floor of the cave, it exploded, showering me with the truth.

Drip.

I was ruined.

Drip.

I deserved it.

Every step on my climb to the top, I'd carried my self-loathing. Been undermined by my lack of worth. So, this was only right – to be expected. Every school playground punch, every sneering teacher's scoff at my dreams, every City boy's insult at the worthless country mouse was true. Why would this outsider, this lump of shit, deserve success? That was for the effortlessly good-looking elite, the charmers. Those with charisma and a dazzling smile.

Drip.

Not for me.

I wasn't good enough, worthy enough.

Drip.

I'm a criminal.

***

Everything at the police station deepened my new reality. I grimaced as my sweaty fingerprints burned their way onto the police database. I cringed as the swab scrapped my cheek for DNA. My beltless trousers hung a little lower than normal, my laceless shoes felt too big as I shuffled on the spot.

I tried to get back into the cave and cut out all the police officers' words, but more drips seeped through.

Drip. *'Arrested for exposure…'*

Drip. *'Section 66 of the Sexual Offences Act 2003.'*

The words *sexual offences* hit me with the force of a volcano erupting, and crashed me back into the stark, grimy police station.

'Do you want legal advice?' a voice said.

I couldn't bring myself to look at any of them, especially the women. Definitely not look into their eyes and see all their contempt glaring at me.

'Yes,' I murmured, but who? I couldn't see some tired, apathetic duty solicitor saving me and my phone wasn't exactly full of solicitor friends. I didn't know who to use, but I visualised Vardah back at her desk, working on all the deal paperwork. She'd know a specialist at the top of their profession, I hoped. Someone who could wave their magic wand and make it all go away.

I gave her name and the office number and I heard the tap of a keyboard as one of the officers made a note.

'Would you like us to tell someone that you're here?'

The crack in the roof of the cave split open and a waterfall of reality poured down. The torrent of it hit me and I swayed and rolled on my feet.

'You alright, sir?' said a voice.

'Can you tell my wife where I am?'

Chapter 9

I sat in the small grey meeting room opposite Jessica, the specialist sexual offence solicitor Vardah had contacted.

Jessica coughed. It sounded like she was buying time to think of the right way to break it to me. 'You've got to understand, there's zero-tolerance towards sexual crimes these days.' She looked like she was in her early thirties but already seemed tired and world-weary.

'You might think that having a woman defend you will help,' she continued.

A little dribble of hope made me nod along.

'It won't,' Jessica said.

'I didn't do it,' I shouted. 'That woman hit me and pulled my dick out.' I looked into her hard, intelligent eyes that had seen it all before.

'No one is going to believe you. You've no evidence to prove you were attacked except a couple of bruises on your ribs.'

'But it's the truth. Did the police find the waitress?'

Jessica shook her head. 'They checked the CCTV from the tube and there's no image that shows her face. They also checked with the restaurant. The address she gave them is a derelict block of flats. It's a dead end.'

'But I'm innocent...' My voice trailed away.

'If you fight this and plead not guilty it will make things much worse. The prosecution have all the people on the train as witnesses, and then there's this.' She held her phone towards me and I could see a paused video on the YouTube app.

I knew what was coming but she pressed play anyway. I dropped my eyes to avoid reliving it but I couldn't shut my ears to the commentary. 'Pervert... He's wanking... Bastard.'

The noise stopped and I heard Jessica put her phone back on the desk. 'No jury will find you innocent,' she said. 'You can't argue that you didn't get your penis out. The videos and all the witnesses prove you did.'

She was right. Who would believe my story? *'Yes, your honour, I was on the Tube when an attractive woman stood very close to me and started pressing against me. I tried to stop her, but she hit me and pulled my penis out.'*

Despite the truth, the judge and jury would see an entitled man sexually harassing a woman who was out of his league and deliberately exposing his penis. The injustice of it burned like acid spilt on my skin.

My innocence was irrelevant. 'How do I beat this?'

She looked straight at me and I could see the compassion in her eyes. 'Your best option is to plead guilty and avoid a trial. You're lucky there were no children in the carriage. It's your first offence so that will help, but the presence of others and your alcohol consumption will count as aggravating factors.'

I stared into space. Jessica was the best lawyer there was and she was telling me I had no hope.

'What happens if I plead guilty?' I asked.

She thought for a while. 'I'm sure I can argue that it's a Category Two offence and then the sentence range is community order to twenty-six weeks custody. The court will probably go at the higher end, but you'll get a reduction for a guilty plea – a third discount. So, your twenty-six weeks becomes seventeen, and as it's under two years, we can ask for a suspended sentence plus community service.'

'So can I go home to see my kids if I plead guilty?'

'Probably. I would guess that seventeen weeks prison sentence, suspended for two years, with the requirement of two hundred hours unpaid work and supervision, plus a big fine and court costs would be reasonable.'

'Reasonable… reasonable?' My mind was back into meltdown mode again.

'That's the best case if you plead guilty.' She pushed some pieces of paper towards me. 'Some of the passengers said they felt scared and vulnerable in their witness statements. They will count against you.'

Jessica paused to make sure I was following.

'If you go to court with this evidence, they *will* find you guilty. You'll be sent to prison, probably for twelve months.'

'It can't be. Twelve months in prison?' I couldn't believe it. I was innocent. How could this be justice?

Jessica waited for me to come to terms with it, but I couldn't. It was as if I had been hit by a wrecking ball.

'I've talked to the police and they're saying they can't risk releasing you if there's a chance of you reoffending. They're going to keep you in custody and you'll see the magistrate tomorrow.'

'I've got to decide now to plead guilty for something I didn't do?' I said as my mind tried to deal with the assumption that I was guilty and would reoffend.

'No. Tomorrow in court. But if you plead not guilty there's a risk they will refuse bail and you'll be held on remand. Plead guilty and you should be home tomorrow.'

I seemed to have two terrible choices. Plead innocent and spend months on remand with the stress and shame on my family, or plead guilty to something I hadn't done and go home.

'One more thing,' she said and the bluntness of her words cut through me. 'You'll have to sign on to the Sex Offender Register.'

'Like a bloody paedophile?'

I couldn't take it. My vision blurred, my pulse racing.

My head spun and hit the table with a clang.

Chapter 10

As my head completed a tour of the magistrates' court, I couldn't see Felicity. I can't say I blamed her, she would be trying to protect our kids from seeing the video of their dad. Their dad on the Tube, their dad on YouTube. They were eight and six, how could I begin to explain it to them?

The public area was deserted except an elderly gentleman in a well lived-in suit and tie dozing in the corner. Whatever fame or notoriety I had all seemed to be online. No press in the court. I blew out a sigh of relief.

The process of the hearing seemed to follow a well-practised flow in which I was almost irrelevant. I stood in the dock and glanced at a man in a suit who I assumed was the prosecution solicitor. I let it all happen around me and bounced between my obsessions: the corrosive injustice of it all, my innocence and why *she* had destroyed me.

Jessica landed a gentle tap of her foot onto her desk and broke into my thoughts in time for my only line.

'…how do you plead?' a voice said.

Today should have been the start of my new life. Financially independent, on top form – an essential part of Salamander Capital, now under the umbrella of KapGroup.

I wanted to scream my innocence at the world. It was all happening so quickly. The system gave me no time to prove I didn't do it – I was set-up.

My head dropped as I replayed Jessica's advice and how badly a trial would go. The extra publicity and the impact on my kids weighed on me. Then there was the risk that I would be held on remand. I looked up at the magistrate and found no warmth or comfort in her hard eyes and pursed lips. I wanted to be home with Felicity and the kids.

'Guilty,' I mumbled.

'Speak up so the court can hear you.'

My head spun and whirled. The situation was too bleak. The contrast from the high of signing to this low was impossible to process. Like I was watching through the wrong end of a telescope, I saw someone who looked like me repeat the word, 'Guilty'.

The rest of the hearing was a daze as my brain gave up trying to deal with all my thoughts, anger and the disbelief crashing through me. It shut down, going into a survival mode where it did the instinctive actions of keeping my heart pumping and breathing. I hoped my brain would give up completely, but it allowed in words like sentencing, custodial, community service. The words *Sex Offender Register* seared into my head and I couldn't shake them out.

***

My brain restarted inside the courtroom with Jessica shaking my shoulder. 'Dan, Dan. Are you OK?'

I knew that Jessica had done her best in the hearing, but it was only damage limitation.

'What happened?' I asked.

She frowned at me, and seemed to be thinking I was making a bad joke, then her face softened.

'I know it can be a shock, but I was right: seventeen weeks, suspended, with two hundred hours and costs.'

'Right, what now?'

Jessica looked up at the now empty room. 'The magistrates asked me to take you to find a probation officer.'

'I'm on probation as well?' I asked. There were so many things I'd half-heard of on television shows and knew nothing about.

'No, they manage the community service.'

Dishonoured

I stood and my legs didn't seem properly attached any more. I grabbed the chair for support.

'Let's go,' Jessica said, taking my elbow and steering me to towards the door.

My feet scuffed and scraped on the cheap courtroom carpet and my walking didn't improve outside.

With a heavy sigh, Jessica steered me to a chair and walked off.

When she came back, she thrust a piece of paper at me.

It was a simple pro-forma letter from the probation office, with the date, time and address of my first appointment.

Clutching the first tangible proof of my new life as a convicted criminal, I thought I had hit rock bottom.

No such luck.

Chapter 11

A squall of driving rain hit me as I stepped outside the courtroom, snatching at my letter and almost tearing it from my hand. I grabbed at it with my other hand, and more screwed than folded it, and stuffed it into my pocket.

Now what? Work could wait. I needed to get home, change and shower to get the smell of the police station off me.

The rain hit me again, stinging and slapping my face like it was an interrogator trying to soften me up before the torture began. It was too late. My self-torture was way ahead of it. Every time I tried to think of something else, a pulse of guilt hit me and I'd be back on the train, wishing people weren't staring at me. Wishing the police weren't grabbing my arms.

I shut my eyes and shuddered. It wasn't only the guilt, but the waves of revulsion and self-disgust. They fed on themselves and sent shudders through me.

While it had taken a few months for Jerry's life to unravel as he hurtled towards homelessness after leaving the army hospital, it had only taken me four Northern Line Tube stops to walk off a cliff edge and plummet from the top of the world to ruin.

The speed of my fall meant that I couldn't adjust to my new reality or even see it. It had to be fake, a dream. A nightmare. I'd wake up soon and find myself in bed, everything back to normal.

More rain slapped me in the face. 'This is normal now,' it screamed.

I started walking, habit driving me in the direction of a signpost to the nearest Tube station, then stopped. I couldn't face using the Tube and even if a cab gave warmth and shelter, what would I say if the cabbie turned to me and said, 'You hear about that banker with his knob out on the Tube?' Worse still – 'Aren't you the guy…'

Dropping my head to avoid showing my face to any casual pedestrian, I walked faster and after I turned the corner, the size of the buildings and their shiny glass-fronted facades gave me some shelter from the rain. Everyone I passed seemed to be staring at me. They couldn't all recognise me. Could they?

Further along the road, I could see a bench tucked into a quiet little alcove, and I headed for it. Running my hand across the dry seat told me that the rain hadn't dampened the surface and I collapsed onto the bench, pleased to have both the support and the ability to huddle and hide from the passers-by.

I pulled out my phone and called Felicity. It rang and rang. The echo of the ringtone filled me with dread.

I smiled and sat up as the call answered, but froze when I heard a click and Felicity's voice, cracked with emotion and tears. 'How could you?' she said. 'It's disgusting. The video is everywhere.'

'But I didn't–'

'Dan, don't treat me like I'm stupid… I have to protect the children. They're getting all sorts of abusive messages and threats at school. I need to protect them and our future. I need time.'

She hung up. It was all too new and raw for her.

'Our future' meant Felicity and the kids, not Felicity and me, I thought.

I shut my eyes and tried to suppress it all, to keep it in, but two separate thoughts hit me. One, she believed that I had *chosen* to expose myself. Two, she had at least answered the phone and said she needed time – there was hope. The thoughts clashed and merged, like water sloshing from side to side in a bucket.

I couldn't blame Felicity for not believing that I was set-up, and as the water stilled, I smiled. She had picked up and that was my first positive step since... since the Tube.

Paul was the next number on my favourites list and I listened to his ringtone. After five, he answered and before I could even say 'Paul', he said, "What the hell, Dad. How could you?' His voice was low and urgent, like he wanted to shout but was in a public space. 'Everyone has seen the video.'

'I—' was as far as I got before he hung up.

The rest of my favourites on my phone were like a judgement on my life choices. Mostly work colleagues, the rest were at best acquaintances, or merely functional – the plumber, gardener, garage. No friends to call, no shoulder to rest on and get comfort.

Nothing.

***

As I trudged along the roads towards home, my grim reality seeped in and started to make itself at home, like a destructive and unwanted house guest. Occasionally, denial came to my rescue and all was well again, but a quick hand into my jacket pocket, and my fingers touched my probation office appointment letter.

The pedestrian traffic had thinned as I got closer to home and I could avoid people's glances and the paranoia that they recognised me from the video footage. Turning into our road, I thought that I had made it safely back, but as I walked towards the house, I saw Belinda, one of our neighbours and her dog coming around the corner. She'd been fun when Felicity and I had first met her and her husband, all late-night parties and laughter, but she had never forgiven me for rejecting her boozy, stumbling attempted kiss and whispered offer late one night.

She was engrossed in her phone and didn't see me until she was a few metres away. 'Ah, our film star,' she spat and turned her phone to show me what she had been watching. Curling her little finger, she said, 'Doesn't look like I was missing much.'

Bertie, her big, happy Labrador, wiggled and wagged from behind her, pleased to see me. He pushed his head against my leg to demand my attention and affection and his enthusiastic, wet tongue licked across my hand.

Belinda grabbed at his collar and dragged him away from me. She spat the word 'bastard' and was gone.

I was learning that the words 'exposure' and 'Sex Offender Register' have the effect of turning your world into post-apocalyptic dust.

Bertie turned his head against Belinda's rough handling and seemed to smile at me. My eyes filled with tears at this first moment of kindness or affection since the Tube.

Perhaps dogs could see the real you.

Chapter 12

I reached our gate and stepped through and up the garden. The house seemed quiet. No sign of Felicity or her car that she never bothered to put in the garage. 'Too much hassle when I'm in a rush with the children,' she would always say.

Standing at the front door, I pulled in a big breath and let it slide out. If I could only talk to Felicity, then perhaps I could somehow persuade her it was all a mistake. Maybe I could still save something from this.

My house keys snagged in my pocket as I wrestled them out and I paused, staring at the very shiny new lock nestling in the door. I pushed my worn key at it, but the lock wouldn't allow more than a few millimetres of my key in, let alone slide home and turn.

Another attempt at calling Felicity went to voicemail.

'Felicity, darling,' I said. 'I'm home and the lock's been changed. Where are you? I need to talk to you… I need you.'

I hung up and waited, hoping she would call me back.

I heard nothing but the rustling of the trees and the background hum of nearby traffic.

Scanning the driveway and the bushes of our garden, I worried that I would find the shredded remnants of my clothes, flung in anger and hurt by Felicity. But all I could see were the familiar shapes of lawn, flowers and hedges – none of them wearing one of my ties. At least the CCTV cameras on the house were battery-driven dummy deterrents and despite their flashing red lights, couldn't record my defeated shoulders slumping and my head tipping forward.

My only hope now was the remote control on my key ring. I pressed the button and smiled as the garage door started folding and lifting, revealing the tiled floor and the nose of my Aston Martin.

Would Felicity have taken her revulsion out on my car if she had spared my clothes?

I pushed under the garage door before it was even half-open and scanned the side of the Aston nearest to me. Its shine blossomed as the door rose and allowed more light in. The silver metallic paint glowed in its usual perfection – not scarred by angry keys scraping along it, no dents, no slashed tyres. Only the wheelie suitcase I used for business trips rested near the boot.

I grabbed the bag's handle and tested its weight. Not the fullest it had ever been. That had been a glorious autumnal trip to the Alps before we had kids. We'd packed for every type of weather and ended up spending the week in bed and walking in the mountains in T-shirts.

Front door lock changed and clothes in a packed bag. As hints went, it wasn't subtle, but I ignored that and popped the door of the Aston open and settled into the cosseting leather of the interior and the embroidered initials DBS. The smell of leather and the elegance of the controls brought some small respite from the world and a brief smile to my face. I wasn't Daniel Craig in *Casino Royale*, but there was no tractor for this country mouse.

Still, it wasn't going to take me far without the car keys and tracker fob from inside the house, so I walked over to the internal door leading from the garage to the kitchen. The door didn't yield when I turned the handle. Trying the usual key from my key ring had no effect on the lock. She must have changed that as well.

I banged on the door but got no reward other than a bit of noise and a sting on my palm. But it dislodged some of my anger. I hit the door again. And again, raining blows on the blameless wood. Finally, I stopped, turned and leant my back against the door and slid down until my bum hit the floor.

My head dropped, defeated by the door, destroyed by the waitress on the Tube.

What now?

I had no idea.

***

I stayed on the garage floor until my legs got numb and the cold of the day seeped into my fingers. When I tried to get up, I rubbed and worked my legs to get the pins and needles out of them. Then I listened to the ringtone on my next call to Felicity. The answering system clicked in and I hung up.

Should I stay and sleep in the garage? I dismissed the thought. *So where?*

My deliberations were interrupted by the soft ping of a message. I grabbed at the phone. Yes! It was from Felicity, but my joy crashed when I saw that the preview of the message started with the word 'Sorry'.

It evaporated when I read it: *Sorry, Dan, but I can't have you in the house and near the kids.*

I shut my eyes and tried to suppress the flash of pain from the words.

Perhaps I could use the money from the deal to rebuild my life and marriage. Get my kids back.

The best place to start was the office.

Chapter 13

Colin stiffened as the revolving door deposited me inside Salamander Capital's office foyer. Gone were his usual nod and smile. The eyes of the people in the atrium swivelled towards me, heads bent in whispered comments. I was relieved that I'd left my suitcase in a storage locker rather than strolling in looking like what I was – a man thrown out by his wife.

'Alright, Col,' I said.

He raised his arm in what I hoped would be his usually welcoming wave, but he stepped in front of me to block my path. He seemed to be pointing me at the tiny office on the public side of the barriers. The office that was always used for bad news – cancelled contracts, redundancy, and firing. Used so that your sour face wouldn't contaminate the rest of the workers on the privileged side of the barriers. Officially, it was Meeting Room G.1, but everyone called it the 'Decontamination Room'.

No way was I going in there without a fight. It was obvious that I needed to talk to Yas.

I took a step towards Decontamination and Colin's shoulders dropped as he relaxed. I took it as a sign and spun around him in the opposite direction. I left him for dead as deftly as any premier league striker left a defender, and headed for the barrier. My staff pass touched on the scanner, but instead of the welcoming hiss of the gates opening, they stayed shut. Colin's hand landed on my shoulder before I could launch myself over the barrier.

Maddie glared at me from behind her reception desk and Colin steered me towards Decontamination. 'Sorry, Dan, but I've got me orders.'

***

Over thirty minutes later, I saw Colin's silhouette move outside Decontamination's glass door. Whoever came through that door would tell me all I needed to know before a word was spoken.

I smiled when I saw it was Vardah, carrying a thick file, but as she inched into the room and had to sidestep into a chair, another figure appeared. The one I'd dreaded. Hannah Taylor.

Hannah stood in the doorway and her eyes crackled with icy fury. She was Human Resource's lawyer, wheeled out to destroy any threat to Salamander Capital. In the past, I'd always been able to aim her glacial intellect at some cringing soul. Calling her Hatchet Hannah worked when you were the one wielding her.

Hannah held our slim Employee Handbook. As one of the founders, I had helped craft it, but Hannah had forged it to be as solid as iron.

In a hostile silence we all sat, but I decided that attack was better than destruction.

'What the hell's going on,' I said. 'I'm an owner of this firm and my pass isn't working.'

Hannah's mouth opened into a hard slit.

'You were an owner, until the deal with KapGroup.' Hannah put the Employee Handbook onto the desk like she was handling some sacred relic. 'You're familiar with the section on Gross Misconduct.'

Here it comes, I thought as the ground under me dissolved and my descent resumed.

'So, you know that a criminal conviction, especially one that so publicly damages the reputation of Salamander, would fit the definition of Gross Misconduct in clause nine point one.'

Unlike Hannah, I couldn't remember the clause number, but the clause itself was clear enough – Gross Misconduct allowed for immediate dismissal. Loss of all rights to bonuses, performance fees, pension payments or the generous benefits package.

'I need your phone and company credit card,' Hannah said, and held out her hand in expectation.

I tossed my phone across the desk and watched her smirk when I dug out my company credit card and spun it across the desk like a Las Vegas casino dealer.

Then Hannah smiled, and I knew there was worse to come.

'I have informed the FCA to have you permanently removed from the Fit and Proper Person register. I'm sure that they will agree that someone on the Sex Offender Register is not suitable for this industry.'

She was burying the hatchet – into me. Not only was I out of work, but the City's regulator would block me from any decent City job in the future.

Surely this was the bottom of my descent? Hannah couldn't do more than she had, but she smiled again.

Shit, what now? My whole body dropped, like I was falling down an endless lift shaft.

Vardah coughed and I spun my head to her.

'There's something else,' she said. 'According to the terms of the sale agreement with KapGroup, you were entitled to receive two-million pounds on signing. You received that yesterday?'

'Yes.' I nodded.

'But,' she said.

Shit, there was a *but*.

'Although that money is safe, the terms of the deal said that your residual payment of forty million is payable in three months.'

'Yes,' I said, panting short, scared breaths. The end of a career was one thing. The money would have sustained the kids.

'But there are certain conditions, which we discussed. Remember?' Vardah said.

'There were lots of conditions.' I squirmed as a hard ball of panic grew in my gut. *Where is rock bottom?*

'The one that matters said that you are only entitled to the payment of forty million if at the time of the payment, you are still a *fit and proper person* with no criminal record, and working at Salamander Capital.'

'And *now* I have a record,' I said, dropping my hands to my stomach to try and control the shooting pains and rising vomit.

'Yes, now you have a criminal record,' Vardah agreed with a soft apology in her tone. 'So you won't receive the money.'

'And you can't exercise the options so you're not entitled to the final fifty-eight-million either,' Hannah added and banged the desk like she was trying to chop through it. It was her trademark move, the one that got her the hatchet nickname.

I gulped as a mouthful of vomit shot into my mouth. I caught most of it, but some of it escaped and sprayed onto the table.

My only speck of joy was the splatter of vomit landing on Hannah's sleeve and her precious handbook.

Chapter 14

'Sorry, Dan,' Colin said again as he walked me away from Decontamination and to the revolving exit door.

I was battling hard to keep a lid on my emotions, but it was like trying to contain a burst fuel line with my finger. As hard as I pressed, highly flammable fuel spurted out.

Twenty years of slog, eighteen-hour days, all the sacrifice and it was all gone – no family, no job, no career, no payout.

I walked out onto the pavement of Cheapside and kept going.

A savage blast of a car horn and squealing tyres brought me back to life. I looked down at the nose of the car that was millimetres from my leg, then swung my gaze up at the red-faced driver.

'Crazy fucker. You want to kill yourself, do it somewhere private. Don't involve me.'

He pressed back on his horn with one hand and waved me out of the road with his other.

A gaggle of pedestrians had formed, staring and filming me on their phones. I turned away from them, sick of everyone's ability to record the darkest moments of my life for their personal amusement and to increase their follower statistics.

I reached the other side of the road and felt in my pocket for my work phone. I panicked for a second that I had lost it before remembering that Hannah had seized it. It felt alien not to have the rectangular shape in my pocket or hand.

How could I call Felicity, or the kids?

There was a phone shop around the corner, so I headed off, careful to keep my face looking at the shop fronts and away from the gaze of anyone who knew me.

***

My personal credit card slid out of my wallet. It was always two slots down in my wallet, one below the now empty slot where my Salamander Capital credit card always nestled. The top to bottom order was set in stone: Salamander card, personal credit card, joint debit, personal debit card. The cards for the gym, health insurance, and everything else shared an inner sleeve in my wallet.

The salesperson did the usual tapping on the machine but it was made more difficult by her massive purple fingernails. 'Put your PIN in, please.'

I did, my fingers following the practised dance between the keys.

'Denied,' she said, and raised her eyebrows into a high frown.

'Can't be,' I said, wondering why it wouldn't work – maybe some random fraud flag set by the card company. 'Can you try again.'

The salesperson's eyebrows stayed high, but then she shrugged and repeated the tapping.

'Denied,' she said after my next typing of my PIN. Her eyebrows lowered, and she gave me a look that said 'you can't afford it'.

I was still in the same expensive suit I had worn to the signing, but I doubted its creases were inspiring the salesperson about my credit worthiness.

'You got cash or another card?' she asked.

Cash? Who has cash when even the cheapest items are available through contactless payment? I checked my wallet. To my surprise, a five-pound note rested in the corner of one of the long pockets.

I gave the salesperson the debit card that was linked to the joint account I shared with Felicity. The same account the £2m had gone into yesterday This one had to work.

But we repeated the same process of tapping, entering my PIN, the card being declined and her eyebrows going up again.

The salesperson started glancing around the shop. I wasn't sure if she was worried for me or if she was looking for security.

I pushed the box containing the newest iPhone and its price I couldn't afford towards the salesperson. My legs gave way under me as my life descended again.

Can't be. CAN'T BE.

***

Standing on Cheapside trying to hide the ATM screen from the person behind me, my stomach twisted and cramped.

The display screen blinked slowly, but my pulse hammered in my skull and I could feel a vein throbbing in my neck.

The balance of the joint account stood at £0.19. The last transaction had moved nearly two and a half million pounds to an account I didn't recognise.

Was this a coincidence? Was I the victim of a bank fraud the same day I got convicted for exposure? I didn't think so. More likely that it explained Felicity's text about protecting her and the kids' future.

I retrieved my now useless card from the slot in the machine and replaced it with the card linked to my private account. I blew out a sigh of relief and some of the stress I'd been holding washed out of me. A dragging, cloying tiredness replaced it.

The balance was £637 – the complete inheritance from my parents. I'd kept it as a testament to their hard work, and to remind me how lucky I was. I hadn't touched it in all those years.

Now, it was all I had.

***

When I went back into the phone shop, the salesperson let out a sigh of frustration, like I was responsible for wasting her life, even though there wasn't a queue behind me.

'What's the cheapest pay-as-you-go phone you've got?' I asked.

Yesterday, I wouldn't have winced at ten times the amount, but today I was faced with a completely new financial standing.

She disappeared for a while, before returning with a small plastic bag. She dropped the bag on the counter and I stared at the 'refurbished' sticker, and an iPhone that was at least five generations past new.

'How much?' I asked.

'One hundred and ten pounds, but you'll need to buy a top-up.' She looked at me, her eyebrows back into their high arched position again.

I placed my personal card on the table and the salesperson let out a 'huh' of surprise when the payment cleared and she gave me my not-so-new phone.

At least now I had a way to contact Felicity. Maybe she'd answer the unfamiliar number and I'd be able to explain. Maybe I'd talk to Hugo and little Victoria.

I dialled Felicity's number and waited. It rang and rang.

***

After paying for the phone and the £20 top-up, I was down to £507. Jerry would have known how to make it last, but to me, it felt like a decent meal with a client, or one night in a nice hotel.

I had enough money to avoid moving in with Jerry on the bench in St Peter Cheap, but I needed somewhere to stay.

The coffee shop by the Tube station would make a nice place to browse, but for the first time in years, the price of a coffee was too much to accept. And I didn't want to waste any of my new £20 balance on my phone surfing. Still, the coffee shop had good Wi-Fi and hadn't changed the password in years, so I did what I had seen others do and rested against the small section of brick wall next to its window.

I searched for a Wi-Fi signal, and sure enough up popped the coffee shop's name and the password still worked.

Browsing to the usual hotel booking website brought up a long list of places available. I shook my head in disbelief at the prices, selected 'Price ascending' in the sort order, and looked at the photos of some of the places that were available.

'Welcome to the real world, Dan', I could hear Jerry saying, but I couldn't adjust to the very bottom of the market. Three pages in, a hotel that was cheap, close to where I'd left my case and didn't look too disgusting, hooked me with the promise of free Wi-Fi and an en-suite shower.

***

The hotel room turned out to look little like the photos. Dark brown wallpaper and ceiling painted in beige gloss paint loomed in on me, making the space feel even smaller. The en-suite was the size of a wardrobe and the shower took real coaxing to let out even a tepid dribble.

A brick wall stared back at me if I stood and looked out of the window. I sat on the bed, the mattress creaking with age and I tried not to imagine how many people had been on it and what they might have done.

I'd given up on Felicity for tonight. Fifteen unanswered calls didn't leave much room for doubt that she wasn't going to pick up. Paul had at least answered and heard my story out. When I finished, I listened to the silence of him trying to find something to say before I heard Suzie, his wife, call him. 'Got to go, Dad. Talk tomorrow,' was all he managed.

My new phone didn't have any of my contacts so I couldn't ring around in search of company or help. Not that any of them had answered my calls from my old phone after the Tube video went viral.

The light faded from the day, and the darkness made the walls feel like they were pressing into the room. The dim single bulb in the ceiling light barely had the power to stretch into the corners of the room.

Was this it? The new me? Stuck in a dark, shabby room. No one to call. No one who cared.

I hoped that Hugo and Victoria would be asking 'where's Daddy?'. Would Felicity lock me out of their lives as firmly as she had locked me out of the house?

I forced my head up from off of my chin and shook my whole body to snap me out of the dark, swirling thoughts. I had only one other number that I could remember off by heart, so I dialled.

On the third ring, Rosalyn said, 'Hello?'

'Hi, Rosalyn, it's me, Dan.'

'Dan, I saw what happened…'

I could hear the surprise in her voice from the non-committal 'I see's, and 'Oh's she gave as I reeled off the story of the woman who had destroyed me.

When I finished, the silence dragged on. Maybe she didn't want to judge me. I wouldn't have blamed her if she had. To most people who had seen the video, I was scum and perverted filth. How could my family think any differently?

After a few more seconds she said, 'I wish Kat was still with us. She'd have known what to do.'

And she was right, Kat had a way of seeing the positives in any situation that could act as the start of something new.

I hung up.

Although it was early, I turned the light off and tried to settle, but each time I shut my eyes I saw short bursts of the last few days: the signing, the waitress on the Tube, the court, the front of the car that almost ended it all.

Each flash of memory was followed by a thumping wave of guilt and shame. I screwed my eyes up tight, hoping to block the memories, but they flashed again and again. Each one, a nail in the coffin of my old life.

As I stared at the darkness surrounding me, I wished I had never got on that Tube train. But it was so simple and normal to get on a Tube train without fear.

That one mistake, and my life disintegrated like rotten and decayed wood.

Chapter 15

The next morning didn't get any better. I had made sure that I was early for my appointment with my probation officer. My reward was more time on the hard plastic chair in the waiting room and a little ticket with the number seventy-three on it. As I looked at the walls of the waiting room, I realised that everything I thought I knew from films and books about probation seemed wrong. The posters aimed at informing me and ensuring that I knew my rights didn't call me a criminal or offender – I was a 'service user'. My probation officer was called a 'case worker' and the probation service weren't even involved. I was in the care of a private Community Rehabilitation Company. All these soft words didn't change the hard fact of my conviction.

My suit, although looking crumpled, made me seem overdressed. Jogging bottoms or jeans with T-shirts seemed needed to blend in, and the other people waiting stared and sneered as if they deemed my crime 'white-collar' and therefore inferior to whatever they had done. Maybe there was some sort of 'crime credibility ranking' that put assault or burglary above fraud or embezzlement. Any sort of sexual offence was going to be near the bottom. My exposure conviction dumped me one level above rapists and child abusers.

At least there weren't many mobile phones on show, but I dropped my head and sat lower into the chair, praying that no one recognised me from an online photo or video.

'Sixty-five,' a man in a blue shirt said, and a woman with long, greasy dark hair pushed herself up and hobbled after the man and along a corridor.

I settled lower in the chair, expecting a long wait, but almost immediately a woman said 'seventy-three' and waited expectantly at the mouth of the corridor.

My hand came up in a little wave of acknowledgement, but dropped when I heard sniggers around me. I stood and avoided looking at anyone in the waiting room by keeping my eyes locked onto the woman's back. She stopped and ushered me into a small room with a cheap wood veneer desk with patches of chipboard to absorb the spilt coffee. I took the nearest of the two chairs. It was more comfortable than the waiting room ones, with stained blue cloth covering foam to form a seat pad.

The woman sat down opposite me, and dropped a small file onto the table. She must have been in her fifties and had a world-weary expression and sag to her shoulders, like she had seen every type of person and hadn't been able to save them all from reoffending.

I hoped that she wouldn't judge me by my conviction.

'Mr Mendoza, I'm Sally Masterson,' she said. 'I'm your case worker and offender manager.'

'Err, hi,' I said, as I suppressed the image of the train that flashed across my mind.

'Your sentence was suspended after you pleaded guilty and you entered a period of probation. You also have a community order requirement of two hundred hours of unpaid work. Do you understand this?'

'Kind of. I get the high level, but not how it works in practice.'

She nodded. 'That's what your sentence plan is for,' she said and pulled out a couple of sheets of paper, pushing one across the desk to me.

She started talking me through the rules of my probation, my responsibilities, and detailing the dates, times and places of our future meetings. She paused and looked straight at me. 'You could go back to court if you break any rules of your probation. For example, if you commit another crime, miss any of our meetings or appointments without a good reason or behave in an aggressive, racist or other unacceptable way at a meeting or appointment. Do you understand?'

I nodded, hoping another court date wasn't in my future.

'Your unpaid work order will be managed under the Community Payback Scheme. Are you employed?'

I relived Hatchet Hannah sitting in the Decontamination Room, telling me I was out of my own firm. I screwed my eyes up tight to blank the memory out and stop the anger boiling up. I caught it in time and took in a deep breath.

'No,' I said.

'OK, then you'll have to do a minimum of eighteen hours each week, over three days.'

Two hundred hours at eighteen hours a week – I'd be done in just over eleven weeks, but I didn't want to spend time alone in my hotel room with images of the train flashing through my head.

'I'd like to work harder than the minimum and start as soon as possible.'

Sally look surprised, like she was more used to people trying to avoid the work. She pulled out a second sheet of paper and crossed out the date on it. 'Tomorrow OK?'

As I nodded, she wrote tomorrow's date on the sheet. 'Here are the details,' she said and pushed the sheet of paper towards me. 'I'll arrange it, and the extra hours. And wear work clothes.'

I picked up the sheet and saw an address and time on it.

'And then there's your Notification Requirement.' She looked straight at me.

No judgement in her eyes, but I wilted from her gaze and tried to push myself through the back of the chair. All I achieved was the front legs of the chair tipping up and I nearly overbalanced.

'Have you reported to the police station yet? You've only got three days from the date of your conviction.'

I was being treated the same way as a paedophile and my body shuddered in revulsion.

***

I pushed through the doors of the police station, with my stomach cramping and twisting in protest.

Shouldn't be here, my brain complained. *It's not fair.* It started off on the all too familiar cycle: *not fair, why me? What happened?*

I should be at work, living at home, my world cosseted and secure. Instead, I approached the desk and whispered, 'I need to report here for the Sex Offender Register.'

The female police officer's eyes narrowed and hardened. Her mouth curled like she had trodden in some dog shit on the pavement. It was the reaction I got from people, but each time it cut into me harder.

I wasn't a paedo or pervert. *I was innocent.*

The officer made a call and eventually, I was escorted through the police station to an interview room with a long mirror, grey table and four basic chairs.

I waited. And waited – I wasn't anyone's top priority.

Eventually, a bored-looking officer came in and landed on the chair opposite me with a grunt. He looked tired, like he was at the end of a long shift and let out a pained sigh. I could imagine that he didn't want to be here either.

'OK, can you confirm your full name and any aliases you have been known by?' he said.

'Daniel Mendoza. People call me Dan.' I wasn't going to tell him that they also called me Mouse.

'Date and place of birth?'

I told him. He went on to ask me for my national insurance number and passport details, which I gave him.

'Details of bank or savings accounts to which you have access?' he asked.

My inheritance account was the only one that seemed relevant so I gave him details of that.

'Date of conviction, court and offence?'

'Yesterday, City of London Magistrates' Court…' I paused, not wanting to say it.

His tone changed to a harder edge. 'Offence?'

'Exposure,' I mumbled.

He looked at me. Cold, assessing eyes. I could see him go through the possibilities – worst would be at a school, but then his face cracked into a smile. 'I saw your video. You're that bloke with his knob out on the Tube.'

His smile sparked my sense of unfairness into roaring anger. I wanted to smash my fist into his face, but I caught it before it got away from me, closed my eyes and took in two long breaths. 'It's not so funny when it's you.'

To his credit, he recovered his professional police face and said, 'No, no. Can you confirm your home address at the time of the conviction?'

I gave him my home address.

'Is that your current address?' he asked.

My voice dropped. 'No.'

'Missus not taking too kindly to the conviction?'

'You could say that.'

'Often the way, mate,' he said, softening his voice again. 'You got kids?'

'Two,' I said and tears filled my eyes. I missed hugging them.

'Ages?' he said, a serious tone back in his voice.

'Eight and six.'

He scribbled this down onto his form where he had written everything else. 'Where are you staying then?'

I told him and the name and address of the hotel went onto the form.

'You'll be on the Sex Offender Register for five years. You must report to the police every twelve months and inform the police of any change in your address. OK?'

OK? No, not OK. Five years of stigma and contempt. Five years of trying to hide the truth.

More than that. Now there was no way back into the City, I needed a new way of earning. My skills didn't leave me a lot of choices other than simple, menial tasks, but even then, I would need an employer who would be caring enough to give a convicted sex offender a chance when others were applying for the job without that poisoned chalice around their necks. Maybe now I had finally hit rock bottom.

What did I have left?

I clung to the hope that I somehow could get Felicity and the kids back.

Chapter 16

That night after checking my dwindling bank balance, I dropped my chin and let water from the grimy shower head wash over me. Wash was too strong a word. Most of the water shot off in random directions, some of it over the limescale encrusted, creaking shower door, some of it over the black mould on the tiles. The rest more or less leaked vertically down. The water had a slight browny-orange tinge to it that had leeched into the once-white shower tray.

At home I would stand under the piping hot torrent of water from my shiny wet-room shower for ages, letting the water soothe and wash away the day. *Nothing like a good shower to ease the mind*, I thought, and the hotel's dribble of water was definitely nothing like a 'good shower'.

Grabbing at the threadbare towel, I tried to dry myself off, but the scratchy material seemed to move the water around more than absorb it. After a lot of rubbing, I wasn't much drier, so I gave up and collapsed backwards onto the bed, arms spread wide. When I shut my eyes, scenes from the last few days flashed into me. My brain chose all the worst bits: the train, the court, my key not working in my front door, people's sneers and contempt. It was like watching a gory, time-lapse film where the director was aiming for maximum shock and destruction.

My brain had done the same thing when Mum and Dad had died rushing to be with Kat and me. Rushing to see baby Paul. It picked out my worst memories and stitched them together into a horror show. It even added how I imagined my parents' last moments, staring into a lorry's headlights that hurtled towards them.

I had endured another film of memories when Kat died. Full of the regrets over our last words and the things we'd left unsaid.

Back then, the sickening pain of reliving those memories had left me covered in sweat with my stomach cramping. I had battled myself day by agonising day. I'd managed to shut down my brain's evil cinema. I'd keep the door boarded shut, everything locked away.

I needed to do the same now, otherwise, I would spend all day, every day in silent self-torture.

***

The night passed in fitful sleep, interrupted by the looping memories of the past two days and the overwhelming shame and self-loathing that each one burned into me.

My eyes were gritty and sore the next morning as I clambered off the van and stood in a ragged line with ten strangers on the verge of a busy A-road. The click-click of the van's hazard warning lights made brief appearances in the gaps from the noise of cars flashing past.

Alan, our Community Payback Supervisor, stood next to the van and waved me forward. He flashed me a friendly smile but then launched into the rules and warnings. 'The orange jacket is so that the public know that Community Payback work is being done. OK?'

'Sure,' I said.

'If you don't turn up for your Community Payback work without a good reason, or you break the rules, I'll give you a warning or a breach of your order. You can only have one warning in any twelve months. Otherwise, it's back to court and prison. OK?'

'OK.'

'Don't forget, Community Payback is a punishment, but it's also a chance for you to learn new skills,' he said with a smile.

As Alan reached through the van's open doors, he grabbed a black bin bag and litter-picker and shoved them at me. The litter-picker had a black handle with a small trigger that worked a 'grab' at the other end. I squeezed the trigger a couple of times and the grab obeyed. This was a new skill for me, and the learning hadn't been too taxing.

'Come and get your things,' Alan called to the rest of the line.

''Urry up,' a man behind me said, 'don't think you're special 'cos you got flashy clothes.' I felt a shoulder crash into me. As I stumbled forwards, my litter-picker caught between my knees and pitched me forward and down onto one knee. The grass gave under my weight with a squelch. I stood and brushed at the wet brown circle on my jeans.

'Serves you right,' the man in his early twenties said, turning to a second young man right behind him. 'What a twat.' They both laughed, sending their round bellies bouncing. The movement separated the bottom of their West Ham United football shirts from the top of their grubby grey sweatpants and we were all treated to a flash of hairy, pale skin.

'Gaz, Tel. Put it away. It's making me puke,' the woman in her twenties said. She was about five foot six with and with long, straight, black hair. She looked Japanese, but her accent was pure Newcastle Geordie.

The man who must have pushed me, grabbed a hand onto his groin and started thrusting his hips back and forth. 'Eh, Tel,' he said. 'Bet little *Emika* is up for a bit of double-teaming.'

Tel looked blank for a second and then laughed and copied Gaz's thrusting. 'Yeah.'

Emika flashed them a finger. 'Just what I need – a couple of fat slobs with an Asian Fetish. Not even in your dreams.' She strolled off and went to stand by a tall, thin man with a wispy goatee.

Gaz stopped thrusting and frowned as he tried to think of a comeback. Tel stopped as well. Everything he did seemed to mirror Gaz with a built-in one-second delay, like he was his bigger, slower shadow.

Before Gaz had worked out what to say, Alan shoved a bag and litter-picker at Gaz and he trudged off, followed by the faithful Tel. They scowled at Emika and then Gaz turned his face towards me.

I wandered a few paces away and stood in the no man's land between the two groups.

Gaz smiled and leered at me.

Oh, shit, I thought.

He dug in the pocket of his sweatpants which pushed them lower and revealed the top of his pants. It looked like the waistband of the pants would have said 'Calvin Klein' if it hadn't been squashed and distorted by his heavy gut.

He pulled his phone out and started swiping and tapping. Every few seconds, he flashed me a glare.

Shit, shit, shit.

'Hah! Knew it,' Gaz said and jabbed an elbow into Tel's side. Tel's head tipped forward to watch Gaz's phone.

Gaz turned his phone so that I could see it. It was too far away for me to see clearly, but I didn't need to. I had the same images replaying in my head all night. 'Our flash twat is that banker.' He dropped his hand to his groin again, but this time, instead of cupping himself, he balled his fist and left his little finger waving at me.

Spinning on my right foot, I headed off towards the edge of the verge and scooped up a discarded plastic bottle. I popped it into my black bag and aimed my litter-picker at a sodden sandwich packet.

'He's that banker,' Gaz shouted, 'and all bankers are wankers. We've got the proof. He had a nice wank on the Tube.'

'Yeah,' Tel added. 'Wanker banker.'

'He got his knob out on the Tube and waved it around. It's all over YouTube. What a twat. What a…' Gaz paused and I could almost hear his brain chugging through his extensive selection of expletives. '… Knob,' he said.

I could hear the disappointment in his voice that he hadn't come up with something better. Then he laughed. 'Eh, Tel. Let's call our little princess, Knobby.'

A second passed and I expected Tel to add a 'Yeah, Knobby', but he couldn't have got the joke as Gaz said, 'You know, Knobby – 'cos he was on the Tube with his knob out.'

This time a second passed and Tel got the joke. 'Yeah, Knobby. Good one.'

'OK, OK, that's enough. Spread out and start picking up the litter,' Alan said.

I sensed movement near me and heard a Geordie accent.

'Ignore them. They can't help it.'

Those few kind words triggered water in my eyes, like when Bertie the Labrador had sniffed and licked me.

I turned away from her and with my voice, huskier than normal, threatening to betray me I said, 'Yeah. Thanks, Emika.'

'Call me Anomaly,' she said.

'OK.'

I drifted away from Anomaly and each time my litter-picker clicked, another piece of litter joined the others in my bulging bin bag. When I had cleared an area of litter, I paused. It certainly looked much better.

A car slowed behind me and I heard a window purr down.

''Ere you go,' a voice said and a McDonald's bag landed next to my foot. It burst open, jetting red milkshake over my shoe and scattering wrappers over my newly cleared area.

'Bloody convicts should be in jail,' the voice said and the car revved up and started to move.

Chapter 17

The day passed at a series of different verges along similar roads. I picked up the same types of litter again and again: plastic bottles, crisp packets, sandwich containers and cigarette packs. All thrown by someone too selfish and lazy to take their rubbish home or stop at a bin. Would they be happy if I threw my rubbish into their garden, or would they run out full of aggression and threats? Probably fists flying, I decided.

Gaz and Tel punctuated the day with verses of West Ham's signature 'I'm Forever Blowing Bubbles', but they always followed it with the same repetitive chant.

'Knobby, Knobby, Knobby,' Gaz would start.

'Oi, oi, oi!' would come back from Tel after his usual delay.

'Knobby.'

'Oi!'

'Knobby, Knobby, Knobby.'

'Oi, oi, oi!'

They'd both laugh and empty plastic bottles would bounce and land around me. They didn't tire of it.

I let it slide. It was the variation of a theme I'd had my whole life. Some bully would find something different about me and pick and pick at the same thread, hoping for a reaction. When I was a kid, I'd react. Punches would fly and I'd find myself back with my dad's arm around me, telling me it was OK to be different.

It had been many years since I had been in a fight, but I doubted the same would be true of Gaz and Tel. They would make it two against one. Not a fight I'd win. Plus, the risk of Alan reporting me to my probation officer, Sally, and me ending up back in court wasn't something I wanted.

Despite all my best intentions, after about the twentieth chant and a half-full Coke bottle hitting my head, it was enough.

I bent and picked up the bottle, hurling it back at them.

Shock flashed across Gaz's face that I had dared to retaliate, but instead of sending the bottle flying back towards me, he glanced at Alan's van.

It was empty.

Gaz turned to me and smiled, before nodding to Tel. 'Grab 'im.'

Even though Tel carried a lot of weight, his young muscles carried him across the open ground before I could get more than a few paces away. He grabbed my arms, yanking them behind my back and spinning me to face Gaz.

Gaz arrived in front of me, his eyes glittering. 'You rich bastard think you're better than us?'

'No–' I started, but Gaz's right fist smacked into my stomach. Tel's grip on my arms held me tight and stopped me doubling over.

'You're a fucking pervert.' Gaz landed a second punch.

Tel's grip loosened, and he said, 'Alan's coming back.'

Gaz's head shot around. 'Shit,' he said, as he lifted his left hand that carried the bottle I had thrown back. 'Let 'im go, Tel.'

Tel did as he was told and as I stepped free of his grip Gaz unscrewed the bottle top and rained the sticky, flat Coke over my head.

Then it rained for real.

Heavy, persistent and cold.

***

As we all spilt from the side door of Alan's van, my hands were blue from the cold. Gaz and Tel both managed not too subtle barges into my side but I was prepared and rolled with them. They grunted in disappointment and headed off with one finger raised. When they got to the corner, Gaz started with the 'Knobby' chant again.

I let it go. No point in wasting any more effort on them, but I hoped that we wouldn't share another Community Payback session.

'Those two are idiots,' Anomaly said beside me. I looked down at her and she shivered in her thin, damp coat.

'I'm frozen. You fancy a coffee in that cafe?' I said, nodding at the nearby parade of shops and the seemingly inescapable franchised coffee brand and the word Starbucks.

She spun and glared at me, 'What? Why would I?'

I took half a step back, not sure what I had said wrong. It wasn't like I'd asked her on a date.

The tall guy came up behind her, like he was her bouncer. 'Easy there, fella,' he said.

'I didn't… Look, I'm cold and I'm offering to buy you both a coffee in a nice warm cafe.' Then the truth slipped out. 'I haven't really talked to anyone in days,' I ended lamely and shrugged.

Anomaly continued her glare, but it softened as her forehead unknotted its frown. She must have decided I was more pathetic loser than sex pest, because she smiled and said, 'You're paying, right?'

'Right.'

***

The three of us sat at a small table in the back of the cafe, hands wrapped around our cups, staring into the steam rising off the dark brown liquid. They sat on one side. I was the untrusted bloke on the other.

'I'm Dan.'

'That you in the video?' Anomaly asked after the tips of her fingers started to regain a more natural colour.

'It's not how it looks.'

'Hard to read it any other way.'

'I was set-up,' I said.

That brought coughed laughs from them both.

'Weren't we all,' she said.

It was too raw for me to talk about, so I said, 'Why did Gaz use another name for you?'

'He uses it to try and wind me up, like. Alan uses it and Gaz heard.'

'So why Anomaly?'

'I was born in Newcastle. I look like my mother and sound like my dad. It freaks people out. Anomaly is how I see myself and it works online.'

'Fair enough.'

Anomaly, something that deviates from what is standard or expected. I could have used it about myself when I was growing up, but the others had chosen names like freak, oddball and abnormal.

I looked at the man who had sat in silence sipping his coffee. 'Sorry,' I said, 'I didn't catch your name.'

He paused with his cup halfway back down onto the table. 'Kev. It's short for Kevin.'

He said it so sincerely, so lacking in all sarcasm that I blinked a few times to cover my surprise.

'Nice to meet you, Kev.'

He ignored me and put his cup down. Not the chatty type.

'Is it OK to ask why you're on community service, Anomaly?'

She shrugged. 'I was set-up.'

'Good one,' Kev said and nudged her arm.

Maybe he was just shy around new people, I thought.

I took a sip of my coffee. Even though it wasn't a full, flowing conversation, at least I wasn't sitting in the hotel room on my own.

'Don't sulk. It's no big secret,' she said and settled back into her chair. 'I used to work in HR for a firm down here, and I'm… I'm very creative with computers.'

'As in computer fraud?'

She crossed her arms. 'No. I'm not a criminal.'

I could have pointed out that any sort of community order might contradict her, but I bit down on the temptation. I was in no position to criticise. 'Sorry, of course not,' I said instead.

'No, since I was a kid, I found it easy to get into other people's computers and have a good look around. Anyway, a friend at work broke up with her boyfriend. He didn't take it well and threatened to post some of their private videos online.' She banged her coffee down and some of the liquid slopped over the rim. 'Revenge porn is an offence, but I got busted for hacking his accounts and deleting the files.'

I started chewing my lip as I thought about it. She'd done the right thing by preventing the boyfriend from posting, but the way she talked, it sounded like she was a good hacker. If she got caught, then maybe she wasn't as good as she thought.

'What?' she said. 'Oh, I get it. I got caught so I must be a rubbish hacker. I can see you thinking it.'

I spread my hands, hoping she took it as half-apology and half acknowledgement.

'Well, my stupid friend got back together with the boyfriend and told him everything. They had no real proof, but she told the police I did it, so I cut a deal. Confession for a fine and community service. I hated the job anyway.'

She dropped her hands to her cup again. 'I'm bloody good.'

We all filled the awkward silence with sips of coffee and theatrical blowing of the steam coming off the cups.

'What about you, Kev?'

'My dad's got cancer and can't get out. This woman in a fancy four-by-four cut across the pavement and almost run me over. She opens her boot, takes a bag of food out and goes inside. I'm skint and there's all these other bags of food there. Thought it would help me dad get stronger, so I lift four bags and have it away.' He shook his head. 'Road's got CCTV.'

'So how were you set-up, Dan?' Anomaly asked.

I talked them through my story of the girl on the Tube, wincing and cringing at how weak and thin it sounded. I expected laughs and 'yeah, right', but they nodded, looking like they believed my story because the world had let them down too.

They seemed easy in each other's company, but didn't look like a natural fit. 'How do you know each other?'

'My case was right after his at the court. We've been on the same work duty and Kev dumped Gaz on his fat arse when he grabbed me on my first day.'

Gaz must have weighed twice as much as Kev. He seemed so calm and quiet. It didn't seem possible, but they both shared a quick smile at the memory.

'Face planted him,' Kev said. 'It was sweet.'

Chapter 18

The next day, I learnt how to scrub graffiti off of walls with another group of strangers. Some were shirking, others working hard like it was a wake-up call and they were going to try everything to avoid coming back. No Anomaly or Kev to chat to, but no Gaz and Tel to torment me. I spent the day with my head down and tried not to be noticed.

In the hotel, I repeated my sad little ritual of a tepid shower, followed by calling Felicity's phone over and over. I missed her. Both her company and the little shared touches and our inside jokes. I'd give anything to feel her hand slide over my shoulders as she walked past me. Anything to see my kids.

Sometimes, I hung up before her voicemail clicked in to save the credit on my phone. Sometimes I let it run so that I could hear her voice. 'Hi, this is Felicity, please leave me a message.' It brought a smile to my face for a second.

I wished that I hadn't objected so strongly to Hugo and Victoria having phones when Felicity had suggested the idea. I could have called them. Told them I loved them. It wouldn't be the same as a big cuddle, but it would have helped. They'd know that I was thinking about them.

I could have drawn strength and comfort from their little voices and, I hoped, from their excited 'Daddy, Daddy'.

I pulled the thin blanket of the bed over me and curled into a ball, pressing my face into the pillow, trying to block the image of the Tube train out.

My brain had other ideas.

'Back by popular demand,' it screamed. 'Your spectacular fall from grace. A story of riches to rags.'

Dishonoured

All the same images flashed into my head and burned into my skull. Even when I screwed my eyes tight, they kept coming.

A relentless wave of misery.

***

The next morning, tiredness weighed down every part of me, making me feel as heavy as Gaz. I hadn't felt like this since Victoria had spent four nights in a row battling chicken pox when she was eight months old. I'd stayed with her. Rocking and soothing her through the night. Getting through the days on zombie-like autopilot.

As I struggled into my orange Community Payback high-vis, I heard a friendly 'Dan.'

Anomaly and Kev waved and looked much too fresh and awake. 'You look like shit,' she said.

'Thanks,' I said, forcing a grin onto my sleepy face.

Then it disappeared as Gaz and Tel came around the corner. 'Look, Tel. It's Knobby, our favourite wanker banker.'

One second passed before Tel said, 'Yeah, Knobby.'

Kev took a couple of paces forward and slid himself in front of me. 'Back off, Gaz,' he said.

If I'm honest, I'd never completely believed Kev's face-plant story. How could he possibly flip Gaz? His muscles barely looked strong enough to break into a bag of crisps.

I waited for Gaz to swell himself up like any alpha male animal about to fight. Making himself bigger and more intimidating, but he ducked his head and diverted around us, Tel half a pace behind.

'That's magic,' I said.

***

The morning passed with more litter clearing. Depressingly, we were back clearing new rubbish from the same verges.

Alan called, 'Drinks break,' as I grabbed a sodden copy of the *Evening Standard* and stuffed it into my bag. *Should be in the recycling*, I thought, *not chucked out of a window. How could things get better when people were so lazy?*

I headed over to the van, took the offered bottle of water and found Anomaly and Kev standing looking at her phone. They straightened when they saw me coming.

Shit, I thought. I hadn't expected them to watch the video. Well, not in front of me.

Anomaly smiled, which made me do a quick double take. Kev's face didn't give anything away.

'Come here, Dan,' she said, waving with her other hand.

She turned her phone towards me. 'This you?'

The screen showed an old story on Salamander Capital's website when we announced the deal to sell to KapGroup. The old me stared out from the photograph. I was standing in the same suit I wore to the signing. That same suit now hung, dirty and crumpled, on a bent metal hanger in the hotel wardrobe. As I looked at Yas and my partners Julian, Ezra and Rupert, I wished I could jump into their happy parallel universe and leave my crappy, miserable one behind.

In the photo, I looked ten years younger than the haggard face that had stared back at me this morning in the bathroom mirror. No dark rings under my eyes.

Clean-shaven and smiling, I was a man with a family.

A man with a future. Only heading up.

What a naive idiot I was.

I shook my head as my brain started showing my film of shame again, and managed to force it to pause. That was real progress. 'How did you find me?' I asked.

Anomaly shifted her weight onto one foot and said, 'Really? I tell you I'm great with computers and you think I can't type "Dan exposure Tube" into a search engine. It wasn't rocket science.'

'No, I guess it was easy.'

I had avoided searching. The results could only be bad. Worse if Hugo or Victoria had done it. I hoped they had real friends at school who wouldn't have shown them the video and gloated.

'The others are all in the news today,' she said and snatched her phone back. After a few fast swipes she passed the phone back.

Now the screen showed a website from one of the City newspapers. Yas, Julian, Ezra and Rupert stared at the camera, big smiles on their faces. It was almost identical to the one from the announcement, except that I had been air-brushed out. Like I had never existed.

The headline read, 'Reorganisation at Salamander Capital'.

My heart banged in my chest and I could feel my pulse echoing in my ears. I read on.

Yasmita Kapoor, CEO of KapGroup, announced today that newly acquired Salamander Capital will now be fully integrated into KapGroup. Since the shock arrest and conviction for exposure of disgraced partner Daniel Mendoza, the funds he managed will be taken on by existing KapGroup money managers.

I had to stop. The banging in my ears was deafening and I couldn't get any air into my lungs. *All my work gone.*

My legs wobbled and I nearly fell, but an arm from Kev, forced its way under mine and lifted me. *He's strong*, I thought.

I coughed and wheezed. Sucking air into my deprived lungs.

Nodding my thanks to Kev, I looked at the screen again and carried on reading.

Insiders have told our reporter that the KapGroup plan had always been to find a way to bring the money fully in-house, but the presence of Mendoza at Salamander prevented that. It is claimed that it was only a matter of time and Mendoza's dramatic fall allowed KapGroup to act faster. The other three Salamander Capital directors will continue in their current customer facing roles and will focus on bringing new investment money into KapGroup.

Somehow, the smiles on the faces of Yas and the three people who used to be my friends seemed wider, like they were laughing at me.

Had they planned it behind my back? Was I always to be a sacrificial lamb?

My legs gave way and I landed on both knees. Cold, wet mud seeped into my jeans and I could hear Gaz and Tel laughing.

Every time I thought I had hit the bottom, the world found another wave to squash me further down.

Rather than restart the film of shame, my brain rolled out another treat. This time it was a mental checklist of everything that I had.

Family – *gone.*

Job at Salamander – *gone.*

Career in the City – *gone.*

Personal dignity – *gone.*

Money – *gone.*

Criminal conviction – *tick.*

Five years on the Sex Offender Register – *tick.*

Self-loathing – *tick.*

I thought it was done, but my brain had one last cherry to put on my cake of ruin.

I had received the £2m on signing and Felicity had transferred it away from our joint account. She'd left me with nothing but the Inland Revenue would treat that money as earnt and tax it at 45%.

The maths was easy: 45% of £2m.

I owed HMRC £900,000 that I didn't have.

Chapter 19

Kev pulled me up off my knees, but my legs still wobbled and shook. The pressure from Kev's arm lessened like he was trying to see if I could stand on my own, but he grabbed me again when gravity proved stronger than the rubber of my legs.

'What's wrong?' Anomaly asked.

'I... I owe nearly a million pounds in tax.'

Anomaly's mouth dropped open and Gaz balled his hands into tight fists. They were the last thing I saw as the realisation shut my brain down, like it was an abandoned graveyard – silent but with that nagging sense of fear and doom. I stood there, alive but empty until my brain started to let thoughts and memories dribble in – of course, it chose only the negative and destructive ones. Then more and more, faster and faster, until a raging torrent swept me away like a twig thrown into the broiling white water.

I let it pull me down, into the savage undercurrent that threw me around and smashed me onto the submerged rocks of my wretched self-worth. From school to City, people had told me I was different, I wasn't worthy.

Was I arrogant enough to doubt them all?

No. They must be right. All my hard work and striving had been battling against my true fate. I deserved this.

It was my rightful destiny and I surrendered to it all, sinking deeper and deeper into the darkness, like a limp, lifeless body tossed from a boat and heading to the bottomless black of the ocean.

My descent slowed and I saw a pinprick of light. Not sunshine, not God – anger. The light grew stronger and I swam towards it. At first tentative, weak strokes, then firmer, harder as the light grew and I could feel its radiant warmth. My brain started to pass on what my ears were hearing and the light of my fury grew and surged. Something in my brain flipped, like a massive anger switch and the light burst like a supernova.

'What's up, Knobby? Crying 'cos you're rich?' Gaz said.

The rubber in my legs mutated into steel, every sinew and fibre burned with repressed rage.

I spun on my toes, body language transforming from meek and dejected cowering to upright and strident. Anger burned out of my eyes and mouth.

Gaz and Tel must have seen it as they both took a step back as my right hand balled into a fist and I pulled my arm back, tensing my back and shoulder, winding it all up so that I could unleash a savage blow into Gaz's face.

'Do it! Smash his face in,' my brain screamed and moved my arm.

Not the surging explosion it wanted, but a slow-motion crawl. I frowned as I saw two hands on my bicep, pulling and slowing my arm. Hands stronger than me. I heard Kev's voice in my ear. 'He's not worth it. They'll call it assault and send you back to court.'

He was right. I slowed my arm, unballed my fist and extended my middle finger. It stopped millimetres short of the West Ham United badge on Gaz's chest.

'You... you.' The anger surged around in me, shaking me as I fought to control it and making any sort of coherent speech impossible.

The shock and fear in Gaz's eyes that had pushed him backwards as I exploded towards him vanished. Now he was the big man again and his eyes glittered as he slapped my outstretched hand away and pushed his face up close to mine.

I flinched at the rank smell from his mouth and flying spittle as he said, 'Fucking rich bastard. Get what you deserve.'

There it was, that same old prejudice I had heard from so many shouting the politics of envy. The City is evil. Bankers are evil. You're not allowed to work to improve yourself. Everyone needs to be equally miserable at the bottom.

'So the rich deserve what they get?'

'Fucking right,' Gaz said, pushing forward again.

'Even your beloved West Ham players? They earn much more than me. Are they rich bastards?'

Gaz blinked rapidly. 'What?'

I wasn't sure if he didn't understand my point, or if he thought I was slagging off his team. 'A lot of your team's players earn more than me, but you cheer them on every week.'

'Yeah, but they give one hundred and ten per cent and they're proper working-class, not like you.'

'My dad was a farm labourer and my mum was a cleaner. How does that make me upper-class?'

Gaz blinked again. I guessed it was his default action when he didn't know what to say.

'As for giving one hundred and ten per cent, all they do is kick a ball around.' I paused and looked at Gaz's clothes – grey and red dust stains, a smear of silicone. 'You a builder, Gaz?'

His blinking stopped. 'Yeah. What's it to you?'

'You work at most an eight-hour shift, less breaks?'

He nodded.

'I've worked sixteen hours a day for years and years,' I continued.

'So, you're still a fucking wanker crying over your tax bill. Give me fucking strength.'

'You work cash-in-hand, Gaz? Most builders do.'

The blinking started again and his eyes dropped towards to grass.

'Of course you do. My tax bill…' I did a quick mental sum, 'is about the same as one hundred and fifty people on the average wage. Then there's all the tax my company pays and the salaries of all the employees. You're taking cash payments so you don't have to pay tax and national insurance. I'm paying a huge amount of tax, and you don't contribute your fair share.'

Gaz blinked again, then smiled. 'Least I didn't get my cock out on a train. Pervert.'

There was no point trying and all the fight flooded out of me, my shoulders slumped and I turned away.

'Yeah, Knobby,' Tel said.

***

Tel's 'yeah, Knobby' rattled around in my head as I lay on my hotel bed. The day had given up and the night stole into the corners of my room. My brain took the hint and replayed my darker memories.

Gaz and Tel didn't care about how much tax I paid or how many people I'd employed. I'd always be a rich bastard. Even now, when I had less than nothing. Always easier to bitch and moan than strive and work and take risks. But where had it got me? All that time with my kids I'd never get back, all those hours in the empty office being the best I could be.

I could have done nothing and been better off.

But no one forced me to work. It was a drive from within. And I'd enjoyed the work, the successes. Each day making the funds grow. Increasing the value of the investment each company or government pension fund made. Sure, I earnt money, but the more each pension fund grew, the more there was for people to live off when they retired. People didn't see it – they thought the banks kept the money for themselves.

But all my thoughts weren't getting me anywhere. I couldn't go back and have my time again. I couldn't hit a global reset switch and revisit every decision with the benefit of hindsight.

I couldn't go back to Bank Station and not get on that train. I couldn't push the Tube away.

If only I could, then I would still have everything I had worked for. That thought pushed me into another downward spiral, like I was on the devil's helter-skelter. At the bottom, I crashed into the thought that had been lurking there ever since Anomaly had shown me the article with Yas and my ex-partners.

This wasn't only me losing – others were benefiting from my fall.

Felicity had the kids and all my money. Yas and my ex-partners had my share of the business, my share of the sale. She didn't need to pay me what was due.

It stung like a slap across the face.

If they benefited from the waitress's actions, was it by accident or was it all planned?

I could picture them all plotting and whispering. Agreeing on the details, putting the finishing touches to their plan to destroy the outsider. To destroy me.

Was I paranoid? Or was it my years of being inferior making me grasp for an easy out and find any way that I could blame someone else for my failings. Avoid blaming myself. Allow me to whine *'It's not fair'*?

Maybe? But my brain let in one memory that I had agonised over so many times. I was back on the train, the waitress mouthing the word sorry, dipping her head and slithering away.

If she was sorry, then why do it?

Unless she was paid to do it. Paid by someone who would gain from my destruction.

The more I thought about it, the more it made sense. What was the old saying? 'Just because you're paranoid, doesn't mean they're not out to get you.'

I faced a fifty–fifty choice – believe that I deserved it all and spend the rest of my life alone and penniless, or fight to get it all back.

'Fight,' I shouted into my hotel room.

Chapter 20

Follow the money.

It's what they always say. And *my* £98m, even split between my three ex-partners would be more than enough to motivate them to set me up, steal my part of the firm and discard me. It was as good a place to start as any.

None of my ex-partners had taken any of my calls since *the Tube*, but Julian's assistant, Sam, had always been friendly when we'd chatted about cricket and rugby. He might get me in.

Definitely worth spending some of my precious pay-as-you-go credit to find out.

I picked up my phone and dialled the number. It rang once before a voice said, 'Salamander Capital, how can I help you?'

'Julian Hall, please.' I knew that Julian never answered his phone and I hoped that Sam was at his desk.

The phone clicked silent as the call was transferred and then rang once again before it was answered.

'Julian Hall's office, this is Sam.'

'Hi, Sam, this is Dan.'

From the tiny gasp and the following silence, I guessed that Sam had recognised my voice and didn't need to ask 'Dan who?'.

'Dan,' he said. 'Er… how're things?'

It's what he had always asked me when we met. A default, polite enquiry, not a serious question. Not *'what the hell do you what?'*. I laughed and lied. 'Fine. Look I need to see Julian, Ezra and Rupert. Can you schedule a meeting?'

He went quiet again. He'd be chewing his lip like he always did when he had some sort of internal debate going on.

'Please. For old time's sake,' I said, trying to sound upbeat and not begging.

'I don't know…' he said.

I waited for the decisive no, but seconds ticked past and then I heard him tap on his keyboard. 'They're all in a meeting tomorrow until 4:30, then another at 5. I'll put you in at 4:30, but I can't promise any more than that.'

***

Community Payback had been two days of graffiti cleaning. The mechanical repetition of brush to bucket, brush to wall, scrub, repeat, became second nature and didn't require any conscious input from my brain. It let my mind run free, and even though it still delighted in running the film of shame, I was fighting back. The viewings now had gaps between them. Sometimes I even managed to shut a viewing down before it finished. Julian, Ezra and Rupert started to take over as I obsessed about what they had done to me.

Alan's van had coughed and spluttered around the multiple roadworks that clogged the route back to the drop-off point, so I hadn't had time to get back to the hotel and change into my suit. Walking up Cheapside, I tried to brush the mud from the knees of my jeans. I got a small, fine dust cloud from each knee, but I couldn't shift the stains. These days I was more Poundland than Armani, but the dirty clothes were like an invisibility cloak from the City workers. I was a builder or workman to them, no one of interest. No one in a video about a banker on the Tube.

That didn't mean I wanted to see my reflection in the glass-fronted shops and offices. It was best not to add another visual image for my brain to append to the film of shame.

As soon as my dirty left shoe hit the shining marble of the inside of Salamander Capital's reception, Colin took a step towards me. 'Building services at the rear. Don't use this entrance again,' he said.

'Alright, Col,' I said.

He did a double take, this time seeing my face and not my clothes. 'Dan. You can't…' he held his arms out wide, like he wanted to shepherd me straight back out.

'I have a meeting with Julian, Ezra and Rupert at four thirty,' I countered.

'Really?' He couldn't hide his surprise. 'Are you sure?'

'Of course, I'm sure,' I said, trying to revive some of my old sense of belonging here.

Colin's frown told me that he wasn't convinced, but he backed away and pointed me towards the reception desk.

I walked over and waited as Maddie dealt with a group of wealthy Italians. The contrast of my clothes to their immaculate suits could not have been bigger. I watched her beam and nod. Her eyes seemed to bathe each of them in the warm yellow of the evening sun. The Italians took the offered passes and headed to the entrance gate.

Maddie looked up at me. Her eyes narrowed and became as welcoming as a Chernobyl winter.

I rushed out another 'I've got a meeting' and she had no option other than to check. A single manicured red fingernail tapped a couple of keys and she frowned her disappointment.

'OK. Someone will be down for you.' A flurry of manicured taps brought the small printer next to her to life. 'Your pass,' she added, passing me the printout.

Settling into a visitor's chair, I waited. And waited. At 5:15, I decided to chase Maddie for the third time but before I could, I saw Vardah step out of a lift, nod in acknowledgement and come towards me.

We had always worked well together, had a bit of a laugh over tedious contracts. She looked the same – same suit, same hair, unaffected by the past few days. Her eyes scanned my dirty work clothes, but seemed more curious than hostile and I relaxed some of the tension in my shoulders. She even held out her hand, and as I took it, the contrast between her soft office hand and my dry and work-roughened hand added another reminder of my fall.

'I'm sorry, Dan, but no one is going to make your meeting.' She pursed her lips and shrugged. 'There's nothing I can do.'

'Not your fault, and thanks for coming down and not getting Col to chuck me out.'

***

What am I going to do now? I thought as I stood outside Salamander Capital. The direct approach didn't work, calling their mobiles hadn't worked.

I tried calling Felicity and listened to it ring then moved my finger to end the call before the voicemail clicked in.

Shoving my phone back into my pocket, I headed to the bakers, bought an all-day breakfast baguette, and went in search of a friend.

Jerry was stretched out on his bench at St Peter Cheap, and he opened his eyes and spun himself upright as my shadow crossed his face. 'Dan, what happened to you?'

'Long story,' I said.

'My diary has an open slot,' he said, although the last words were muffled by the huge bite he took from the defenceless end of the baguette.

Joining him on the seat, I gave him a highly edited rundown of my last few days. The story lasted as long as the baguette.

Jerry wiped his hand over his mouth and said, 'That's a crazy story. I'm sorry, man.'

I shrugged. Resigned. Defeated.

'You OK for cash?' Jerry asked and waved at another bench in the garden. 'The West Wing is free. You can always move in with me.'

I laughed the first real laugh for days and for a second, I forgot. We were two mates chatting on a park bench.

Jerry closed his eyes and let the sun rest on his face. He seemed to have gone to sleep. I sat in silence and watched a couple of pigeons pluck up the courage to dart in and grab some spilt crumbs from Jerry's baguette.

He opened his eyes. 'You can't go after the firm, 'cos they'll roll out loads of expensive lawyers and bury you in cost and time delaying tactics. That ain't going to work for you, so you need a more personal approach. Two tactics would work: Divide and conquer, and ambush.'

My head spun towards him. 'What?'

'Military brain,' he said, tapping his finger on his temple. 'There are four people who could have stitched you up. Julian, Ezra, Rupert as an inside job, and Yas as an outsider. Course, some or all of them could have got together. You need to get something to apply pressure with, then sniff out the weakest link, ambush them and get them to crack.'

'Makes sense.'

'Or I can steal a chainsaw or nail gun, storm the office and wreak bloody havoc. Hack bits off each of them until they confess.'

My mouth gaped open.

'You should see your face. Priceless,' he said.

The glint in his eyes made me think he wasn't completely joking and I wondered what he had done to survive in combat and if he slept with nightmares and his own film of shame.

'Find some leverage and apply pressure,' Jerry said.

But what form could the pressure take?

There might have been all sorts of emails, calls and texts. The cops could prove something, but they wouldn't try for me. Wouldn't even believe me.

You got what you deserved, my brain said.

I shook the thought away. What I needed was access to computer records, mobile phone traces, call logs, bank statements plus everything else.

I had nothing.

Chapter 21

Jerry and I chatted for about an hour and hatched a crude plan. It wasn't based on proof or evidence, only on shock and pity.

My target was Rupert. He was the youngest partner and crucially, the softest. He was kind, great fun to be around and we'd shared many an enjoyable meeting and meal.

He was a partner because of his amazing network of friends and more importantly, wealthy friends of a friend. He could get us in front of a different league of investor. The sort of people the rest of us could only dream of accessing. Rupert would open the doors and arrange the meetings. We'd do our pitch and then we'd leave it to Rupert to talk and soothe fears. He knew the right buttons to press for each person. With some it was greed, some craved something new, others feared missing out. Whatever it was, Rupert knew how to find it. His failing was that in meetings he always went along with the loudest, strongest voice. Usually Julian. No real input of his own. No real ideas.

He was the easiest to isolate.

So, I waited on Gutter Lane and the time ticked by. He usually left between seven and eight in the evening, heading to a bar or restaurant to meet a client or prospect. When he wasn't at work, he was still working.

I tensed and listened every time the large dark-grey roller door next to me started to move. A few months ago, he got himself a shiny, shouty AC Cobra replica with vivid blue paint and no roof. He only drove it on sunny, dry days. Like today.

His car was loud, so most times as the door jerked and started to rise, the lack of the deep exhaust note bouncing off the walls made it obvious that it wasn't Rupert. I watched a stream of silent electric Teslas, or purring luxury saloons leave.

Only once was the approaching car noisy enough for me to drop down and peer under the rising door, but I saw the red nose of a 1970s Ferrari and lost interest.

The gate twitched again and started to move. The booming, reverberating noise of a car grew louder. Dropping down, I could see large chrome bumpers with the number plate '1 RUP'.

The car idled as the gate rolled higher, then Rupert blipped the throttle, maybe signalling his impatience to get moving, or simply enjoying the pulsating echoes of noise.

When the gate got about a metre above the ground, I leapt forward and rolled under it. The nose of the car would have hidden me from Rupert sitting at the wheel. I crawled along the passenger side of the car, careful not to get too close to the heat radiating from the massive chromed exhaust that came out of the front of the car and passed along and under the car's door.

I jumped up and grabbed for where I thought the door handle would be. My fingers only found blue paint. Then I remembered when Rupert first showed us the car, and his long, detailed spiel about the purity of lines of the Cobra's body and that outside door handles were sacrilege.

Side windows must also be a sin since the car didn't have any, but it made leaning in and yanking the door handle nestling on the inside of the passenger's door easy. The door popped open and I jumped in, slamming it behind me and grabbing for the seat belt. Partly to make it harder for him to try and push me out, partly in case he panicked and floored the accelerator and sent us flying through the door and onto the road.

Rupert's eyes were wide open, his mouth a round O. His arms came up in front of his body in some form of defensive gesture like he thought he was going to get mugged. His body relaxed for a second as he recognised me and his brain must have told him, 'It's only Dan'.

Then his brain must have changed emphasis, 'It's *Dan*!!' and his eyes flew wider open and his right hand started to scramble for his door handle.

I spun in my seat, my right hand reaching up and pushing down on Rupert's shoulder. My left hand snaked around in front of my stomach, my fingers mimicking a litter-picker as they slid over Rupert's left bicep. I squeezed until Rupert yelped in pain and my fingers nearly met.

'Relax, Rupert. We need a little chat.'

***

I got Rupert to reverse back into the car park, and although any space would have done, he parked bang in the centre of his allocated place. The car's engine throbbed in the confined space.

'Kill the engine,' I said.

Rupert turned the key and the echoing throb was replaced by the clicks and ticks of the car cooling. It was the perfect place to talk, free of distractions and nosey passers-by.

Rupert's eyes narrowed into a suspicious glare and he rubbed at his arm where my fingers had been.

'Why did you do it?' I asked.

'Julian said we shouldn't go to the meeting and he'd send Vardah instead.'

'Not missing the meeting.' I could hear some of my festering resentment seeping into my voice and Rupert's eyes widened again. *Good.* I let some more out as I said, 'Why did you set me up?'

His eyes widened again, and I dropped a hand onto his knee.

'Why did you *destroy* me?' My fingers tightened and wormed into his leg as I said the word destroy. Rupert yelped and tried to back away.

'What? I didn't... wouldn't.'

His eyes pleaded. He looked more like a wounded puppy than a cunning master criminal. Not that I totally convinced myself that Rupert had planned the whole thing. He was a follower, not a leader, but he could have acted as an agent for one of the others. Done all the smoothing and soothing, all the running around, brokered the deal.

'So, who did?' I squeezed deeper into his leg.

Rupert jumped away from me and I heard the seat belt's safety lock click and stop him disappearing backwards out of the car.

'I don't know anything. We're mates – I'd never stitch you up.'

One more look into his puppy eyes and my anger evaporated. There was no mistaking the warmth in them. I loosened my grip on his knee and patted it. 'Sorry, Rup. I know.'

He relaxed back into his seat, but I crumpled in on myself, my head dropping into my hands and the images of the waitress screaming 'pervert' on the Tube blinded me.

Rupert's hand touched my shoulder, but not with the firmness and aggression that I had shown him. His was soft and caring. 'It did seem way out of character when... you know, the train... What happened?'

'I had one drink, but it felt like ten. I felt pissed. Then on the train, the waitress came up to me–'

'The waitress? What, from the party?'

'Yeah, I'm sure she spiked my drink. Then on the train, she backed me into the corner. I tried to push her off, but she was strong.' I screwed my eyes tight shut to try and diminish the clarity of the images in my head as the whole thing replayed, scene by agonising scene. I could see my missed opportunities to escape if only I could have focused and seized them. 'Then she hit me and grabbed my penis. By the time I knew what was happening, she was backing away and the passengers were screaming.'

I heard Rupert blow out a long breath. 'Shiiiit,' he said.

I could hear his concern and sympathy in the way he dragged out the end of the word, and his 'it could have been me' realisation.

'She said sorry as she stepped away. That bit goes around and around in my head. I've never seen her before, so why pick me? If she was just some weirdo out to get anyone, then why say sorry? There's got to be more to it.'

'So, you think someone paid her to spike your drink and ruin you.'

I lifted my head and banged it. *Stupid, stupid, stupid.* Thankfully the images stopped and a little of my old clarity returned. 'There's enough money at stake.'

'I feel for you, Dan.'

'So why didn't you answer any of my calls? I needed a friend.'

Rupert looked away. 'I'm really sorry, mate, but as soon as the video went viral, someone recognised you. Everything kicked off at work and I got a call from Hannah saying that we mustn't talk to you. It was all about damage limitation and distancing Salamander and KapGroup from you.'

Typical corporate legal thinking – it was all about protecting shareholder value.

I was toxic – fit only to be cast adrift in a neat package onto a sea of humiliation and pain.

Chapter 22

Today's Community Payback was more litter duty, and I attached myself to Anomaly and Kev, clicking and picking a few paces from them, hoping for inclusion in their group of two by association and familiarity.

We were close to the Heathrow flight path that came over London and approached the airport from the East. My little Community Payback group would seem like tiny ants to the people in the planes. Every time I glanced up, the stream of planes was all neatly spaced and shuffled into their approved landing order. They looked way too close together for one to land safely and taxi, and then get out of the way of the next before it landed. But it must be safe, otherwise the airport would be buried under a pile of crashed planes.

The sun caught on the silver nose of one of the planes and reflected a bright flash of light. It tripped my mind back to happier times, getting off a plane in the Caribbean and being hit by the heat and the promise of a welcoming rum punch on the beach.

The planes I could see were arriving into Heathrow, but somewhere to the West, another queue of planes were taxiing, waiting their turn to settle, and then accelerate and blast their lucky travellers towards their far-flung destination.

What I wouldn't give to be on a plane, looking down on a different version of me. A different life, full of places I could go. Not locked in the UK by my sentence. Technically the law allowed me to travel abroad during my sentence, but my parole officer had emphasised the words 'only in exceptional circumstances'. The police were less bothered about my sex offender status. All I had to do was tell them I was going. I could be some disgusting paedophile heading off to shatter children's lives, but the law didn't restrict me. Out of sight out of mind. Someone else's problem.

A plastic bottle of sour milk bounced on the ground near me and broke my thoughts.

'Get on with your work, Knobby,' Gaz said.

Tel aimed a second bottle at me but it fell no nearer to me than Gaz's attempt.

'Your aim is shit, like your superstars.' I dipped my hand into my rubbish bag and felt for the paper. As soon as my hand touched it, I pulled it out and unfurled the headline I had seen when I picked it up: *Wasteful Hammers ship six.*

'West Ham lost six–nil last night. Did your players give one hundred and ten per cent? Did they earn their salaries?'

Gaz went red in the face and started clenching and unclenching his fists. He stole a glance towards the van, but saw Alan watching. A vein started throbbing in his neck. 'I'll fuckin' have you, Knobby.'

***

I'd slipped further along the line of pickers, and away from Gaz and Tel as the afternoon dragged by. The monotony and simplicity of the job gave me way too much time to think and rewatch my film of shame.

I tried to divert my thoughts towards proving my innocence and rescuing my family and life, but every time I came up against my self-doubt. It was like a huge metal door decorated with ornate engravings of my failures. There wasn't a handle and pushing the door got me nowhere. In the middle of it, the word FATE stood proud of the surface.

Had I become what I deserved? What fate had always intended was my natural position? Or was it all a direct consequence of every decision and action I had made? Whatever the reason, it didn't change where I was.

Why would the world like me when I didn't even like myself?

But as much as the world pushed down on me, some stubborn streak in me resisted and rebelled. There's no such thing as fate. I could change my world. Like I had after Kat's accident.

But it was a long way back. Too far to plan the complete path. I'd have to take the first steps and see what happened.

I had crossed out Rupert. Julian and Ezra were my next targets.

'We're done for the day,' Alan said as he sat in the van's open door and waved us over to deposit our bags and litter-pickers.

My phone rang and stopped me dead. Was it Felicity? No.

'Oh. Hi, Paul,' I said, smiling that he had called, but not managing to keep my sadness that it wasn't my wife out of my voice.

'Sorry to disappoint you, Dad.'

'No. No.' Why did simple things have to turn into arguments? 'I'm really pleased to hear from you. How're things?'

'Same. Wanted to check on you? You need anything?'

Other than a new life? A chance to settle into his spare room rather than my crappy hotel room would be nice, but I didn't want to ask. He and Suzie had talked with such enthusiasm a few weeks ago about the transformation they had planned for the room. Gym-come-yoga-room they had called it. I'd wait until I had no other choice.

'No. I've got everything,' I said.

The obvious lie and the sheer enormity of the underlying truth made the line go silent. Once we were past trivial pleasantries, we'd have to talk about the real details. I'd have to convince him I was framed.

'Dan, Dan. We're all waiting,' Alan called.

'Look, Paul, I'm at Community Payback so I can't talk now. Can I call you later?'

'I've got meetings then dinner – usual Friday, but I'm at home tomorrow.'

'Call you then.'

No way was I going to carry on a call in the van with Gaz and Tel listening in.

***

The van's seats squeaked as it chugged along the busy road, surrounded by buses and cars on a typical London afternoon. It stopped at the usual metal lamp post that acted as our drop-off point. Anomaly and Kev walked a couple of paces away towards the bus stop with adverts for the NHS. Someone had smashed the glass side of the bus stop, and the safety glass had shattered into a million glittering little cubes. Before, I would have assumed it had been done as a mindless act of petty vandalism. Now, I could see that it could have been someone banging out their frustration at their life. Someone searching for an affirmation that they still had the power to change something in their world. Even if it was destructive, it proved they existed.

Anomaly's boot crunched onto the broken glass and she stopped, turned and seemed to wait for me. Kev didn't appear to notice the glass.

This time Anomaly smiled when I said, 'Coffee? I'm paying.'

I might've been buying my friends, but it was a small price to pay.

We headed towards the parade of shops, all the same global brands you saw everywhere. A small newsagent was tucked between the Starbucks and the McDonald's. They leaned in on the shop, like two corporate giants trying to squeeze out the hard-working local. I didn't turn into the Starbucks, but headed around the corner to a small cosy-looking coffee shop I'd seen that morning.

The owner smiled, all teeth and big glasses and welcomed us in. 'Get yourselves settled, I'll come over.' It was nice to meet someone who cared, rather than the disinterested shift-workers from the big chains.

We chose the comfy-looking sofa and armchairs that were pushed against a neat brick wall. The rest of the place had warm deep-red walls covered in all sorts of photos. Not a bought-in package, but genuine local photos of the cafe over the years and smiling faces. I peered at one and saw a proud couple with a little girl between them with teeth and big glasses. Mum and Dad's place, now run by their daughter.

The only other customers were a young couple busily exploring each other's mouths while their hot chocolate steamed forgotten on their table. We ordered and I splurged some of my dwindling funds on a blueberry muffin for me, a chocolate one for Kev and an apple turnover for Anomaly. The muffin was pure heaven: light, fluffy and gorgeous. The coffee was dark and bitter. Perfect. All of it was better and cheaper than Starbucks, but the place was nearly empty and Starbucks had been busy. It made no sense to me that people bought brand over quality.

We enjoyed our food, laughing at the crumbs escaping each other's mouths. It felt more natural. Not three musketeers yet, but not two guarded people wary of the stranger. Progress.

The couples' drinks had cooled and they were oblivious to anything outside of the joy of their own entwined cuddle. The girl's hand dropped onto the guy's upper thigh. A casual, relaxed gesture, not with any intent, but it flashed the waitress's face into my brain.

It must have shown on my face as Anomaly frowned. 'You alright, Dan?'

'Flashback,' I said.

Her face softened and seemed to understand, like she had her own version of the film of shame, that replayed and haunted her. It didn't feel right to pry, so I decided to wait until she was comfortable enough to share. Instead, I talked them through my failed ambush of Rupert and looked at the cold dregs of my coffee.

'What ya gonna do?' Kev asked.

I shrugged. My warehouse of workable ideas had cobwebs covering the shelves and a quick mental stocktake generated a total count of zero ideas.

Anomaly twisted the right side of her lower lip into her mouth and behind her teeth. I could see the cogs whirring as she churned something over. Finally, she stopped and reached for her coffee cup. She sipped the liquid and grimaced.

'Were you set-up for real?' she said.

'Of course.'

'If I find you're lying, I'll chop it off and make sure you can't do it again.'

She delivered her words in a flat tone. No histrionics or drama. The steel in her eyes made me want to cover the threatened area with my hands, but I stopped myself in case the action was misinterpreted.

'I'm still connected, despite what my community order says. And you know I love a bit of revenge,' she said.

I shook my head. 'You can't risk it for me.'

Anomaly looked at Kev. They seemed to hold a silent conversation and Kev nodded.

'Look, I told you, the only reason I got caught was my friend telling the cops. I'm not going to get caught.'

'Why would you risk it for me?'

They both laughed.

'We're not in it for love. We want a cut of any money you get back,' she said. 'And some expenses to tide us over.'

Chapter 23

Anomaly interlinked her fingers and pushed her hands forward, palms away from her face and cracked out some of the stiffness. Hours on the keyboard always made her hands and shoulders ache and grumble at the repetitive actions. She'd rescued her tiny desk from the bin store of her block of flats. A perfectly good wood effect IKEA item, but surplus to someone's requirements and easier to leave it in the bin store than have the hassle of an eBay auction, with time wasters and God knows who turning up and looking around your flat for the entry fee of their winning £5 bid.

She'd lost her job after her conviction, but unlike Dan, her fall started and ended there. She'd been careful with her money, and had enough to see her safely through the year before she needed to look for work. Even if she helped Dan only get back a small fraction of his £98m, the fraction of a fraction would do very nicely.

'What you think of Dan?' she said to the Alan Shearer poster on her wall. It showed him smiling, wheeling away from the St James' Park faithful having scored yet another goal and sending the black-and-white-striped Toon Army into ecstasy.

She nodded. *You're right, Al. Wait and see*, she told herself. Wait and see what her searches unearthed.

Her laptop screen had blanked at the temporary inactivity, and Anomaly zigzagged her finger over the mouse pad to wake it up. Her screen filled with a close up of a Jimmy Choo shoe. Pink, high-heeled and glittery. Real Jimmy, she knew. From the man himself, and not the corporate giant that used his name and spat out shoes, bags and even perfume.

Her searches had started with simple background checks, searches using Dan's name, scanning for the most interesting stories and drilling down. Down far enough to find lots of articles with Dan and Salamander. Back to stories calling it career suicide when the partners set out on their own.

She had backed up out of his work, and followed his personal life. Photos with his wife, Felicity, and the kids on holiday. Smiling pink faces of Hugo and Victoria making snow angels in France, or covered in sun-cream in Antigua. Then she followed another set of stories and it got bleaker. Stories of a tragic fall down the stairs and a funeral for his first wife, Kat. Dan standing in the rain with his son, Paul, in a black tie and school shorts. A police report of a car crash with grandparents rushing to see their first grandchild and never making it.

It looked like Dan had survived Kat's death and fought for a future for him and Paul. She found that they'd moved to London and Dan got his first chance to trial a junior traders job.

She looked up and stared out of the window. He'd been put through the wringer back then and again now. How can some people be lucky enough to sail through life unblemished and others have to fight and battle for every breath?

Now Dan was back at the bottom, but did he deserve it? That's what she was going to find out.

Anomaly flicked to an open document window and made some notes under the heading *Dan – Family*. Paranoia of losing her work made her press Save twice, then she scrolled down until she got to the name Julian Hall.

She did all the same sorts of searches she had run on Dan, followed different paths and stories and added notes as she found anything interesting.

Then she repeated it all with Ezra.

Her document grew as she added notes and names of people who caught her interest. Hours later, her eyes were gritty and her shoulders and fingers ached, but she had the information she needed.

***

Anomaly stopped at the door of her block of flats and checked her heart rate and fitness tracker. A good 5k run, not her best time, but she was aiming more for consistency of pace than personal best. And it always cleared her mind and reset her body after a long session on her laptop.

After a quick shower, she put on her favourite leggings and Motorhead T-shirt, dumped a glass of water next to the laptop, sat and tucked her right foot under her left knee. Her running coach told her it was terrible for her knee, but it was so comfortable.

She repeated her finger crutches and settled over the keyboard. Time to go a bit deeper and darker. She logged on to a hidden server, then another. Jumping countries and jurisdictions, swimming under the radar. She dived deeper, past the restrictions the court had placed on her. Not that they'd check. Her one previous minor offence didn't warrant the budget needed for any type of active monitoring of her.

It was strange that for all the years that Dan and his partners had worked together, all their socialising seemed to have been work-based. Restaurants and hotels, mostly with clients. Sometimes Felicity had come to the meals, but they never met at each other's homes. Dan only knew the areas the others lived in. Hampstead for Julian. He got vaguer as the distances grew. North London for Ezra. Essex for Rupert.

Time to find out the details. The next website she visited allowed the online searching of the electoral register. Anomaly liked her targets' names when she saw the results. Not so common as to generate hundreds of matches. Each one generated a nice manageable list that she cross-checked with social media and other searches to find the one she wanted.

She shook her head as she worked. Always amazed how much personal detail people gave away online: a photo of a car with the registration number showing allowed an easy lead to the DVLA database, photos posted of them watching school sports with the location of the photo automatically saved and available if you knew how, tweets about birthday parties. Everything and anything casually tossed onto a social media platform without any thought how someone might use it against them.

Each time she found something, she would flip to her document in other window and add the details. And press Save twice. At the end, she had home addresses, names of partners, kids and pets. Mobile numbers, school names, favourite restaurants, cars driven, the garages they used, birthdays, national insurance numbers, credit scores.

A good starting point even if there wasn't anything definitive. She'd found affluent, successful lives with all the trappings of success. The more you have, the bigger your data footprint. And these guys had plenty.

Did it prove Dan was set-up? No, but it also didn't prove he wasn't. For some people there was never too much money or too many things. Even though Dan's partners had more than most, they wouldn't compare themselves with normal people. Maybe the partners craved more, maybe someone they knew was rubbing their noses in the dirt. Maybe having last year's anything was too much to bear.

It was way past midnight when she decided to call it a night. The notes were encrypted and saved onto a removable data pen. She scoured the laptop of her search history and backed out of all the steps she had taken to hide her true location and identity. She felt safe and secure from the risk of getting caught, let alone convicted, but that didn't mean she was careless enough to email Kev the addresses.

Instead, she pulled a single sheet of paper out of her printer and strolled into the kitchen. After picking up her chopping board, she put the paper on top of it and wrote out the three names and corresponding addresses. The board and single sheet would ensure there was no involuntary copy of the addresses written into a pad of paper by the pressure of her pen denting the sheet below, especially when the board would be straight into the dishwasher.

She folded the paper over and over until it was small enough to fit into her palm easily.

Chapter 24

The Saturday morning sunshine leaked through and around the threadbare curtains of my hotel room. It brightened the brown wallpaper to seem merely unpleasant, rather than its night-time despair. No community service for two days and I didn't think that I would survive being locked in this room that long.

All the negatives remained, but even if I wasn't on the up, at least I wasn't still falling. There was a good chance that I could reopen the lines of communication with Paul. Anomaly and Kev were promising to help, and I'd managed to block out some more showings of my film of shame.

I knew my next big issue was facing the people I knew and loved. I had to re-establish contact with Felicity and the kids, but that was the worse bit. How could I face them and defend myself? It was asking so much of them to take a leap of faith and believe in me when the courts and social media told them I was guilty.

Since the Tube, the people I talked to usually had one of two reactions. Either pity and contempt, like the police and social workers who looked at me like I was damaged, or the hatred and anger, like Gaz and Tel. I understood both. I recognised my reactions to the others on the Sex Offender Register. I would have thought the same about me. Most of the time when I looked in the mirror, I still did.

Other than Bertie the dog, only Vardah, Anomaly, Kev and Rupert, even after my failed ambush, had looked at me like I was approaching normal.

I had a choice: a weekend hiding away in my hotel room, or face the people I cared most for.

***

Dishonoured

The metal gates to Hugo and Victoria's school were open and the car park was dominated by huge black and grey cars. A normal-sized car wouldn't do here, everyone wanted bigger, higher tanks that were too big for the parking spaces and rammed with complex and expensive four-wheel drive systems. The most taxing terrain most of these cars would ever see would be the King's Road, Chelsea or a grass car park at Royal Ascot races with the back packed full of hampers and champers.

The long walk from the hotel passed with me bouncing between looking forward to a hug from the kids and paranoia that they would run from me. Squeezing past one of the tanks that the owner had parked across the pedestrian entrance to the playing fields, I recognised the private number plate on the car. The owner strutted around like they weren't simply *entitled* to do whatever they wanted, they *deserved* it.

I walked past the fence segregating the Head's house from the rest of the school and as I skirted the uniform brick wall of the new science block, I could hear shouts, cheers and the occasional whistle. Saturday afternoon was for sports and both my kids would be playing football. Or a kind of heavily sanitised and controlled version of football that was sympathetic to eight- and six-year-old bones and stamina. The younger years played on a normal pitch split into three separate games with small portable goals on each side and lines of tape to mark the touchline and provide a walkway for parents.

On the game furthest away, I could see Hugo chasing around after a ball, socks around his ankles. He'd inherited Felicity's colouring and mud splattered his pink legs and knees. Felicity watched from behind one goal in her blue wellies and matching Barbour wax-cotton coat. She kept pushing a loose lock of black hair behind her ear as she chatted with a couple of other mothers.

I didn't fancy approaching Felicity when she wasn't on her own. It needed to be in private; I didn't need more public humiliation.

Victoria was in the game nearest to me, her dark hair half in and half out of a ponytail. The ball came to her and she sent it flying towards the other end of the pitch and then seemed to lose interest. She skipped a couple of strides and jumped, both feet together, into a puddle, giggling at the mud splattered across the grass and up her football boots.

'Good kick, Vick-ster,' I said.

She looked up from the mud. 'Daddy!' she yelled and launched herself at me. I dropped down to scoop her up and into the biggest and best cuddle in the world. I pulled her close and rained kisses on the top of her head. She squeezed back and it unblocked all of my self-control. Tears ran down my face and I sobbed and sobbed. I had one arm under Victoria so she used it like a seat, her little arms stretched around my neck.

Victoria lifted her head away from mine. 'Don't cry, Daddy,' she said and then replayed my own saying. 'I'll kiss it better.' She planted a big wet kiss on my cheek.

'You shouldn't be here,' a woman said near me.

'Clear out. We don't want your sort near our kids.' A man's voice, hard and aggressive.

I looked around me, wiping my face with my spare hand.

About five parents had formed a tight knot in front of me. Raw anger and fear in their eyes, hatred in the curls of the mouths, hostile jabbing fingers.

'Fucking pervert,' one of them shouted.

'He used the F-word, Daddy,' Victoria said as she frowned her disapproval.

I took a step back to try and shelter Victoria, looking for the best route to safety, but they kept coming.

More heads turned to see what the fuss was about and I seemed to be a magnet, pulling them all towards me. Next to Hugo's pitch, Felicity turned and her gloved hand moved to cover her mouth. Her eyes couldn't hide her shock. Hugo started running towards me.

I heard rapid, short blasts on a whistle. 'Stop, stop,' the voice of Mr Evans, the geography teacher called. He was in a Welsh rugby jersey and shorts, and running towards me. His face wrinkled into a frown as deep as a gorge in his beloved Brecon Beacons as he switched from football referee to peacekeeper and stepped between me and the angry mob.

'Please, please,' he said, 'let's all calm down and give them some space.' He took a pace towards the parents, but they didn't yield.

'Get that bloody kiddie fiddler away from our children.' This was from Frank, father of one of Victoria's friends. A family we had been on holiday with, but all that was gone as he snarled and tried to get past Mr Evans' arm. 'Jesus, my Katie stayed at their house.'

The whistle blew again, long and hard, then Mr Evans bellowed. 'Enough'.

It silenced the pack and, like a form of muscle memory, they reverted to obedient school children and took a step back.

'Thank you. Now I suggest you go and look after your own children and stop frightening Victoria.'

With some reluctance, they turned and started moving, muttering and complaining. Hostile glares were thrown at me as they went.

Much more vicious than Gaz and Tel could ever be. My so-called friends.

***

Mr Evans had shrugged a 'no problem' when he let me lift Hugo into a big hug. I felt if not complete, then almost like it had never happened. Hugo in one arm, Victoria in the other walking off the field, their muddy boots rubbing against my legs. Only this time, my jeans with their stained knees didn't get any dirtier.

Felicity followed behind, having not said a word to me, but having the grace not to prise the kids from me in full view of the group of hostile parents.

'Take a few minutes in my classroom,' Mr Evans said and led us along the familiar corridors with pictures of school teams mixed with fire extinguishers and the latest batch of finger painting.

In the classroom, I sat with one child on each knee. Not on the little chairs which I doubted would take our combined weight, but on one of the hexagonal desks. The room wasn't so different to my school, with the map of the world, and the ageless water cycle diagram with sea and clouds and hills. Except that everything was newer and in better condition, and in my day, there wouldn't have been a whole section dedicated to graphs of the carbon emissions of the different counties.

Felicity sat at Mr Evans' desk, frowning and rubbing her hands, looking like a worried teacher eager for the class to be over. She didn't say anything as I chatted with the kids and caught up on their days, cuts and bruises and who said what.

'Why can't Daddy come home, Mummy?' Victoria said, her voice full of confusion.

'It's complicated, darling,' Felicity said, and was saved from any embarrassment by Mr Evans returning. 'Mr and Mrs Mendoza, the Head would like a word in her study. I'll take Hugo and Victoria to tea.'

The kids jumped off my knee, sold on the idea of cakes and biscuits.

I watched them go and made no move. I needed the time with Felicity and the head could wait. 'Felicity, please, let me explain–'

Her head shook from side to side and she wouldn't look at me. 'No, Dan, I know what you're going to say. I heard it again and again on all those messages you left. Give me time.'

'Felicity, you know I wouldn't.'

'Did you have a drink?'

'Only one like I promised. Someone must have spiked it.'

She stood up and headed for the head's study so quickly that I had to jog after her.

'Darling, please.'

At the study door, she stopped and knocked. 'Not here,' she said before pushing the door open and disappearing. I stood for a second doing a good impression of a goldfish with wide eyes and my mouth open before I followed her inside.

Chapter 25

Kev walked along the wide pavement as it curved up a gentle hill. He was sure that he was on the right road, but there weren't any house numbers, just long, complicated names. He hadn't seen the name he wanted and kept walking. It took ten or so paces to go from the driveway of one large house to the next. Every house had more than one car to decorate its drive. A lot of Porsche and Mercedes cars, all looking new and shiny.

Pushed deep in his pocket was the piece of paper Anomaly had given him with three names and three addresses. He didn't want to let her down, so he took the paper, unfolded it and checked the names.

And turned around.

He had been looking for the wrong house name. Ezra's house name was second on the list, but he was on the first road where Julian lived. He had already seen a sign with the right name on it earlier.

With the paper refolded and back in his pocket, Kev backtracked for seven houses before he stopped and smiled.

'Knew it,' he said to himself.

He pulled the phone out that Anomaly had given him and pretended to check something on it, but his eyes were scanning the road and the high fence that bordered the property. The tall green fence was made of vertical rows of long, narrow metal pieces with a three-pronged spike on the top. No easy cross rail to put a foot on and help boost himself over. Each upright piece was held tight by smooth, rounded bolt heads that you couldn't get a spanner on. Kev knew from experience that the other side would be secured by a fitting that sheered in half when it was tightened. No easy entry there, it would need a noisy drill or grinder.

The gates to the property were decorative metal hung from two sturdy brick pillars that the ends of the green fence were buried into. No gaps, no wriggle room.

The good news was there were no cameras on the house itself.

Kev crossed the road and lifted his phone. He kept his finger on the button and took a stream of photos of the entrance and fence.

A man peering through the gates behind him called, 'What are you doing?'

Kev turned and smiled. 'I'm doing work for the council's planning permission violation department.' He pointed at his tracksuit. 'Just my disguise.'

The man blinked and scuttled away.

Nothing like the threat of the planning department to send the rich into a spin Anomaly had told him.

***

After some time on the Tube, Kev walked along a different road, looking for Ezra's house. This one was wider with trees planted into the pavements. The fences were mostly wooden and not metal, but just as high. Lots of gates and fences had 'Neighbourhood Watch' signs attached to them. Although the houses weren't quite as big, the cars seemed the same, like there were unwritten rules about what people were allowed to drive if they lived here.

He found Ezra's home, with white rendered walls overlooking a trim green lawn and low bushes. The wooden five-bar gate was low and easy to climb over, and Kev couldn't see CCTV cameras on the corners of the house. He filled some more of his phone with another burst of subtle photos. No interruptions this time and he turned and headed back towards the Tube station and his longer trip to Essex.

***

Rupert's house was altogether different – a new house on a new road. Tall, fake pillars fronted the house with a yellow stone facade and a block paving drive. Little plants twisted their way out of black pots along the path that led to the white front door. It could have been straight from an episode of The Only Way is Essex.

Next to a large black Audi, a low blue and chrome sports car shimmered in the sunshine.

The boundary was the easiest of the three. There were gaps between the thin spindles of individual plants that would eventually grow and intertwine to knit together a solid barrier. The gates were wide open, even though there were small metal plates where the gates pivoted and Kev could see a small grey box that would contain the controls for the gate motors. Maybe they hadn't been finished yet, or maybe they were broken. All very accessible except for the alarm box high on the front wall and the CCTV cameras. Kev could see a camera of each corner of the house and another camera pointing at the gates from a black pole inside the garden. It was much easier to run the cables to the cameras on new-build homes, and Kev imagined the recorder that the cables would be connected to and moved on to hide from the unblinking gaze of the nearest camera.

Taking photos was easy as Kev could see a couple taking a long video of the front of a home further up the road. He looked like another tourist.

Kev tapped on the only number in the phone's contacts. It purred for two rings.

'Kev, what you got for me?' Anomaly said.

He talked her through the general layout of each house before she said, 'Problems?'

'The CCTV cameras I can take out with a splat from my paintball gun, but the alarm is a good make and Julian's fence is difficult.'

'OK. Give me a sec.'

Kev strolled up to see what was special about the house the couple were filming, but the building looked like an identical twin of Rupert's. Same colours, even the same plants in pots, the only difference was the lack of cars visible on the drive.

'Can you get back to Ezra's on Monday?'

'Yep.'

'I've found an easier way.'

Chapter 26

The head's study wasn't a room any academic work was done in. The wooden panelling and dark red carpet were meant to reassure prospective parents that the school was traditional enough to ensure that it honoured its history and the virtues of private education. The modern chrome and black armchairs and glass side tables showed that it was progressive and modern in its teaching. It got the balance just about right, and any doubts the parents had were swamped by the weight of the immense fees per term. Surely, they guaranteed small class sizes, top-quality teachers and the best start for their offspring. It had worked for Felicity and me, along with the promise that neither child would have to leave home and board.

The room's other use was for meetings with existing parents. Only ever very good news – your child has won a scholarship to a top senior school, or very bad – we need to talk about a different school for your child. I was sure that this was going to be bad.

The head sat in one of the armchairs with Felicity and myself opposite her. She was thin and prim in a dark brown suit. Her legs were tucked neatly to one side of her and her bony hands rested in her lap. My legs mirrored hers. Since the Tube, I had made a real effort to emasculate myself when I sat so that I avoided any hint of 'man-sitting', or accusations of overt 'crotch display'.

'Mr Mendoza, in light of recent, um…' The head coughed softly. 'Recent incidents, I must insist that you refrain from entering the school until further notice.'

I jerked upright in my seat. 'But it was all the other parents swearing and causing the problem.'

'They would argue that your presence is an unnecessary provocation and a threat to the well-being of the school and the children. I must say that I agree with them. A parent convicted of a sexual offence and appearing on the Sex Offender Register cannot be tolerated.'

'But my conviction doesn't have anything to do with children.'

She pursed her lips and failed to suppress a small shudder. 'At the moment.'

I grabbed the sides of the chair. 'How dare you suggest that. If I presented any risk to children then the courts would have put restrictions on me. But they didn't.' I looked at Felicity for support, but she had her head down and was pinching the bridge of her nose. Her silence wasn't helping my case.

'Well I've made my decision, and I can't comment on the failings of our legal system and its overly lenient sentencing.'

She stared at me. If she had been my judge, she'd have been reaching for a black cap and sentencing me for an immediate appointment with the hangman. Instead, she reached for a small brass bell on a wooden handle and gave it a little shake.

The door to the study opened and the frame filled with the bulk of Mr Baker, Head of Games. Retired professional boxer.

'Mr Baker will escort you from the premises.'

'Felicity,' I tried, but she twisted in her chair away from me. I stood when I felt Baker behind me. I didn't want the scene of me being forced out of my chair adding to my film of shame. I walked ahead of him through the school, and out into the car park. Some of the tanks were gone and I could see Felicity's little red Fiat parked in a corner. Sets of hostile eyes tracked my progress from the remaining cars.

The car nearest to me beeped and flashed its indicators as it honoured a command from a remote key fob.

'Stay away from our children,' hissed a woman. 'I'll call the police if I see you here again.'

***

I could have let the venom from the other parents poison my trip back to my solitary hotel room, but I clung on to the memory of Hugo and Victoria's embrace, and their unconditional acceptance of me. Felicity had taken the money and could have easily turned the kids against me. But she hadn't. It made me want to return home even more.

My wife might not be ready to talk to me yet, but she had been more distant than hostile at the school. Clutching at more straws, I let myself imagine me winning her back and settling in again at home. The smile it brought to my face appeared to confuse the man who was always at the hotel reception. I had always been downcast and miserable before.

His glum stare tracked me past the reception desk. 'What you smiling at?' He made it sound like a crime.

I dropped onto my bed and bounced a couple of times, enjoying the groan of the springs and the creak of the bed frame. If I got my money back, the parents would forget all about today and would revert to asking me for market recommendations and seeing if I was free for golf. The veil covering their true feelings had been pulled back and exposed them for who they really were. I'd be civil if I had to at the side of a pitch or parents' meeting, but I'd cut them out of my life.

My other major broken relationship was with Paul so, I picked up my phone and called him. 'Hi, Paul,' I said when he answered. 'How're things?'

'Good, Dad. You?'

'Better today. I saw Hugo and Victoria before being run off the school grounds by Mr Baker.'

I heard him give a half laugh and then silence.

It dragged on, neither of us sure how to get past the change in my life.

'You know I love you, Paul.'

'I know you do, Dad.'

More silence.

I decided to go back in time and try to reconnect that way. 'I know it was tough for you when Mum died.'

He gasped like he always did at any mention of Kat's death. I pressed on. 'No kid deserves that, then the move to London and the new life. I feel guilty for leaving you with babysitters after school. I missed so much of your life, but I did it for you as well. The effort I put in in those early years was to afford the future you deserve.'

'I know, Dad.' More silence, but then he said, 'It's OK, I understand. You can't undo the past.'

Chapter 27

My weekend was the best since the Tube. Paul and I had chatted and it felt almost back to how it was – talking about sport, his progress on the spare room transformation and work. Always work.

It was our common ground since I'd recommended him to Pierre Dufrais two years ago. Pierre was a one-time colleague a decade ago and we'd been competitive back then, pushing each other to post the highest returns. He'd jumped ship to another firm, and when he needed an unpaid intern, I recommended Paul. It had gone well and my son was now full-time and earning strong money.

Sunday morning passed quickly with me fantasising about all the different ways I could get Felicity and the kids back. They all worked in my head, but I knew reality was going to be harder with her parents. Monty and Babs would be chirping in her ear: 'he was never good enough', 'I always knew there was something wrong with him', 'you're better off without him'. And so many more. My imagination could turn all those cool greetings, shallow conversations and their shared sly glances into a million insults.

However hard I tried, the lack of self-worth I learnt as a child was always lurking around the corner, ready to pounce if I faltered and acknowledged it. I wasn't good enough for myself, so I couldn't be good enough for Felicity.

I never felt better if I let these thoughts run, so I jumped off the bed, grabbed my coat and shoes and headed out into the daylight. Pale sunshine greeted me on the pavement, along with traffic noise and fumes. Old vans pushed out black clouds of diesel, car after car passing with their engines running. Not the sort of air quality you wanted to suck greedily into your lungs.

Yet, it felt better to be outside – in the world, rather than in my head. I set off, aiming for the nearby small square of green the locals called the park.

As my stride lengthened and I looked at the passing people, I felt lighter. I realised people weren't going to recognise me from the video and scream and run. I wasn't scared to be outside.

***

Monday's community service was graffiti removal. Kev wasn't working and Anomaly only had time to squeeze my arm and whisper, 'Made progress. We've got a plan,' before Alan waved her into a separate group with a different set of walls to clean.

The word 'plan' set my heart running and pushed a smile onto my face as I watched Anomaly's departing back. What could it be? Was it the step onto the first rung of the ladder back up?

'Look, Tel. I reckon Knobby's got the hots for Emika,' Gaz growled behind me.

'Grow up, Gaz,' I said and walked off to collect my bucket, gloves and brush. Then I aimed for a section of wall small enough that Gaz and Tel would have to work somewhere else.

I started scrubbing at a blue 'tag' on the wall and pressed hard into the back and forth action until I could see a tint of blue in the water. Dropping my shoulder to send my hand into the bucket for more water, I swirled the brush around. As I stood, I sensed a shadow flashing towards me. I tried to duck away from it, but the hard edge of a brush caught me on the eyebrow. 'Shit,' I shouted, and my hand flew up onto my face, fingers exploring the point of impact. No blood, but the soft skin was starting to swell.

Gaz and Tel's laughter told me what had happened before my head turned enough to see them. 'Good shot, Gaz,' Tel said as he slapped Gaz's back.

'Don't get in my way with Emika.' Gaz's eyes blazed – part pride at his throw, part hatred of me. Definitely pleasure in having inflicted pain. He looked like he would detest anything and anyone that didn't fit his point of view. And enjoy hurting them.

I took a couple of paces forward, starting to pull my arm back, but my brush had barely moved before Tel started running, he tucked his right foot behind his left calf and mimed out a dramatic trip. His bucket, newly filled with chemically enhanced liquid, shot forward, sending a long stream of water towards me. It hit the tops of my thighs, drenching my jeans, turning the light blue fabric a soapy black.

Tel dropped his bucket and roared with laughter. 'Oops. I slipped.'

Gaz walked forward and made no pretence. He pulled his bucket back and threw the whole lot at my chest. 'Wanker,' he spat and landed a punch into my side. Then he leaned in closer. 'Your type needs a fucking good kicking. Not here with Alan watching. Somewhere private. We're going 'ave you.'

Chapter 28

Kev was back on Ezra's road wearing a hoodie over his tracksuit, but not carrying any tools to break in with, or using darkness to cover his approach. At ten in the morning, Kev strolled up the road, visible to anyone who cared to see him.

The houses were all set back from the road to give their owners privacy, so they might get a glimpse of him as he walked across their driveway, but no one seemed to bother. Even the Neighbourhood Watch wouldn't be too paranoid about 'man walking on road, empty-handed in daytime'.

The only change to the road since Kev was last here was the lack of cars in the drives. Kev guessed that they'd be at train stations or office blocks or supermarket car parks. The usual Monday morning routine, but they weren't his target. Slowing his pace as he reached the edge of Ezra's garden, he scanned along the fence, then the wooden five-bar gate and on to the start of Ezra's neighbours' hedge.

'No need to break in,' Anomaly had said. 'It will be waiting for you outside.'

She was right.

Kev flicked his hood up over his head and peered over the fence. The bushes planted on the inside of the boundary line blocked some of his view, but he could see the drive was clear of anyone who might scream. He walked on, straight and true, aiming for a spot to the right of the gate. As he got there, he twisted his head to make sure that anybody looking from the house would only get a view of the back of his hood. He stretched his hand, grabbed his target and pulled.

The wheelie bin trundled after him, jolting over the bumps on the pavement. Once he was across the openness of the driveway, he took a couple more paces and stopped.

He could hear Anomaly in his head. 'Cleaners tend to empty internal waste bins into bags first, then put the whole bag in the wheelie bin. Feel for anything soft, like paper.'

The lid of the bin flipped up and over. On top were some broken down Amazon delivery boxes, then a layer of wine bottles, then another layer of cardboard. *Ezra must have had a piss-up at the weekend with lots of deliveries*, Kev thought. He pushed his hand down to the bottom layer of the wine bottle sandwich and lifted. He could see bags underneath the bottom cardboard layer, but he wasn't going to get them out and keep the bottles inside the bin. So the top layer of Amazon boxes came out and Kev put them next to the bin, then the bottles, then he pivoted the bottom cardboard layer up and yanked out two white bags of recycling. Both felt soft and he peered into the little gap the drawstring left at the top of each bag – shredded paper in one, envelopes and letters in the other.

Result.

After all his time picking up litter, Kev couldn't leave the bottles and cardboard out, so he dropped them back in the bin and flipped the lid shut.

He sauntered back down the road, a white bag in each hand.

***

Kev typed a flat number into the entry system's keypad and pressed a button next to a picture that looked like a mouth. Lights on the panel came on and Kev stared into the camera. The door buzzed and he pushed his way inside and headed to the lift.

Four storeys later, Kev walked along the corridor and into the open doorway of Anomaly's flat. 'In the lounge,' she called.

He pulled his trainers off by the door, not wanting another bollocking from her about the germs on the soles of his shoes, and padded his way to the lounge, his big toe poking out of the large hole in his left sock.

Anomaly was waiting. Her small orange sofa was pushed back against the wall and she'd rolled up her rug and propped it against the sofa. It had bent and folded over like a traffic sign hit by a car.

In the rug's place was a large clear plastic sheet, a roll of black bin bags, decorator's silicone gloves and face masks.

'It's bags of recycling, not toxic waste,' Kev said.

Anomaly looked at the two white bags that Kev dropped onto the plastic sheet. 'That's it?' she asked.

'Unless you wanted Amazon boxes and empty wine bottles?'

'Let's start. You take one, I'll do the other,' she said, snapping on some gloves and fitting a surgical mask.

Kev shrugged, tugged the drawstring of one of the bags open and pushed his bare hand inside.

'Ewww,' she said and opened her own bag.

Half an hour later, they had separated and graded their prizes: shredded paper, a week's worth of newspapers, a lot of discarded junk mail, most of it not even opened, a tin of baked beans, two tins of chopped tomatoes and an empty bottle of Tabasco. No personal letters or bank statements.

'Shit,' Kev said, looking at the pile of shredded paper. It wasn't like in the CSI programmes he had seen where they pieced together thin strips of paper back into a full document that proved who the killer was. This paper was chopped into tiny little diamond-shaped pieces, like recycled confetti. 'We're never going to piece all that back together.'

Kev reached towards a glass tumbler.

'Don't touch that,' Anomaly shouted.

Chapter 29

Anomaly made Kev help clear up all the rubbish back into the bags. Her mask and gloves went on top, then she shepherded him towards the bathroom.

He reached out for the shining tap, but before he could get there, Anomaly smacked his wrist.

She turned the tap on and picked up a bottle of liquid soap. She nodded him towards the water and watched him wet his hands before she squirted soap into his palms. 'Ewww,' she said again as he rubbed and a black tinge appeared in the water under his hands.

He rinsed the soap off his hands and looked for a towel.

'Again. And longer.'

She squirted more soap and Kev rubbed again. More black water ran down the drain. Finally, she relented and passed Kev the towel.

Then wished she hadn't. 'Kev,' she shouted.

'What?' he said.

She yanked the towel out of his hands and turned it so that he could see the grey smears on her clean white towel.

'It's a towel.' Kev shrugged, not seeing a problem.

She gave up. 'Get the bags and drop them in the bin store.'

Kev nodded.

***

You've let Dan down, Anomaly told herself as she went through her finger clicking ritual. She'd thought that Ezra's bin would have something interesting in it, but Ezra was clearly cautious enough to have got a good quality shredder and thorough enough to use it on everything.

She opened a Google search window and typed in Ezra's name, like on all her previous searches. She wanted to check that there wasn't anything new today, before she was forced to delve any deeper. And there it was.

She picked up her phone and dialled the number Dan had given her.

'I know where Julian and Ezra will be on Wednesday.'

'Brilliant,' Dan said. 'You really are the master hacker. Did you bug their phones and take control of their laptops?'

'Kind of,' she said.

'Where are they going to be? Can I get to them?'

She could hear the excitement in Dan's voice.

Anomaly leaned closer to her screen and scanned the web page that Google had popped up for her.

Impact Investing Conference – Breaking News: Julian Hall and Ezra Lara, partners at Salamander Capital have been added to the panel discussion on 'Inclusive Capitalism and sustainable finance in a Carbon Neutral World'.

'They'll be at the Kensington Conference and Events Centre from 3pm.'

'Wow,' said Dan. 'Anomaly the super-hacker strikes.'

'Something like that,' she said.

Chapter 30

Tuesday had its ups and downs. The highlights were no Gaz or Tel and agreeing with Alan that I didn't have to work on Wednesday. These positives were offset by working outside in a cold, biting wind, and heavy rain showers.

At least on Wednesday, as I made the long walk from the hotel to the conference centre, the dark clouds kept the rain for themselves.

I was worried that Anomaly hadn't been able to give me any real evidence to throw at Julian and Ezra. I'd have to be more creative than I had been with Rupert. Grabbing Julian by the balls and squeezing wouldn't work.

My first issue was getting into the building. With a conference on anything finance-based, the firms always paid for their staff to attend. Banks had deep pockets and conference organisers weren't stupid or shy of charging top-whack. I'd checked the ticket prices: £1,800 including VAT for a two-day pass. It would have seemed steep, even if I was still at Salamander. Now, I was getting dangerously close to the bottom of my bank account, having paid for more days at the hotel, food and some travel money for Kev. The ticket price was way beyond me.

Two things helped me. I had my suit and tie from the day of the signing. They had rested under my mattress overnight to try and press some of the creases out and it didn't look too bad. The other was that I was arriving halfway through the afternoon. These events didn't usually attract gatecrashers. No one nudged a colleague on a quiet afternoon and said, 'Let's have some fun, skive off work and sneak into a conference and learn about companies working to generate a measurable, beneficial environmental impact as well as a financial return'.

Event staff might be alert at morning registration, but by the afternoon, most didn't care about a delegate coming in without a conference lanyard around their neck.

I climbed the steps to the Kensington Conference and Events Centre, noticing that more people were leaving than arriving. Maybe they were heading off for a cheeky short day while pretending to still be at the conference, maybe back to the office for meetings.

Inside the centre, there were banners and signs for the conference and I stopped at a board with the conference agenda on it. I ran my finger down the timings. The conference was split into twenty-minute chunks – a series of panel discussions or keynote speeches on an important topic, mixed with longer 'networking' breaks.

The slot I was looking for started at 3:15pm. I had ten minutes to spare.

'May I help you, sir?' a man in a black suit said next to me. His suit was too shapeless to belong to a delegate, so he must be one of the venue staff.

'I'm OK, thanks.'

I made to head in the direction of the Great Hall, but he held out his hand. 'You don't have your delegates badge on.'

'You got me,' I said, trying to make a joke of it. 'I work with Julian Hall at Salamander Capital. He's on in ten minutes and I noticed a bad error in his presentation.' I tapped my trouser pocket. 'Got the amendments on a data pen. He'll sack me if I don't get them to him.'

'Wouldn't want that, sir,' the man said, and dropped his hand.

Act like you belong, look like you belong and you can go a long way.

***

I waited in the gents' toilets in the centre stall, trying to ignore the noises and smells coming from my neighbours. I'd ducked into the toilets when I had seen Pierre further across the foyer. I didn't want to be recognised now, but the toilets were getting busy as people took the switch of speakers between sessions as a perfect time to get rid of some conference coffee.

I ignored several rattles on my locked cubicle door and waited until Julian and Ezra's session should be coming to a close before making my escape. The corridor was nearly empty and I pushed the door to the Great Hall open. Pausing inside the door, I looked across a sea of suits sitting on gold upright chairs. At the far end of the room was the raised stage with a lectern and a table with four chairs facing into the room. Julian was standing at the lectern, half-turned away from his audience as he waved his hand in a small circle at the massive drop-down screen. A little red dot from his laser pointer danced around a number on the screen that Julian clearly thought was essential for the audience to understand.

His amplified voice played over loudspeakers so that even at the very back of the room, I could hear him over the muttering and side-conversations of the delegates. The aisle seat of the back row was vacant and I headed for that.

Julian finished his speech, and he returned to the table and sat down next to Ezra. A woman in a stylish blue suit who must have been the moderator thanked Julian and asked a follow-up question. She'd been well chosen as the question showed deep insight and I could see Julian thinking hard before he answered.

When he finished, the woman looked at her watch and said, 'We've got time for some questions from the floor.'

My hand shot up, but she pointed at someone at the front. There was a pause as one of the event staff ran to the person in the audience and gave them a battery-powered microphone.

I kept my hand up during the question and the woman nodded to me. I was next.

A male voice asked a pretty routine question that seemed to be a thinly veiled advert for the company he worked for. Ezra batted the question away with ease and the woman pointed towards me. 'At the very back,' she said to help the staff member running with the mic.

I took it and stood up. Julian and Ezra straightened in their seats, glanced at each other, before looking back at me.

'In this time of ethical investing,' I said, my voice bouncing around for the whole audience to hear. 'I'd like to ask the panel their view on the ethics of two partners ruining a friend and stealing his money?'

The room went silent for a second, the crowd unsure if they had heard my question correctly. Then faces spun towards me and the room burst with noise. This time I didn't mind the phones pointing towards me and filming. Julian and Ezra looked less pleased. They still had a professional standing with lots to lose.

That went perfectly, I told myself as I pushed my way towards the stage. When I reached the bottom step of the stage, I looked up. Julian's face had turned a very pleasing red and Ezra's jaw clenched tighter than seemed healthy.

'Alright, boys,' I said.

'What are you doing here?' Julian hissed.

'You need to answer my question.'

'Not here,' Ezra said, looking out at the sea of phones pointed at him.

***

Julian and Ezra led the way out of the Great Hall, ignoring the questions that were thrown at us and all the phones shoved in our faces. I walked a pace behind them, wearing a broad smile.

People could easily interpret their obvious anger and their silence as an admission of guilt.

Julian barged a man standing in the doorway out of his way and strode across the foyer towards the stairs. He seemed to know his way around and I followed him up the stairs, across another carpeted foyer and into a bland meeting room with 'Committee Room 3' on the door.

He spun to face me, the anger still visible in his face and Ezra closed in at his side.

'How can you come here and accuse us like that in public?' Julian said.

'That's nothing compared with what you did to me,' I said.

'Don't kid yourself. *You* got your knob out on the train. Don't go blaming us,' Ezra piled in.

I looked at my old partners, seeing their anger at my accusations. They seemed genuine, but they were good at spinning a story and making it believable. Were they angry because I'd humiliated them in public for no reason? Or because they were trying to deflect me away from the truth?

'But you'll both get a split of my share.' This time my anger came out and I prodded a finger at them. 'Deny it.'

Julian's face cooled a little, going from dark beetroot to more like bad sunburn. 'Well, that's true.'

'So will Yas,' Ezra said. 'After all we've been through together, you've got to believe we wouldn't do anything to hurt you.'

But I didn't.

Chapter 31

For today's Community Payback, Alan had driven us away from our usual litter and graffiti sites and unloaded us at a youth centre. The sky was heavy with low, dark clouds, and I could feel the threat of rain in the air. The car park looked litter free and the outside walls were covered with bright, swirling colours and murals, so I wondered what we were doing here. Given that the forecast was for torrential rain all day, I hoped that we'd be inside.

When Alan led us through and into the building's main open space, we were greeted by the sight of paint, rollers and plastic sheets. All the sofas and other furniture, including a vivid purple pool table, had been pushed into the centre of the room. The walls were chipped and scratched, and darker rectangles showed where posters had been and how much the old paint had faded.

Trust was the word that occupied my mind as my hands were busy rolling beige paint onto a wall. Did I trust Julian and Ezra? Or Rupert?

While I didn't exactly trust Rupert, I pushed him to the back on my list of suspects. Would he take the extra money? Absolutely. Would he have gone for such a vicious plan that destroyed me? I couldn't see him signing up for that, even if he was pressured by the others.

Julian and Ezra were different. Where money was concerned, they were as ruthless as great white sharks fighting over meat. And once Salamander was sold, would a split of my £98m motivate them? You bet it would. It made sense that I was the target. They needed Rupert's contacts, but they could think that my skills in investing the money and making it grow could be transferred to KapGroup. Not as well maybe, but good enough to make grabbing my share of the sale tempting.

That left Yas. She'd save a lot of money not having to pay me my salary, bonus, and all the other payments in the deal that were due in the future. Maybe she'd squeeze out my ex-partners as well. Maybe they were feeling the pressure and they had agreed to do the conference as an impromptu attempt at self-marketing in case they were pushed.

I looked at the wall and realised that in my frustration and anger I had been painting jagged and patchy strokes over the same piece of defenceless wall.

***

As we waited for the coffee shop owner to bring us our drinks, Anomaly, Kev and I settled in the usual sofa and armchairs. I picked and prodded at the little beige paint dots the roller had splashed onto my hands. I couldn't get them off, so I headed to wash my hands again, worrying why Gaz and Tel weren't working today, and imagining them waiting for me somewhere on my route home, desperate to give me 'a good kicking'.

The owner placed a large black coffee in front of me and smiled. The bill chipped another piece out of my bank balance, but the shop was the easiest and closest place to sit and chat.

I dialled the number Anomaly had given me. Yas' mobile rang again. And again, there was no answer. She must have blocked me.

'Try the office,' Anomaly said.

'Yasmita Kapoor, please,' I said when the call was answered.

'Putting you through,' a polite voice said.

The call clicked and then rang again. 'Ms Kapoor's office.' The assistant's voice was just as polite, although with a little more Essex accent in it.

'Can I speak to Yas, please.'

'Who's calling?'

Even though the front line KapGroup receptionists had no reason to know my name, Yas' office would. Her lawyers would have reacted in the same way as Hannah and ordered an immediate shutdown on communications. A made-up name had no hope of reaching the busy chief executive of KapGroup.

'It's Julian Hall from Salamander,' I said, pinching my throat a little to try and mimic Julian's voice.

There was a moment's silence. 'That's clever,' the assistant said.

'Sorry?'

'Well, if you're Mr Hall, then somehow you're sitting in front of me in one of Ms Kapoor's visitors' chairs, reading a magazine while at the same time talking to me on an invisible phone. I've noted your number and will inform the switchboard to refuse all future calls.'

The line dropped and I shook my head. 'We need a different plan.'

In response, Anomaly showed me her phone.

'I don't think calling from a different number is going to make a difference,' I said.

She frowned and said, 'Look at the screen. It's Yas' home address.'

The screen showed the familiar Google Maps app, with a little round marker pin in the centre. The pin rested in the middle of a thick white line that represented a road, with an expanse of featureless grey surrounding it. I wasn't sure what to do with the information.

'Look.' She jumped up from her armchair, skirted the table and dropped next to me on the sofa.

She pressed something on the screen and the image changed to Street View with actual images of the road and two big arrows. Anomaly pressed on one of the arrows and the image changed so that, even though it wasn't live-streaming, it looked like we were actually walking down Yas' road. 'Looks quiet there. Lots of fields and no neighbours,' she said.

Her fingers moved around and the image turned, and we headed back along the road and stopped at a large set of solid wooden gates.

'That's her house.'

Chapter 32

Kev sat on the wall inside the blue metal gates on Austin Friars. He liked how the little cobbled lane in the centre of the City of London sounded like the Austin Powers films. He had been waiting there an hour, and now it was getting darker, the cold seeped through his tracksuit. Across the narrow grey section of Throgmonton Avenue, he could see the big metal-clad pillars and revolving doors of the KapGroup entrance.

They'd planned out some possible scenarios in the coffee shop. Kev's role was to wait and follow.

Other than the cold, he was well prepared with a photo of Yas on his borrowed phone and Anomaly's Oyster card to make getting through the Tube barriers easier. If Yas jumped in a cab, it would get difficult, but Dan said she got car sick in taxis and only used them if she was running very late.

He waited and after another forty minutes or so, the revolving doors spun again. This time, Yas stepped out onto the road, pulling a black coat over her business suit. By the time she had settled the coat on her shoulders and buttoned up the front, two other people came out of the doors. All three headed along Throgmonton Avenue and through its blue gates.

Kev pushed himself off the wall and followed. Yas and the others formed a tight group with Yas doing a lot of talking and arm waving to emphasise her points. The other two nodded and hurried to keep up with her. They didn't notice him, and anyway, he looked much less suspicious than the two furtive smokers huddled in the corner of the KapGroup building.

Kev followed a safe distance behind, hidden by the other people on the streets. Yas turned right onto Throgmonton Street, left onto Bartholomew Lane and past the line of stone columns and the entrance to the Bank of England Museum. She paused at the entrance to Bank Tube station to give her last instructions.

Kev was ten paces behind her as she headed down the steps.

***

Kev felt warmer as he hung on to an overhead strap of the Tube train. Yas was half a carriage away next to the double doors. She'd followed Dan's guess – Bank to Oxford Circus on the Central line, then change to the Bakerloo line for the train to Paddington.

After the train left Edgware Road and started slowing for Paddington, Kev shuffled closer towards the door. Yas looked around and towards him, but he was moving towards the door like a lot of other people in the carriage. It would probably empty at the next stop.

The train stopped and the doors opened. Yas eased between two slow tourists and skipped onto the platform. Kev's route was blocked by the desperation of the people waiting to get onto the train not allowing enough room for a man with a big suitcase to get off.

Shit, Kev thought. By the time he had pushed and shoved his way off the train and into the narrow corridor between the station wall and the waiting passengers, Yas had gone.

He reached the bottom of the escalator. 'Move to the right if you're going to stand,' he swore at the slow man who was blocking the escalator.

Kev pushed by and run up the escalator, brushing past people with bulky rucksacks. Still no sign of Yas. Anomaly would scream at him if he lost her.

The open space of the overground station was busy, announcements and chatter buzzed under the high domed ceiling. Kev tried to move towards the board with the details of the train departures, but each person seemed to be on a mission to slow him as they dithered or stopped abruptly to look up.

The display showed the platform numbers and departure times. The train he thought Yas would aim for was due to leave in six minutes. Kev started to run, skipping past and around slower people who were all heading towards the platform.

When he got to the barrier, he stopped and saw Yas take two steps and climb onto a carriage with a big number one painted on it.

Now people were swearing at him for blocking their route. Anxious voices afraid that the train would leave without them. 'Sorry, mate,' Kev said as he stepped back and away, uncorking the flow of passengers behind him. The beepers on the train doors sounded and caused more panic from the travellers. They sprinted for the doors trying to get onto the train. One didn't make it, but he kept pressing the door open button. 'Why don't the doors open?' he shouted. After over a minute of fruitless pressing, the man gave up as the train started to move.

Pulling out his phone, Kev dialled. When it answered he said, 'Train's leaving now.'

Chapter 33

The engine idled on Anomaly's car, sending a pooling cloud of hot exhaust gases up into the cold night air. She'd left London and battled to get to the M4 before Kev had reached Austin Friars. Dan didn't know Yas' schedule or routine, so she could have left at seven and headed straight home, worked later or even gone out for the evening before heading home. Anomaly didn't want to race Yas' train through the London traffic, so she had chosen arriving early and being bored. And cold.

She turned the temperature gauge up on the car's heater, then clicked the fan up to maximum. The whooshing noise of the fan drowned out the sound of the car's engine. After the inside of the car had warmed enough, she turned the engine off to save fuel. She dipped her hand into the open bag of crisps on her lap. She'd been picking at it as a way to kill time and the bag was down to the last small remnants. The bag rustled as she pulled the crisps out, tipped her head back and dropped them into her mouth.

Her phone rang through the Bluetooth connection on her car and she clicked a button on the steering wheel to answer. 'And?' she said.

'Train's leaving now,' Kev said.

She wiped the flavour 'dust' from the crisps off her hands and steering wheel with a wet wipe. 'Thanks, Kev,' she said and hung up.

The train app was already open on her phone and primed with the next possible departure. Anomaly clicked on the Live Tracker button, and the screen redrew with London Paddington at the top and the words 'On time' under it. Running down the screen were all the stations the train was due to call at and the corresponding estimated time of arrival. Forty minutes to Thatcham, then a fifteen-minute drive.

Anomaly opened another bag of crisps and waited.

＊

Her car's hazard warning lights clicked out a relentless rhythm as Anomaly drove past Yas' gate. The house itself was hidden from the road by the solid wooden gates. The high hedges flanking the pillars clicked orange and black in time with the lights and then flared red as Anomaly put her foot on the brake. She reversed and the car emitted a low whine as she edged in backwards across the gates. After some see-sawing with the steering and shunting the car back and forth, she had the car neatly across the gates and completely off the road.

She reached up and adjusted her rear-view mirror so that she could see the road behind her. Although the car's rear lights and the dim lights on the pillars only showed the first few metres of the road, it had been arrow-straight for at least half a mile before she put her hazards on. The glare from Yas' headlights would be visible in the clear night air before the lights themselves appeared.

The clock on the car's dashboard said that Yas should be about one minute away. 'Game time,' Anomaly said, before turning the engine off and dropping her hand to pull the lever that released the bonnet catch. She turned, grabbed her coat off of the heap of blankets that covered the back seat and got out. The cold cut into her after the warmth of the car and she rushed to tug her coat on.

As she lifted the bonnet to expose the cooling engine, she unclipped the support and propped the bonnet open. Rubbing her hands against the cold, she ducked her head under the bonnet like she was trying to fix the car. The click of the car's hazard lights was the only thing to disturb the quiet of the rural countryside.

***

Away in the distance, she could see car lights seeming to create a white fog-like glow in the sky. Then a car crested the rise and two sharp beams of light bounced along the road. Anomaly pushed herself deeper under the bonnet, not wanting a random passer-by to see her and stop. She knew this was a risk, but had decided that as it was cold and dark, a car parked outside a house suggested that the owner was already inside getting help and a warm drink. And most people seemed to prefer not to get involved unless forced to.

The light and noise of the car got closer, then the pitch changed as the car started to slow. Its horn blared.

Not the action of a concerned passer-by, Anomaly decided. Much more like the action of a tired person, longing for home after a hectic day, seeing a car blocking their entrance.

The horn blared again as the car stopped. 'You're blocking my drive.'

Must be Yas, Anomaly thought.

Anomaly waited, she needed the woman out of her car.

'Hello?' Yas said, then Anomaly heard the car lurch into park and the door open. 'Unbelievable, bloody breakdown on my drive.'

Anomaly listened to the crunch of footfalls on the drive. Out of the corner of her eye, the distorted shadow of a woman blended with the shadow of her car.

The noise of feet stopped. *She must be checking inside the car*, Anomaly thought.

The feet moved again and sounded closer to the front of the car. Anomaly snapped the torch of her phone on, spun away from the engine and shone the light straight into Yas' face.

Chapter 34

I didn't want to give any hint where I was, so I kept my breathing shallow and my body as still as possible.

Then I heard Yas scream, 'What the… who are you?'

That was my cue. I pushed off the blankets that covered me and sat up on the back seat of Anomaly's car.

I could see Yas standing by the car's front wing, her hand in front of her face to stop the light from Anomaly's phone from blinding her. Grabbing and yanking at the door catch, I pushed the door open and stood up behind Yas.

'Stop shining that light in my face–' Yas said, but at that moment, I grabbed her upper arms and pulled her backwards as hard as I could. She screamed, but on the empty road, there was no one to hear her. Or help her.

She struggled and twisted so hard that I almost lost my grip, but I shifted my hands to bunch and grasp the fabric of her coat, hauled her back past the open rear door of the car, then bent my legs. As I pushed up through my thighs, I lifted my hands and pulled Yas upright. Despite her being a good six inches shorter than me and much lighter, my heart was pumping hard and the muscles in my arms were complaining about all those missed gym sessions.

Before Yas could reorientate herself, I put my hand on her head like I had seen in all those US cop shows and pushed down. Her head dropped and I shoved her bum with the side of my hip and sent her sprawling across the back seat.

I took a breath and looked towards the front of the car. Anomaly had the bonnet shut and was climbing into the driver's seat.

It was difficult for me to get in the car next to Yas, but I crouched and perched my knees on the edge of the back seat and shoved her in further. Yas made a lunge for the door handle, but before she could get a grip, I hooked my left hand around her right arm and pulled to stop her getting the door open.

I heard Anomaly's door slam and from the corner of my eye saw her flicking buttons on the car's centre console screen. 'The kiddie locks are on,' she said and adjusted the rear-view mirror so that she could see Yas.

Releasing my grip on Yas' arm, I slid onto my bum and pulled my feet into the car, then my right hand flapped around for the door handle, and I pulled it shut.

The door locks clunked closed.

Yas slid her bum along the back seat and straightened into a normal seating position. Her hands flew at the door handle and she yanked at it. The door stayed locked and Yas' eyes stared at the disobedient door handle willing it to open.

'I've got money in the house, don't hurt me,' she said.

'Have you got ninety-eight million pounds?' I asked and Yas turned her face towards me for the first time.

'Dan?' Her eyes were wide and I could see her body shaking. I thought it was fear, but then she screamed. 'Dan, how *dare* you attack me?'

'We haven't attacked you, you're just in the car to answer a few questions.'

'I've been kidnapped.'

'You're right outside your gates. That's not kidnapping,' Anomaly said.

Yas seemed to notice her in the car for the first time. 'Who... the... fuck... is... that?' She emphasised each word with a punch to my arm.

I saw Anomaly's eyes flare in the rear-view mirror and her head shook.

'A friend,' I said.

The click-click of the hazard lights seemed to grow louder as the inside of the car went silent.

'And turn those bloody lights off,' Yas said as she glared at Anomaly's back.

I wasn't sure what to say. This wasn't how it was meant to play out. I decided on a more conciliatory approach and twisted in my seat so that I faced Yas.

'On the day of the signing, I was set-up. It allowed you to fire me and steal the rest of the purchase price from me. Not to mention keeping all the performance fees. You made a lot of money by destroying me.'

She did me the favour of keeping quiet while I talked.

After she considered my words, she laughed. 'I think you can say the same about your partners.'

'They denied it and that leaves you. I want my life back.' I delivered this with a much louder and more forceful tone than I ever had at work.

Yas blinked a couple of times. 'Didn't know you had it in you.'

'Well, I do.'

'What happened to you was like hitting a lemon with a sledgehammer. I operate with more finesse. If it was me, it would have been more like a dissection.'

The coldness in her voice cut through me and silenced my complaint at being called a lemon.

'There are so many ways I could have squeezed and tormented you before I chopped you out of KapGroup. I could have taken the four hundred million price, cut all of you out, and walked away with your firm for six million. But I didn't, I actually wanted to give you some of my money to run.'

She ended on a sigh, sounding like she really did regret it. 'Go back and look at your partners.'

Then she straightened and pulled on the door handle again.

'Now open this fucking door and move this pile of shit before I call the police.'

Chapter 35

Yas stormed out of the car, pausing only long enough to swing the door shut with a vicious bang that set the car rocking. When she reached her car, she blared her horn the whole time as Anomaly edged backwards and forwards, trying to get back out onto the road without hitting the gates or Yas' car.

Finally, we swung on to the road and turned in the direction that Yas had come from. Anomaly and I kept our eyes straight ahead and let the drum of the tyres on the road fighting with the noise from the heating fan wash over us.

'Can you stop?' I said finally. 'I feel like a kid sitting in the back.'

She flicked an indicator and pulled over. As soon as she stopped, I jumped out of the rear passenger door and settled in next to her.

'Yas was scary,' Anomaly said as she pulled away. 'When she talked about dissection, all I could think of was her standing over me with a scalpel and a deranged grin.'

I'd got nowhere with Rupert, been brushed off by Julian and Ezra and barely escaped Yas.

And as for Anomaly, Kev and me being able to prove anything or recover any of the money – we'd proved how pathetic we were. Any dreams of us being the Three Musketeers were cancelled and replaced by a farce starring the Three Stooges.

I was too broken to cry, too empty to talk. The miles rolled on and Anomaly kept looking straight ahead, like she didn't want to be contaminated by my mood.

The black night sky provided the perfect backdrop for the extended director's cut of my film of shame. The images were brighter, the colours more vivid and the sounds deafening. It scorched its way into my soul.

***

Anomaly may have ignored me on the way back, but she did go out of her way to drive me back to my disgusting hotel rather than dumping me and making me walk.

In the room, I turned the TV on, hoping to find something to lift my spirits. The news didn't help, nor the reality TV where people shed more and more self-respect to win votes. I channel-hopped all the way to an American-style evangelical preacher who ensured me that 'God loved me.'

I didn't believe that for a second. I knew that God had it in for me.

After my parents died, I'd asked the local vicar, 'If there's a God, why do bad things happen?'

'It's a test of your faith, Dan,' the vicar had said.

I'd buried my faith along with my parents, but God kept testing me over the years.

Before the signing, I had dared hope that my days of being tested were behind me, and I could live happily with Felicity and the kids. Then the Tube came and gave me another test from God: *I'm going to destroy you, Dan. It will be fun to see how you cope.*

I toyed with the idea of provoking Gaz and Tel on Monday at Community Payback, goading them into going too far and landing some vicious kicks to my head to put me out of my misery. But I didn't deserve anything so easy. I'd end up surviving and living with brain damage or permanent disability. Another test from God.

Then I saw a note on the floor that I hadn't noticed when I came in and got off the bed to see what it said.

If you want to stay, you need to pay.

The hotel insisted on payment in advance so I was safe over the weekend, but how much longer could I justify a hotel?

'Oh, shit,' I said after checking the balance on the banking app on my phone. £37.62 in credit.

It was all I had. It wouldn't stretch. Every time I thought I was at the bottom, something pushed me lower.

From the top of the world to homeless inside two weeks.

My mind flipped and I was in a swimming pool. The rancid water of my self-worth poured into the pool. The stench made me gag and the thick, dark water edged towards me. I tried to run but the tiles at the bottom of the pool grew over my feet and locked me in place. The water touched my leg and rose to my knees. Then waist. Up to my chest. I opened my mouth to scream.

The water reached my neck. My eyes bulged in panic. My scream died as the foul water flooded into my mouth.

Chapter 36

The hotel room had been my cage for most of the weekend, broken only by rare trips to the local supermarket to buy reduced, out-of-date sandwiches. My film of shame was always showing as I drowned in the inexorable waters of my own self-loathing. Now my body floated, face down and legs stretched out, looking like a suicide victim floating in a pool.

A hard, bang-bang on the door jerked me back into the brown gloom of the hotel room. I rolled onto my side, feeling the wet drool on my face from where my open mouth had pushed into the creaky old mattress. 'What?' I called.

'Check out is at nine tomorrow if you don't pay in full before,' said the hotel manager. His tone didn't leave any room for negotiation.

I didn't have any money, and in the morning, I wouldn't have anywhere to live.

I looked at my phone and thought about Paul's spare room in the middle of its conversion to gym-cum-yoga room.

What was stopping me calling? It wasn't self-respect. Any that I once had lay in tatters on the floor. Pride then? No.

When I finally looked at the question face on and acknowledged it, it was my stubborn self-reliance. When things went wrong, I worked out a way to fix it. I worked longer, or harder, or differently, until I overcame it. But where had my recent attempts got me? Nowhere.

Now I had to choose. I could be stubborn and sleep on the rain-drenched streets, or I could ask for help and sleep on a dry yoga mat. It should have been easy, but saliva flooded my mouth.

Call Paul, the logical, rational half of my head said. Despite all the evidence to the contrary, the other half of my brain shouted, *No, you'll find a way.*

Rational thought tried to move my fingers to dial the number, but it felt like surrender. The ultimate betrayal of who I was. My lowest point yet.

You will find a way to help yourself, logic said, and then got sneaky. *By calling Paul.*

It was the perfect self-delusion. I was proving I was self-reliant... by begging for help. Before I could stop them, my fingers moved and I listened to the ringtone.

It rang and rang, before a sleepy voice said, 'What?'

'Paul, it's Dad.'

'It's... after midnight.'

I could hear Suzie's voice in the background. 'Who is it?' she said.

'Dad,' Paul said. The volume of his voice was lower as he must have turned to Suzie.

Then all I could hear was rustling, like an animated mime conversation was going on.

Finally, Paul said, 'Can't it wait until tomorrow?'

'Not really. Look, Paul, I hate to ask...' I paused because the noise on the other end of the call changed. It was subtle, but there seemed a tiny bit more echo with the background noises stronger.

He's put me on speaker, I decided. Now my begging for pity was to both of them, and I shelved the emotive father to son words I had been going to use and kept it short and to the point.

'I'm skint and I can't stay at the hotel anymore. Can I stay in your spare room?'

The question hung in the silence and I imagined the whispered conversation going on. Suzie saying no and Paul fighting for me. Surely my need would prevail.

'Sorry, the room is such a mess... and the decorators are coming. I can't put them off.' He sounded embarrassed more than sorry.

'Sure, I understand.' I tried to sound upbeat, like I had other choices, but the back of my throat closed up. The truth was that having capitulated so completely to even ask, getting a 'no' was flogging me when I lay helpless on the floor.

Every instinct told me to put the phone down, but I couldn't avoid my other pressing need. 'Could you spare some cash for your old dad?' I croaked.

I listened to another silence and imagined more conversation.

'You know we're saving up for the wedding next year and Suzie needs a new car... Look, if you come to the office tomorrow I can give you some cash.'

Suzie's car was two years old so she couldn't *need* a new one. It was difficult to fight the wedding. They had booked some huge venue off of Park Lane, with hundreds coming. The budget was probably close to a small nation's GDP.

I couldn't bear the conversation any longer. 'Thanks. See you tomorrow.'

***

Packing my bag only took a few minutes and I tried to convince myself that it was one of the benefits of travelling light. Pulling the zip closed, I realised that my lack of bank balance was forcing me to see everything differently. The £600 I had paid for my Tumi bag had been justified as I *needed* a quality stylish bag for short business trips. Now I was looking at it wondering if I could get £50 for it and put my stuff in a bin bag. I needed the money more than the bag, but how long would it last me? And what next? £20 for my £400 shoes.

I wasn't exactly flush with things to sell. Then what?

Since the Tube, every time I thought my feet touched the bottom of my fall, the floor caved in and down I went again.

I looked at the time display on my phone. 08:44. Sixteen minutes until I was homeless.

Felicity would be in her Fiat, driving the kids to school. I could call and talk to her and the kids. At least that is what I told myself – it wasn't like was I repeating the humiliating call with Paul and begging for money and somewhere to stay.

Was I? Of course not, and if I was on the phone and casually dropped it into the conversation that was completely different, right?

No. But I called anyway.

Each ring-ring sounded like 'you've-failed'.

'Daddy,' Hugo shouted and I smiled. He was the self-appointed DJ on car journeys and probably had Felicity's phone in his hand with the cable snaking to the car's radio.

'Daddy,' screamed Victoria.

'Hi, kids, how are you both?'

The conversation flitted back and forth with chit-chat before Felicity said, 'We're nearly there, Dan.'

'Wait, Felicity. I've got no money left and I'm homeless. Can we talk about me coming home?'

'It's too soon... too raw. I don't know what to think.'

'I've got nothing but family now.'

'I worry about the kids... I need all the money I can get. You're not going to be able to work in the City again and you know how small my salary is.'

When we first met, this rising-star of an architect had blown me away with her appetite for life. The only baggage she carried was from her time at the boarding school that Babs and Monty had packed her off to. It made her determined to keep Hugo and Victoria close. Local day schools only. Definitely no boarding.

And it meant a local job. She'd gladly swapped her prospects for making partner for a small local firm who couldn't afford someone as talented as her. She struck a deal with them: tiny salary in return for complete flexibility around school holidays and only working school hours. Her career had started working on huge landmark buildings, but now she fought for a few more metres on a home extension.

She worried about the kids and I made the money. That was our partnership. And now I couldn't uphold my end of the deal.

She'd left me with nothing, but I knew what her thought process would have been. *Dan's not going to be able to provide the money on a day-to-day basis, so I'll take the lump sum as a pre-payment of his obligations to the children.*

She could have left me something, but every penny made the kids' future more secure. Her brain didn't recognise the concept of enough when it came to keeping the kids safe and secure.

'You still there, Dan? Get the money from your partners. They owe you.'

***

My Tumi bag trundled after me as I walked along the high street. As I passed the coffee shop that had become my regular, I waved at the owner. Reflected in the glass I saw a scruffy labourer with a nice bag. My designer jeans had become work-wear, encrusted with dirt, mud and paint.

Ahead of me loomed the bulk of Gaz and I slowed. He had his back to me and his mobile phone pressed against his ear.

'No, Mum,' he said in a soft voice. 'I'll clean up tonight.'

Now I was right behind him and I could hear the squawk of a shrill voice laying into him.

'Sorry, Mum.' He must have sensed my presence as he snapped his head around. 'Wait a sec, Mum.'

Gaz winced as I looked at his phone that still emitted the shrill, demanding voice, then he pumped himself up. His body language transformed from meek and cowering into the Gaz I knew – the strident bully out to intimidate and belittle everyone. Hatred sparked in his eyes.

I stepped into the road to avoid the kick he aimed at me, making a cyclist swerve and swear at me. As I ran around Gaz, he pivoted and his gaze followed me. He made a V with his fingers and pointed them at his eyes before flicking them at me in an 'I'm watching you' gesture.

When I'd gone about ten paces past him, I glanced back at Gaz and he seemed to have deflated back into a little boy cringing under his mum's harsh tongue.

I had thought Gaz hated me because of envy or some misplaced jealousy about Anomaly, but maybe it was the only way he could get power and control if he was bullied at home. It didn't matter. Understanding him wouldn't stop his boots and fists, and now I was sure that he would want revenge for me seeing his weakness.

I rushed on, eager to get away from Gaz and into the safety of company.

Anomaly and Kev were chatting, but stopped as they watched me approaching.

'You know you can't go out of the country on holiday,' Anomaly said.

'Funny,' I said, taking my trailing hand off the case.

Kev looked at the bag. 'Hey, it's sitting next to him. It's like bring a pet to school day.'

I did a double take. This was the first time Kev had said anything that suggested he understood sarcasm. Then I saw that he wasn't smiling and meant it literally.

Gaz stormed over, his eyes still glittering with hate and kicked my bag. He sent it skiting and rolling, the small rigid wheels not built for fast travel over rough surfaces. It flew off the edge of the kerb and fell. 'Today ain't gonna end well for you, Knobby.'

I ignored him and went to fetch my bag. I rubbed at the front. Some dirt came off but a long scratch now scarred the shiny surface.

When I got back, Tel had come over to stand by Gaz's shoulder. 'First, you cry about getting kicked out by your missus. Now you bring your bag, so what? You out on the street?' Gaz said as he skipped from foot to foot, a little dance of gloating, his eyes still punching into me.

I said nothing, but I couldn't hide the defeated slope of my shoulders.

'Fuck, he is. Tel, we're richer than Knobby.'

Tel beamed. 'Yeah.'

'How's that feel, Knobby?'

This new-found social status energised them, and they headed off on a tour of bragging as they told all the other workers. It was about pushing me down, not bigging themselves up.

'You really out?' Anomaly said.

I shrugged. I'd had my fill of asking and getting slapped down. I might be moving in with Jerry after all.

Gaz and Tel completed their lap and headed back towards me, big smiles on their face. Kicking people, literally and figuratively, when they were down seemed to rank one notch below watching West Ham.

'Knobby fuckin' homeless! Brilliant. What he deserves,' Gaz said.

Then Anomaly grabbed my arm and pecked me on the cheek. 'He's not homeless, *Gary*. He's moving in with me.'

Gaz's smile froze, and his head snapped back and forth between us. His neck grew darker and darker red. 'That fucking wanker,' he spat. As he stormed off he added, 'I'll get you later.'

I couldn't speak and my mouth dropped open. Partly the threat from Gaz, partly at Anomaly's spontaneous act of kindness. I didn't know it, but she had started another test from God: *Dan, you know that no act of kindness goes unpunished, don't you?*

When I managed to get my mouth to work again, I said, 'Are you sure?'

She shifted her weight onto one foot and crossed her arms across her chest.

'No, I'm not sure, but I couldn't bear Gaz's smirking.'

Nothing I was going to say would convince her, so I waited and watched her thinking.

'I'll give you a two-night trial, but I've got two rules. One is you keep the place spotlessly clean.' She flashed a glance at Kev but it seemed to fly straight over his head. 'At least I've seen you wash your hands on your own, but no dirty marks, no smears. Clean as you go.'

'That's OK. What's the second rule?'

'No flashing your dick around.'

Chapter 37

Anomaly moved two big cushions into their perfect positions on the sofa and snuggled into her favourite corner.

She sighed, still not sure what moment of madness made her offer her spare room to Dan, so she compiled a list of reasons to convince herself:

1. Gaz was an arsehole.
2. Dan had taken a lot of heat from Gaz that she would have got otherwise.
3. Gaz was an arsehole.
4. Dan seemed OK.
5. He seemed genuine about being set-up.
6. She hated seeing Gaz happy.
7. She felt sorry for Dan.
8. He had nowhere else to go.
9. Did she mention that Gaz was an arsehole?
10. It was only for two days.

Even though all Dan had done was put his bag in her spare room before he headed out again, it still felt like an invasion. The place wasn't completely hers. Then she remembered that he'd had a piss in her toilet. She jumped up. If it was grim, she'd kick him out.

She rushed to the bathroom and steeled herself as she peered around the door.

One furrow in her forehead loosened. The toilet seat was down. She lifted the upper lid. Good, no hairs or marks. She lifted the whole seat and saw the sparkling bowl and rim. She looked at the floor for signs of a careless aim or lazy drips. Nothing. Her frown all but disappeared.

The sink was clean and it looked like he had even wiped the water marks away with the micro-fibre cloth that hung next to the hand towel.

She had to give Dan ten out of ten as the towel was neatly folded and the damp marks from where he'd dried his hands were the only sign he had been there.

Anomaly turned to go, then saw Dan's phone on the small shelf in front of the mirror. He must have forgotten it when he went off to tell the probation and police his new address.

A tap on the screen and the phone prompted her for a code. It was too crappy to have face ID or even fingerprint recognition.

Her laptop with her notes was still in the drawer of the IKEA desk in her spare room, and when she opened it, she skimmed through the notes she had made on Dan. What would he use? A birthday? Maybe Felicity's. She typed in 0509 for the 5th of September, but the phone buzzed and prompted for a code again. The kids then, but which one? Both she decided and ran her finger down the page. Hugo was 6th of July and Victoria was 25th November. She typed in 06072511 and the phone unlocked.

Sometimes it was too easy.

She clicked on the little email icon on the phone. Partly because she liked to have a good nose around other people's electronic worlds, but mostly because she had invited a man into her house who was on the Sex Offender Register. It wasn't too late to throw his bag out and keep the door firmly shut.

Starting with the sent items, she scanned Dan's personal email account. Mostly emails to Felicity, some begging forgiveness, some hoping to see her. All of them protesting his innocence. The emails to his ex-partners had started with pleas for help, and then deteriorated into rants, full of spelling mistakes and expletives.

It was all consistent with his story, but didn't prove anything.

Dan's inbox was thin of emails from the days after his conviction. No replies from Felicity, nor the partners. Before the conviction, there were loads of emails. Invitations to social events, queries about whether a certain company's shares were a good idea to buy, confirmation of lots of purchases. One day he was in the middle of a hectic social whirlwind, the next he was standing in a ghost town with tumbleweeds bouncing off his legs.

One email stood out. It was from his Salamander Capital work email account and forwarded to his personal one on the day of the signing. The subject said: *Deal paperwork*.

The email didn't have any text in the message, just several big attachments that would need time and a bigger screen to read properly.

She hadn't been stupid enough to give Dan a key to her flat or even the code to the outside door, so he'd have to buzz to get back in. She'd get plenty of warning of his return.

The files would take ages on the 3G network that Dan's phone showed, plus make a large dent in his phone's data credit, so Anomaly connected the phone to her home's Wi-Fi before forwarding the email to her account. She waited until her phone pinged with the announcement of a new email before she deleted the email from Dan's sent items folder. Next, she disconnected from the Wi-Fi and clicked Forget This Network to avoid him knowing she had used his phone.

On the way back from putting Dan's phone back in the bathroom where she had found it, Anomaly picked up her laptop and resettled on her sofa.

The email downloaded, and Anomaly clicked on the first attachment and began reading.

An hour later, she was on her third reading of the document with the main details of the sale of Salamander Capital to KapGroup. Dan hadn't lied about the £98m. It was a huge number and she couldn't grasp what it would mean to have it. 'Twenty-eight per cent will go in capital gains tax – over twenty-seven million pounds to the taxman. I hope they spend it on the NHS or something worthwhile,' Dan had said.

That would leave Dan a little over £70m. Did one person need that much money? Of course not, but he had worked all his life for it. That week's EuroMillions lottery prize was estimated at £105m tax-free and required no more effort than picking a few numbers. That felt much less deserved.

The intercom buzzed and she leaned on the door release button when Dan said, 'I'm back.' She left the front door of the flat on the latch and headed back to the sofa and her laptop.

'All done,' he said when he came into the lounge. 'But they make you feel like filth when you tell them you're on the register.'

Anomaly smiled. Dan had even left his shoes by the door without needing to be asked.

She looked back down at the document open on her laptop.

'Do you trust your wife?' she asked.

Chapter 38

Anomaly looked at me without any hint of malice or sarcasm.

'Do you trust your wife?' she asked again.

It seemed like a genuine question, but not one I'd expected to walk into having spent time at the probation office and then the police station. I suppose I could have waited to tell them my new address. Waited until I was sure that I was going to stay at Anomaly's flat longer than two days, but I didn't want any risk of being in breach.

'What do you mean?' I said, not wanting to commit until I knew what she was getting at.

'You left your phone in the bathroom.'

I patted my pockets in reflex. I hadn't even missed it. No one called me anymore. No one even emailed me. So, what's the point? I didn't want to waste my credit by burning data watching pointless Facebook updates or surfing the next wave of bile crashing through Twitter. 'Why does leaving my phone make you ask about trust. Did she call?'

'No, but I had a little look around your phone.'

'What?' My cheeks flushed with anger but I took a breath – I needed somewhere to stay and a massive fight with Anomaly might see me heading out the door. 'How? It's locked.'

'Oh, come on. Your passcode is your kids' birthdays.'

When she said it like that, it was obvious. Maybe not to someone like Gaz, but this was Anomaly, the self-proclaimed super-hacker.

'You shouldn't look at other people's stuff.'

She blew her lips out in a short huff. 'You didn't care when I was looking for dirt on your partners or finding Yas' address.'

I said nothing. Of course I was pissed off she had gone through my phone, but I was also happy that she had got all that data on the others. I was a hypocrite when it came to stuff that was personal to me. Like most people.

Her eyes didn't leave me, like she expected some sort of comeback, or was trying to work me out. Then she dropped her gaze to her laptop, 'So, do you trust your wife or not?' she asked.

'I trust her with the kids absolutely.' Did I trust her feelings towards me? I had hoped she'd take me back, but I wasn't sure.

'What about money?'

When Felicity and I shared a joint account, everything went through without either of us questioning the other. She got the things she needed – so did I. We didn't argue about it. We were a team.

Now the joint account was empty.

'I used to,' I said, still not wanting to commit. 'What's this about?'

Anomaly patted the cushion on the sofa next to her. 'I'll show you.'

Doing what I was told, I sat next to her and looked at her laptop screen. My anger flared again in red hot spikes. How dare she open my deal emails!

I told myself to breathe.

Calm down and see where this is heading. I put my hands on my knees to keep them still and waited.

Her finger moved to a point on her laptop screen. 'This is the two-million pounds that you told us about. Right? The money Felicity took.'

I nodded.

'And then the forty million you lost because you got fired, gets split between Julian, Ezra and Rupert. Right?'

'I really don't want to relive it all again,' I said, pushing my knees tight together to try and control the surge of anger and frustration that thinking about it sent through me.

Two of her fingers hit the keys at the same time and a new window showed. 'Bear with me, it'll be worth it.'

That caught my interest.

'I'm only trying to make sure I've got it all straight,' she said.

'OK,' I said.

My shoulders always rode up when I was tense, so it released them, feeling my shoulder blades slide down and the tension drop away from my neck.

'You've got this email confirming that you own all these shares, but they don't have any value.'

'Yeah, they didn't want us to have anything we could sell straight away.'

'But the email confirming your put options means that you can sell them back to KapGroup for fifty-eight million?'

That brought my shoulders straight back up. 'It did, but when I was fired Yas got to keep it.'

'I don't think so.'

Her smile almost split her face, but I was sure she was wrong. 'Hannah said they were worthless. She won't have made a mistake.'

'Hannah wanted you to believe that to save the firm fifty-eight million. Look…'

This time when Anomaly's fingers moved, the window showed the deal terms and conditions. It was a big document, full of indemnities and ownership clauses, and page after page of legal stuff. Vardah had tried to walk me through it with the other partners, but it was heavy going and getting it right was her job. She'd managed to ram the important stuff into us.

'This clause is the key,' Anomaly said after she had scrolled down for a long way.

I leant over to read it.

17.5 The Executive shall have the right and option (the 'Put Option') to sell any or all of the Shares then owned by the Stockholder to KapGroup for a minimum total value of £58m. The earliest date that the Executive may exercise their option is three hundred and sixty-five days (365) after the date the KapGroup shares were distributed to the Executive.

'So, in the clause, *Executive* means you, and it gives you a year before you can sell the options.'

My excitement vanished. 'That's no good on its own. There's a clause further down that cancels it.'

Anomaly's smile remained. 'Yeah, I know.'

She paged through the document before she stopped and pointed at the screen again. 'This one.'

I looked at the clause.

24.6 In the event that the Executive is no longer employed by the Company by reason other than the Executive's death, disability, or retirement in the ordinary course, the option price will be zero.

'Exactly,' I said. I wasn't dead or disabled or retired, so the options allowed me to sell my shares but receive zero for them. 'I get nothing if I'm sacked.'

There it was. Checkmate, but Anomaly didn't seem defeated.

'You need to look at the definitions,' she said as she scrolled all the way up to the front of the document. 'There.'

I read the screen.

Executive means Mr Daniel Mendoza, Permitted Transferees, and their respective estates or heirs as applicable.

'You see the words "Permitted Transferees"?' she said.

'Yeah, but…' I saw the words, but not the significance.

Her little finger hit the Page Down button and she said, 'There.'

Permitted Transferee means a) a member of the Option holder's immediate family including child, stepchild, parent or spouse, or b) a trust or charitable foundation.

I read the definition. 'So?'

She sighed and the sound reminded me of Mrs Shakeshaft, a nasty teacher in tweed who liked nothing better than to humiliate you if you didn't understand by smacking the back of your legs with a wooden ruler.

'You look like you've swallowed a wasp,' Anomaly said. 'You should be pleased.'

I was sure that Anomaly didn't have a wooden ruler to hand so I said, 'I don't get it.'

'It says that the Permitted Transferee can be your spouse. Right?'

I nodded as she scrolled.

'Felicity is a valid Permitted Transferee, so the words make her an Executive too. It means she can take your options.'

Anomaly went on about the clauses again.

I wasn't sure, but she seemed convinced I could still get the £58m.

Chapter 39

Anomaly's spare bed was a million times more comfortable than the hotel's, so I should have slept like a baby, but I tossed and turned, dozed and then snapped awake, then repeated the whole process. Settling was impossible when stuck in a looping nightmare of running through a field, my arm stretched out, chasing a fluttering piece of paper with £58m written on it, never quite able to reach it. Then closer and closer. Nearly. My fingertips brushed the paper. Then a scarecrow grabbed the paper from me and cackled. It morphed into Hannah and she ripped the paper into a thousand pieces and threw it to the wind and out of my grasp forever.

I gave up trying to sleep when my phone said 07:30, pulled some clothes on and padded towards the kitchen to get a drink of water. A hammering pain moved into my head and banged a throbbing pulse into my temples.

The water didn't help. Risking the touch of the tips of my index fingers on each temple, I rotated and massaged. The hammering was a bit quieter by the time I reached the lounge.

Anomaly was already up and looked ready for the day, with her fingers flying over her laptop keyboard.

I collapsed onto the sofa next to her and tried to look at the screen, but she twisted it away from me. 'It's private,' she said.

She's a hypocrite too, I thought, but even that little effort was too much and started the jack-hammer up again. I shut my eyes and rolled my head to try and ease the tension.

'Didn't sleep?' Anomaly asked, without pausing the speed of her typing.

'No,' I groaned. Even the click of the keys seemed too loud. I heard her close her laptop, stand and leave. The quiet along with keeping my eyes shut helped, and the banging eased a little.

165

Her hand clasped my right hand and raised it, breaking me out of the trance.

'Here,' she said and put the handle of a steaming cup in my hand. 'It will help.'

I sat up, pulling the cup to my nose and sniffed. Not coffee or English breakfast tea. Some floral smell I didn't recognise. It wasn't unpleasant so I risked a sip. Nice. After the whole cup, I started to feel better.

***

The big disadvantage of working in the City were the hours. Early starts and late evenings made for little sleep. I was often in the office by 6am. The legal team strolled in at a tardy 7am for their daily team briefing. By eight, you felt like everybody should be at work and accessible, but normal people didn't start until 9am or later.

It worked better the other way around, I decided. My phone said 08:15 and I knew that on a Tuesday morning Vardah would have been at work for at least an hour. I had plenty of time before Anomaly and I needed to head off to another session of scrubbing walls or picking up litter.

We were sitting on the sofa again. My head had cleared and the noise from her typing didn't bother me.

'Can I borrow your phone?' I asked.

Her eyes narrowed in suspicion. 'Why?'

'I'm going to test your theory on Vardah and she won't recognise your number.' She wouldn't recognise the number of my new crappy phone either, but I didn't want to use any credit.

The small uplift of Anomaly's mouth told me that she had probably run the same thought process, but she held her phone to her face to unlock it and passed it to me.

After calling the switchboard and asking for Vardah by name, I listened to it ring, hoping she was out of her morning meeting.

'Vardah's phone,' a voice I didn't recognise said.

'Can I speak to her?'

'She's getting a drink… here she comes.'

I heard the phone being placed on a desk, then a background hum, before Vardah said, 'Hello.'

'Hi, Vardah.'

'Dan?' she said in almost a whisper. I could imagine her cupping the receiver with her hand and looking around.

'I need your expert advice,' I said.

'You know I don't do criminal law.'

The casual assumption that I was in more criminal trouble hit hard and knocked the words I had planned from my mind.

'Dan?'

Recovering, I said, 'No. This is about the deal.'

I listened to silence again and looked at Anomaly. Her eyebrows were up, anxious to know if she was right.

'What about it?' Vardah said.

'Have you got the document with all the terms and conditions?' I asked, and nodded to Anomaly. She took the hint and turned her laptop so that I could see my copy of the document.

'Bear with,' Vardah said, and I heard the click of her keyboard and mouse. 'Got it.'

I talked her through Anomaly's assertion that Felicity was a Permitted Transferee in the definitions section. 'She is permitted,' Vardah confirmed.

'OK. So, assuming I make a transfer to Felicity, everywhere the word Executive was used in the agreement, then that would apply to Felicity. Right?'

'Yes, but there's no point transferring valueless shares and options,' Vardah countered.

'Ignore that for a minute and look at clause seventeen-point-five.' I waited for Vardah to find it before continuing. 'Where it says "The Executive shall have the right and option to sell" that means Felicity has the right. Correct?'

'Well, yes.'

'Now look at clause twenty-four-point-six.'

I waited as Vardah scrolled again and read out the key clause, 'In the event that the Executive is no longer employed by the Company by reason other than the Executive's death, Disability, or retirement in the ordinary course, the option price will be zero.'

'It says that if the Executive is no longer employed because they die, or are disabled or retires then the option keeps its value—' I said.

Vardah interrupted my flow. 'Yes, but you didn't do any of those. You were fired.'

'I know that,' I said. 'But the clause uses the word Executive, and if I transfer Felicity my options, that's her not me. Correct?'

'Yes,' Vardah said, sounding certain.

The next bit was the key point. Taking a breath in, I said, 'The words "no longer employed" can only apply to someone who has worked at Salamander. Right?'

'Yes…' she said, but now I could hear the hesitation in her voice.

'But Felicity has never worked at Salamander so this whole clause can't apply to her. That means if I transfer my shares and options to Felicity, she can exercise the options in a year for the full price. Right?'

Vardah went quiet. Each second of silence dragged into a lifetime and Anomaly leaned in closer and closer. She had her fingers crossed.

'I can see that you might make that argument. It has some merit,' Vardah said. It was as close as a lawyer could get to agreeing with us. 'I'll email you the transfer forms.'

I beamed at Anomaly jumping up in celebration.

The last thing Vardah said before hanging up poured cold water on us. 'But Hannah will contest it.'

Chapter 40

Despite having the words 'Hannah will contest it' still ringing in my ears, I leapt up and embraced Anomaly. It was the first real step towards recovering some of the money that had been stolen from me. Enough to rebuild my family. Enough for me to stay at home and be around as the kids grew. I could go to their school plays, help with their homework, do all the things a good dad should do. It was an opportunity to avoid all the mistakes that I had made with Paul.

As we collapsed back down onto her sofa, my phone pinged with an incoming email. As I checked the screen, my smile broadened. The mail was from Vardah with the subject line *Transfer Forms*. I turned the phone towards Anomaly for her to look, but she snatched it from me. 'Hey,' I complained.

Her fingers flew over my screen and I heard the little whoosh sound of an email being sent.

'Ever hear of privacy?' I said.

She shrugged. 'Do you want me to print the transfer forms or not?'

I hadn't thought that far ahead. I would need to explain this to Felicity in person and obviously, she would need to sign them. 'Thanks,' I said, making it sound like half-thanks, half-apology.

Anomaly picked up her laptop, tapped a few keys and I heard the printer in the spare room starting to spool and do its thing.

'I can't thank you enough,' I said.

Her eyes flicked up towards the ceiling and her mouth compressed. I could almost see her brain turning over.

'I can think of a million ways of saying thank you,' she said.

'What…' I started to object and I could feel the anger rising and burning in my voice, but then the more logical part of my brain clicked in. Without her I'd have no chance of recovering the £58m, so a £1m fee was more than fair. 'What a good idea,' I said in a more upbeat voice, hoping that she hadn't caught the shift in tone.

Her sideways look told me that she had, but I ploughed on before it could become an issue. 'You're definitely worth it. I'd be nowhere without you.' Then I patted my pockets. 'I don't have it on me at the moment. You'll have to wait until the options are exercised and Felicity gets the money.'

'Too right I'm worth it,' Anomaly said before heading off towards the spare room.

The money from the options was a long way from safe. Even though the transfer couldn't be blocked, there would be legal battles when Felicity tried to exercise them. Yas wouldn't want to pay £58m if she could find a way around it.

Money, money, money. Being set-up had to be about the money. The second payment of £40m was gone, and unless Yas found a way of clawing it back from Julian, Ezra and Rupert, they would each benefit from my destruction by £13.3m.

They all denied setting me up. But what else would they do? Especially when I had no proof or witnesses.

All I had done was charge around, blustering from failed confrontation to failed confrontation. I had been too obsessed and shocked to process anything properly. It was time to think more logically.

Do I believe I was set-up? Yes.

Did Yas or my partners have a motive? Yes, the money was more than enough motive for any of them.

Did they have the means? Certainly.

What about the opportunity? Not the actual act because they weren't on the train, but the opportunity to set it up? Definitely.

There was only one thread left to pick at. It had been staring me in the face but the image of the waitress stepping off the Tube train had stopped me thinking about her in a positive way.

She was my witness. She was my link to whoever had done this.

I had to find her.

But how? She could be anyone.

***

I made the mistake of opening my call to Felicity with: 'We need to talk.'

'Dan, not now,' she said and I could hear the stress in her voice. Partly because she was on the school run again and the kids were squabbling in the back of the car, partly because she wasn't ready to talk to me.

'I have a way to secure the kids' and your future,' I said, aiming straight at the most important thing to her. 'But we have to meet so I can explain it.'

She was quiet, and the car's microphone relayed the kids' argument about who had kicked the other at full volume. Finally, she said, 'OK, but not at home.'

'I'll text you an address,' I said.

I'd borrowed £10 from Anomaly and now I was sitting in the coffee shop wearing my Community Payback work clothes. My usual coffee sat on the table, along with a brown A4 envelope. There was no sign of Felicity and I fretted away the minutes thinking about trust and money but didn't get any closer to a conclusion. My shoulders tightened and I looked down at my hand. I had scratched a red gouge into it.

Anomaly had asked me if I trusted my wife. I did. Or more accurately I had, until she had taken all the money we had. If she got the £58m, would she let me back in or cut me out?

The sound of the door to the coffee shop opening broke my thoughts and I saw Felicity standing in the doorway. The wind outside had pulled her hair out of place and her face glowed red with cold. A hand gripped my heart and squeezed as I remembered how much I missed that look. She tried to push some hair back into place in fast, sharp movements. She hated being late for anything. Even me.

I raised a hand in a shy, small wave, feeling as nervous as on a first date rather than meeting my wife of ten years.

She nodded in acknowledgement and walked towards me. Her usual jacket was zipped up to her neck and she pulled at her gloves. Her ensemble was completed by a frown and sad, wary eyes.

Seeing her made up my mind. If we could work things out, we'd end up sharing the money to give us a future. Of course there was a risk that she would betray me and keep everything, but if I didn't transfer her the options, then I definitely wasn't going to get the money.

The chance of something was always better than a guaranteed nothing.

'Hi, darling,' I said.

A smile flashed across her face and was gone almost before it had arrived. If I hadn't been staring at her I would have missed it. There was no missing the defensive crossing of her legs and folding of her arms that stayed firmly in place as she gave her coffee order.

The beam from the overhead light hit her hair and seemed to project a halo around her head. I closed my eyes for a couple of seconds to slam the lid back down on my emotions.

I preferred how I used to be. Everything logical, emotions buttoned down. I felt too much like a victim when my emotions could betray me at any moment. 'Thanks for coming, I missed you.'

'I came for the kids… How could you?' She shook her head as she said it. 'You promised me only one drink. You know you can't take it.'

'Did you listen to any of my messages? I was set-up… She'd spiked my drink.'

'But you still let her do it.'

There it was – the inescapable truth.

If I told myself I was set-up and that the drugs in my drink made me helpless, then I was a victim. If I acknowledged that I could have fought harder and stopped her, then it was all my fault.

I sank a little lower into my sofa and shrugged. I wished I could hit the rewind button to leaving the party and choose a different path. I watched myself wave down a cab and flop into it instead of heading to the Tube. I shook my head. It was an old habit from when I arrived in London for the first time and had to stretch every penny to the maximum. Taxis were expensive and wasteful compared to the Tube.

'I can't roll back time.'

Felicity sniffed and dug into her bag, pulled out a tissue and dabbed at the corners of her eyes so it picked up tears without smudging her make-up. 'It's not like it's the first time. Mum's not forgiven you for New Year's Eve.'

Another low point. Two tequilas had been much too much for me. Babs hated swearing and my raucous lecture on all the different variations on the word 'fuck' had bombed.

'Don't give up on us,' I pleaded.

'All our plans…' she said. 'I don't know…'

The conversation was spiralling down to a place where I was on my own forever, so I tried to turn it around. 'Look, I can't change anything in the past and I can't earn enough to provide for the kids–'

'You said you had a way,' she interrupted.

'It's not certain, the forty million pounds are lost, but you might be able to get the fifty-eight million in options if I transfer them to you.'

When I saw her frown, I explained all the clauses in the deal paperwork and the possibility that she could exercise the options.

'I want us to be a family again. I love you and I love the kids, so it's best if I transfer the options to you,' I said.

'I can't afford to pay the tax on fifty-eight million.'

'There's no tax on a transfer between spouses. The tax would be due when you exercise the options and get the money.'

Felicity nodded and smiled. 'It will make the kids secure.'

I pulled out the forms that Vardah had sent to allow me to transfer the shares and options to Felicity. 'I've filled in all your details. You just need to sign.'

She picked up the papers and read the forms – always cautious, she wouldn't sign anything without reading it first. Then she nodded, took the pen I offered her, and signed.

'No guarantee, but it gives us a future,' I said.

As I slid the papers into the envelope, she picked up her coffee and took a sip. Her eyes flicked up and she held mine for a moment.

That look and the fact that she hadn't objected to my use of the word 'us' gave me hope.

Chapter 41

Felicity and I spent the rest of the time it took her to finish her coffee talking about the kids.

Then she looked at her watch. 'I need to go.'

'Can I come over and see the kids at home?'

'Maybe, let me think about it,' she said as she stood. I couldn't guess if she meant that as a positive, because her eyes were turned away from me as she reached for her coat draped over the back of her chair.

She slipped into her coat and I stepped forward and hugged her, pecking her once on each cheek.

My hope doubled.

She hadn't hugged me back, but hadn't flinched away. Plus, she hadn't completely dismissed the idea of me seeing the kids.

The bell chimed as Felicity pulled the door open and stepped back into the wind. She grabbed at her hair to stop it flying away.

'Yes,' I said to myself. Other than the beginning, the meeting had gone better than I dared hope, and I decided to celebrate by waving at the cafe owner and picking up my empty cup. She nodded, and I heard the crunching growl of the grinder attacking coffee beans.

I pulled out the transfer forms and turned them over. It was worth the risk and the transfer would show Felicity I was serious about the kids' future. After scrawling my signature on the forms, I pushed them back in the envelope and wrote Vardah's name on the front.

They were too important to trust to the postal service so I pulled out my phone and called her.

'Can I drop the transfer forms over to you now?' I asked after the opening hellos.

'That was quick,' she said. 'I'll be here.'

'Does Hannah know?'

'I had to tell her about the clause and the transfer.' She sounded reluctant, but I knew she had no choice. It would have been unprofessional and she would have left herself open to attack from Hannah.

'And?'

'She swore about ten times in a row, so I think you can say she's worried.'

'That's great.' I punched one arm into the air. If Hannah reacted like that, then she must think that Felicity might be able to exercise the options and collect the £58m.

The hope from my meeting with Felicity grew as it fed on itself.

I was on my way back.

***

The hope of getting some of my money back in a year didn't change the fact that after paying for my two double espressos and Felicity's cappuccino, I only had £4.14 left of Anomaly's £10. No way could I face asking Felicity for money, so swallowing my pride and taking some money from Paul was my only option.

Paul's office was only about ten minutes' walk from Salamander, so I could drop the transfer forms in, say hi to Jerry and then head off to see Paul. I could pay Anomaly back and finish the evening ahead of where I'd started. First, I had to get the forms to Vardah.

The walk took nearly an hour, but I had the time and didn't have the money for anything else. My film of shame was on hold and for the first time, I noticed an unexpected positive. Hours and hours at my desk, staring at a screen didn't burn as many calories as the client lunches and dinners piled on. The

Community Payback work wasn't strenuous, but I was much more mobile and my limited budget didn't stretch to large portions or rich, exotic ingredients. The end result, judging from the hang of my trousers, was that I must have lost some weight.

The day was getting better and better.

I pushed the door of Salamander's office open and said, 'Alright, Col.'

Colin rushed towards me, arms out wide, barring my entrance. 'Sorry, Dan, you're not allowed in the building. Hannah's orders.'

'I want to give this to Vardah.'

He shook his head and kept his arms up. I could see Maddie's eyes watching from behind her desk. Col couldn't help me under her gaze even if he wanted to.

When I was back on the street, I could see Colin standing close to the door. At first, I thought he wanted to block any hope I had of coming back in, but his head jerked to the left and his eyes opened wider. He repeated the head jerk and eye flaring until I understood and walked away.

Around the corner, I went through the open doors and into the building's loading and unloading bays. It was full of all sorts of vans, some with big water cooler bottles, others with reams of paper. All the needs of a busy office. A man in a yellow high-vis jacket popped his head up from behind a clipboard. I answered his silent question by waving the brown A4 envelope and he nodded towards the back of the bay.

I followed the direction of his nod into the mailroom, and waited for a courier with skin-tight Lycra, bulging calves and a big bag to sign for some parcels. He stuffed the parcels in his bag and rushed out.

'What you got, mate?' the man on the other side of the counter said.

'Letter for Vardah Ansari at Salamander.' I offered the envelope, watched him take it and, with a practised flick of the wrist, spin it onto a pile of other envelopes.

***

'You should have called if you wanted to stay,' Jerry said when he saw me walking along Wood Street and into St Peter Cheap. 'The West Wing is dirty and the cleaners have let me down again.'

'Looks like the pigeon beat me to it anyway,' I said, gesturing towards the bird pecking at a discarded crust.

'Bloody squatters.' Jerry waved an arm and the pigeon flapped away, but only a few metres. It started to inch back to the crust as soon as Jerry turned his back.

'Sorry, breakfast baguettes were all sold out.' I hated to let him down, so I had taken a chance. 'Tuna melt OK?' I said and passed him the piping hot sandwich. It was an end of day special and all that I could afford. I was down to 15p.

'Been trying to eat more fish,' he said with a smile. 'How did it go with Rupert?'

While he tucked into the tuna, I filled him in on my failures, before finishing on Anomaly's discovery.

'She sounds smart.' He rubbed at the end of his leg, where his knee should have been.

'You OK?' I asked.

'Usual. Hurts like buggery sometimes.'

He rarely mentioned his pain, but it was always there, visible in his drawn, grey face and the winces he tried to hide. 'No point complaining to you, Dan,' he had said when we were still getting to know each other. 'Not like you're a doctor, is it?'

I watched him rub and massage, thinking that I could have helped him if things were different. I'd earmarked some of the sale proceeds to see if I could get him into a prosthetics programme and back on his feet – in both senses of the phrase. My stomach knotted with regret. I could have done more. Should have done more. A daily sandwich and a chat seemed pathetic now.

'Cheer up, mate,' he said.

'I wish I'd helped you more...' I started, but he waved me down.

'Don't beat yourself up. You *did* something real to help me. The chats and nosh made me feel half human again. All I get from the others is bloody leaflets.'

He pointed at the bin by the tree. On top was a logo of a charity I hadn't heard of that helped ex-service personnel.

'Can't eat a bloody leaflet, can I?'

Chapter 42

I huddled around the corner from Paul's office, not wanting to bump into Pierre or anyone else I knew. Desperate to avoid answering the 'what happened', or 'what are you doing now' questions that would inevitably follow a meeting.

Did I manage to pull off the look of an office worker on a quick break? Probably not. My clothes told their own story. They said I was more tramp than City worker.

Had it come to this? Skint dad waiting outside his son's office for a handout like Oliver Twist asking for more.

For the moment I had to survive my economic truth and I needed a job to start earning again. Get through the year and smile at Hannah as I stood next to Felicity when she exercised the options and we shared the £58m. That was the dream I needed to turn into reality. Then I'd be back, and I would be able to deal with the questions and looks.

When Paul came around the corner, I could see him scanning for me. He might have been expecting me to wait for him inside the shiny, bright reception area, but I would have been too exposed there.

'Paul,' I called and pushed my right foot against the wall and stood straight.

He waved and headed towards me, his hands in his coat pocket.

We did our usual hug: brief contact of side of chest to side of chest, one arm around the back, two quick pats and break apart. He'd been much cuddlier before Kat died, but understandably, the loss of his mum so young had driven him into himself. Maybe one day, he'd manage to break himself out.

'How's it going, Dad?' he asked, but the £200 he held towards me seemed to answer his own question.

'Thanks, Paul. Really appreciate it.'

To cover the awkwardness of the moment, he stamped his feet and said, 'Getting cold.'

'Yep, but I'm on the way back,' I said with a smile.

His eyes opened with surprise. 'How?'

Before I could give him the good news about Anomaly finding the way around the clause on the deal paperwork, I heard, 'Paul? Paul, you there? We need to go.'

'Shit,' I muttered as Paul turned.

'Be right there, Pierre.'

I ducked my head to try and hide behind Paul.

'That you, Dan?' Pierre said.

Shit, shit, shit. Continuing to hide would only make it worse, so I waved. 'Hi, Pierre.'

He sauntered over to us, wearing a spotless cashmere coat. The glint from the shine polished into his shoes was a trademark. It went along with his 'you can tell so much from a man's shoes' saying.

He stopped next to Paul and, as he always did on meeting someone, flicked his eyes down. Today, he was right. My shoes, scuffed and paint flecked, gave me away and his smile broadened.

'Paul's been keeping me up to date. So sorry, Dan.' He didn't even sound as sincere as an insurance broker apologising to a client that their claim was being refused, and I could see in his eyes that he hadn't even tried.

The bastard was enjoying it. Finally, he was doing better than me.

'Paul's doing well here with me.' He slipped an arm over my son's shoulder. It was casual, but designed to look paternal.

I bit my tongue to stop me shouting, 'He's my son, not yours.'

His sideways smile and the way his eyes closed into a slit as he watched me, sent a chill through me. It struck me that I should have thought about him more. Was his need to be the best strong enough for him to crush me?

Of course it was.

***

On the long walk from the City back towards Anomaly's flat, I thought more and more about Pierre. I spooled through my memories, assessing each cold sneer at me, each look he gave Felicity or Paul. Had he always been planning and searching for a way to get me?

How could I possibly prove it?

I had no idea and my track record of investigative failure didn't give me any real hope. He'd simply deny it all like the others.

Two streets from Anomaly's flat, I tried to focus on the positives. I'd received an email from Vardah confirming receipt of the transfer forms. When the transfer went through, I really would be on the way back. The thoughts lifted my body taller. Prouder – that was a word I thought had been lost to me.

I glanced at the window of a fast-food restaurant and saw the reflection of a flash of light coming straight at me. A man on a blue moped, with learner plates and a big box strapped to the back, careered across the pavement. I jumped backwards and felt the noise of the moped fly by me. The moped's front wheel hit the shop front and toppled to one side.

'Watch out,' the driver said, half-holding the bike up. 'You made me crash.'

'You shouldn't be riding on the path.' How was it my fault? I was walking on the pavement and he flew at me.

He gave me the finger, accepting no blame for his own mistake.

It wasn't worth the energy of getting into an argument, so I returned his one-fingered salute and walked off.

'Wanker,' I heard called after me. When I turned to swear at him, the driver was disappearing into the shop and I saw Tel close behind me.

His eyes glinted, but not as much as the big metal knuckleduster on his right hand. He looked more alive than I had ever seen him. His nostrils flared like a hunting dog smelling his prey and he bounced as he walked.

My heart rate accelerated and I shot frantic glances around for Gaz. My first thought was, *Good, just Tel*, but then it struck me. When did Tel ever doing anything without Gaz? That meant Gaz was close by, but where?

Needing to get away from Tel and safely behind Anomaly's front door, I walked faster. Away from Tel, but every sense I had screamed, *Where's Gaz?*

He could be hiding behind any of the parked cars, so I stayed as far from the edge of the road as I could and half raised an arm to protect myself in case he jumped out. A couple with arms interlinked strolled past on the other side of the road. Would they help me if Tel attacked me? No.

I started to run towards the corner where I would turn into Anomaly's street. Twenty metres, ten metres. No Gaz.

A snatched glance back over my shoulder showed Tel rolling after me, but I'd opened the gap a little. He jogged after me with enough spare lung capacity to shout 'Wanker banker.'

Once I was around the corner, I had another fifty metres to go to the front door and safety. The road looked deserted, maybe Tel was on his own after all. Maybe Gaz was blocking the far end of the street in case I came from the opposite side.

Run faster, my brain screamed. *Get inside before Gaz comes.*

Dipping my head, I pushed my legs and arms harder, but still watching each parked car I passed, waiting for Gaz to jump out at me.

My pulse rate was sky high and I could hear it surging around my temples. My chest heaved and burned.

Nearly there.

Then I saw the shape next to the front door. Short, wide and wearing a claret and blue shirt with crossed hammers on his chest.

I slammed on the brakes, eyes jagging left and right as I looked for an escape route. A large panel van parked opposite the entrance to Anomaly's block prevented access to the road. Gaz may have been big, but a couple of fast, short paces left him blocking the pavement. Even running at full pace, I didn't think I could run through him.

Tel was closing from behind.

There was only one way open to me, and I ran down the alley to the side of the building.

And regretted it instantly.

'Dead-end,' my brain shouted. The alley only led to the bin store. High brick walls flanked its sides.

I remembered watching a football coaching video with Hugo on YouTube. I could hear the coach's voice. *Position your body to send your opponent where you want them to go*, she had said. Gaz watched football all the time, it would be second nature to him. He'd blocked my path and I'd gone where he wanted.

Down a quiet alley with no way out.

Chapter 43

My head snapped from side to side looking for an escape as I prayed for a miracle. For someone to walk along the road and save me or to appear from the bin store. No one did.

I backed up as Gaz and Tel stepped into the alley. They seemed too wide for it, and an idea flashed into my head. *Maybe they'd get in each other's way and I could jump around them.*

My back touched the metal bars of the bin store door and I spun around and yanked at the handle. I banged the handle up and down, but I knew it was kept locked to stop non-residents dumping their rubbish in it. When I'd emptied the bins in the morning, I had needed Anomaly's fob to open it. A fob I didn't have now.

I slipped my phone out of my pocket and rested it on the bars of the door, then turned to face Gaz and Tel.

'Been looking forward to this, Knobby,' Gaz said as he rolled his thick neck and shoulders.

'You're gonna get a good kickin', Knobby,' Tel added. His knuckleduster slapped into his palm.

My school fights had been a flurry of weak punches and name-calling that were over before they started. I tried a bit of boxing a few years ago when a friend of Felicity's said it was a great way to get in shape, but the long hours at work meant I only managed two visits. Gaz and Tel looked well-practised and I doubted they were constrained by rules or concerns about fair play.

What had I learnt at boxing that might help? Basic protective stance with my hands up, arms tight to my head and sides to protect me, but I'd been up against one other man in a ring.

Gaz and Tel stopped a couple of metres short of me and waited, beaming when they saw the panic in my eyes.

I took a pace forward, not because I had any real plan, but because the gate pushing into my back restricted me.

Gaz frowned in surprise. I think he was waiting for me to collapse into a cowering ball and take the kicking.

Then I took another step forward, almost to touching distance. 'Look, Gaz, Tel, we don't have to do this,' but as I finished, I knew that attack was my only hope. I pulled my head back, and flashed my head forwards, aiming to bury my hard, bony forehead into the soft bridge of Gaz's nose. If I could send Gaz down, Tel might pause and give me time to escape.

Too late, I saw Gaz smile and tip his head forward. Now my nose was hurtling towards the hard, unforgiving top of his head. He must have seen my clumsy move in a million street or pub fights, executed better and faster than mine.

My nose smashed into his head and pain exploded through my face. The sharp crack of my nose breaking was the last thing I heard before a flash of white filled my eyes and my mind blanked.

Slowly my mind rebooted, and I wished it hadn't. My face was on fire and I gagged and heaved.

I kept my eyes shut, willing the world to stop swimming. The motion calmed and stopped.

I opened my eyes. I was lying on my side and four legs with lace-up boots and jeans waited about a metre away.

'He's back with us, Gaz,' Tel said and I groaned.

'Good, 'cos I want him to feel everything.' One boot hitched back and flew towards me. I tensed as the toe smashed into my ribs, driving the wind out of me and adding a second area of my body screaming with pain.

I curled into a ball as boot after boot crashed into my back, side and legs. Gaz and Tel were laughing and joking as they worked. 'Wanker', boot, 'Banker', boot.

The pain now seemed to come from everywhere on my body at the same time. As the flurry of kicks continued my brain ignored the rest of my body. It had one message for me: 'Keep your hands and arms over your head. Keep me safe.'

Then the kicks stopped and I could hear Gaz and Tel sucking in large mouthfuls of air, getting their wind back and preparing to attack again.

But they didn't. I felt hands on my legs and they pulled me around so that my legs pointed along the alley. I kept my head hidden in my arms. Gaz leaned in.

'You know what really pissed me off,' he said. 'You and little Emika. I reckon I could have been in there.' He sniffed. 'She was up for it, but you came along and then I'm out.'

I didn't carry a wallet anymore. Little point when you don't have any money. The cash Paul had given me was still in my back pocket and I felt Gaz's hands rummaging through my pockets. He would have seen me if I had tried to hide it and then I would have lost the money and my phone.

'Cheers, Knobby. Drinks on you tonight,' Gaz said. 'And don't tell no one about this, otherwise we'll send some friends who aren't as nice as us.'

The rank smell of his breath faded and I felt two hands on each of my legs, pulling them apart.

'You're not going to be much use to Emika tonight.'

I thrashed and kicked but the arms held me tight. Struggling woke up all my other bruises and cuts. My nose exploded with pain again and I couldn't keep up the fight.

One hand holding my right leg loosened and I braced for the incoming boot to my groin.

It smashed into me, almost through me, driven by anger, loathing and Gaz's certainty that I had stolen Anomaly from him.

Vomit erupted from my mouth and scorching pain engulfed me.

***

Sometime later, my body was able to cope with the pain levels and I started to come round. At least when I prised an eye open, the alley was empty. The searing, pulsing pain in my groin was like nothing else I had ever felt. It made the agony from a football straight into the nuts at school feel like a wasp sting. Then my nose joined in, then my ribs and all the other places a boot had landed.

Pulling myself up onto one knee, I waited for the surge in pain to dip, before risking bringing the other knee up. Then, with one hand on the brick wall for support, I forced myself up into a crouch. Light flashed in my head and hard bolts of pain shot through me and I heaved, jetting more vomit onto the alley.

When the spinning in my head finished, I risked a step towards the bin store. Then another. Every movement aggravated the sickening ache from my groin. I grabbed the wall to stop myself falling. My eyes wouldn't focus properly, so I leant in close to the gate, hoping that Gaz and Tel hadn't seen me hide my phone. The movement made my head spin and lurch again, but when it stopped enough for my vision to clear, I could see the soft sheen of its screen.

I picked it up in my right hand and looked at my reflection. My eyes looked puffy with dark rings of bruising. My nose seemed fatter with a cut running across it. Blood smeared the bottom half of my face. I raised my left hand, letting the fingers glide over the swollen mass of my nose. Not too bad, but the bridge of my nose crunched and cracked as I touched it and started a firestorm of pain again.

Pace after agonising pace I walked along the alley, stopping to let my head recover and another mouthful of vomit to land on the alley. By the time I reached the front door to Anomaly's block, I had nothing left inside me.

Pressing the call button to her flat forced the light from the entrance camera on, and I stared back at the reflection in the glass.

'Hello,' she said.

I dipped my head to the camera and said 'It's Dan' but it sounded more like 'TTThhhs Dan' through my blocked nose.

'Jesus,' she said and buzzed the door release.

Repeating the slow walk, I shuffled to the lift. The doors opened as I arrived and Anomaly's hands reached out to grab me and guide me in.

'What happened?' she asked.

The lift started moving and my messed-up brain couldn't cope. I slumped against the wall and gulped in air through my mouth to stop myself heaving again.

When the lift arrived on her floor, Anomaly hooked her shoulder under my arm and ushered me towards the flat. She propped me up against the wall as she unlocked the door, re-hooked her shoulder under me and edged me towards the spare bedroom.

'Sit,' she said.

I did as I was told, but my legs didn't obey and I crashed onto the bed, with my back and bum on the bed and legs sprawling. Anomaly lifted my legs and spun me onto the bed, before pulling my vomit splattered shoes off. 'Gross,' she said.

She lifted my head as gently as she could but it still re-sparked the pain. It was like watching the New Year's Eve fireworks over the London Eye.

She left me for a while and my brain enjoyed tormenting me by switching its focus from one area of pain to the next.

Anomaly came back into the room and perched on the edge of the bed.

'I need to clean you up,' she said. 'It's going to hurt. OK?'

'Go,' I said, and braced.

She brought a wet flannel into my eyeline and said, 'Here we go.'

The flannel touched my cheek and moved.

Fireworks fifty times brighter than before erupted, too bright to deal with and I blacked out.

Chapter 44

The loud beeping of a lorry reversing cut through my dark sleep. First priority was a mental stocktake. The pain from my nose had subsided and all the places that Gaz and Tel's boots had landed ached and throbbed.

They weren't bad enough for me to worry about broken bones or internal bleeding. The kick to my groin seemed to build a direct connection from my balls, through my stomach and on to my mouth. Every low, sickening pulse of pain generated a spasm that travelled north and hit my throat.

As I forced my eyes open, I saw Anomaly sitting on the side of my bed with a bag of frozen peas and a box of paracetamol. 'Breakfast of champions,' I said.

She rolled her eyes as she snapped two of the tablets from their packaging and passed me some water. Once they were swallowed and she'd taken back the water, she wrapped the peas in a tea towel and held it towards me. 'For the swelling,' she said.

I took the peas and rested them on the blanket over my aching balls, waiting for the cold to do its magic.

'No, for your nose,' she said, grabbing the peas. She rearranged the towel and rested it on the bridge of my nose.

The cold seeped into my nose and cheeks, numbing the pain. I closed my eyes and dozed.

Anomaly's hand on my shoulder woke me. 'Times up. Twenty minutes max,' she said and lifted the peas from my face.

'Thanks,' I said, knowing that she hadn't been sure about me staying at all, let alone nursing my cuts and bruises.

'Let me guess. Gaz and Tel?'

Remembering Gaz's threat, I said, 'They jumped me before I could see their faces.'

She crossed her arms, looking unconvinced.

'Why have you got my phone?' I asked, seeing one of her hands wrapped around it.

'Checking your email.' She smiled and ignored my frown. No such thing as privacy with her around. 'You got an email from Vardah confirming that the transfer forms have been checked and sent on to be processed.'

It brought a smile to my face. Only a week ago, I had been shouting at Julian and Ezra and getting nowhere. Now there was hope of getting back some of the money.

If a journey was simply a series of steps, I had taken another on my long trek back.

***

The walk to Community Payback had started as an old man's shuffle. All groans and aches, but the stiffness eased a little as the movement got reluctant muscles warm and more mobile. Things south of my nose were feeling almost normal by the time we reached the pickup point. I scanned the faces of the usual suspects waiting for Alan to arrive with his van and take us off to whatever today's work was.

When I didn't see Gaz or Tel, I wiggled my jaw, crunching some of the tension out of it. Then I loosened the other places that I always tensed: a stretch of the fingers, a roll of the neck, a conscious relaxing of the shoulders to push my shoulder blades down.

'What happened to you?' Kev asked, pointing at my face.

'Walked into a door,' I said.

Kev nodded. 'Most accidents happen around the house.'

Then, all the tension I had released, surged back as I clenched and tightened when I saw Gaz and Tel arrive.

They sauntered over towards me, no sign of remorse. Instead, their smiles grew broader and broader as they got closer.

'You look pretty, Knobby,' Gaz said. 'Wearing some of Emika's mascara, are you?'

'Mascara's for the eyelashes. Idiot,' Anomaly said.

Gaz glared at me and bunched his hands into fists. It looked like he was wishing he had gone much, much further last night. And he was planning another meeting.

***

The day passed, and Gaz and Tel threw stones and the occasional 'wanker' at me as they muttered and plotted. Then a bottle fizzed over my head, trailing a shower of yellow liquid that splashed a wet, foul-smelling stripe onto my shirt.

'That's enough you two,' Alan called and waved Gaz and Tel to follow him to the other side of the work area.

I doubted I could get back the £200 that they'd taken and that left me skint again and pushing the boundaries of Anomaly's kindness. It was one thing providing a bed, but nursing care and no contribution for food was going too far. I'd have to beg Paul again and that wasn't a call I wanted to make.

During our next break, I procrastinated with my thumb over the Call button on my phone, then I swallowed the last scrap of self-respect that I ever had and called.

'Hi, Dad. I'm at the airport. We're about to board so don't have much time,' Paul said.

'Look…' I stammered, 'I hate to ask but I got mugged last night and they took the £200. Any chance you can lend me some more?'

I heard an announcement asking business class passengers on the flight to Frankfurt to begin boarding and Paul said, 'Really? Are you OK?'

'Been better.'

'Can't meet you obviously, but I can transfer £200 later. Where do you want it to go?'

Before I could answer I heard Pierre's impatient voice say, 'Paul, come on, we can't miss this flight.'

'Text it to me,' Paul said and the call dropped.

The way he had said 'really' made it sound like he didn't believe me, or maybe I was feeling oversensitive and it was simply a surprise. Either way, I needed to prove I wasn't making it up, so I found the camera app and adopted the selfie pose. I moved my arm in and out until my broken face took up the whole screen, took the photo and selected the button to forward it in a message. Under the picture with dark purple bruises beneath my eyes, I added the details of my bank account.

I sent the text.

His reply flashed in. 'Shit. Looks bad. Talk later.'

My legs started shaking with relief that I didn't have to walk to Paul's office and back again. I could lock myself away in Anomaly's flat, safe from Gaz and Tel's boots.

***

The remnants of the two frozen lasagnes lay before us on Anomaly's small white dining table. Another meal to add to the list of debts and favours I owed.

We were in the post-meal silence when the banking app on my phone flashed a notification. As I pressed the message, I let out a sigh. I hadn't been sure that Paul would have had the time or security details to arrange the payment, but when I checked my balance it was just over £200.

The temporary liquidity would ease things.

'I owe you £10 and I want to contribute to the food. What are your account details?'

She nodded and told me. After a few seconds on my banking app, I confirmed a payment, and unseen computers moved £40 from my bank account to Anomaly's.

Now to address the question that had been hanging over me all evening. 'Err, when I came you said I could stay a couple of nights. Tonight would be three.'

Perhaps she would do a check round to ensure that I hadn't left a mark anywhere. Whatever I expected, it wasn't her casual shrug and the words, 'You're good for a bit longer. Can't feed you to Gaz.'

To prove that I was a valuable asset to the household, I scooped up the dinner things and did the washing up, wiped down the kitchen and then cleaned the table. Only my nose throbbed at the exercise, the rest had moved from painful to a dull ache.

I had got away lightly. No cracked ribs, no concussion, but I felt shattered and now that I knew I had a bed to sleep in, I said goodnight and headed off to the spare room.

The bed felt even better than I thought possible. I picked up my phone and found the selfie I had taken. I looked like crap and thought about Paul's reaction. It might gain me some sympathy from Felicity and help to open up our text communication again, so I forwarded her the picture.

A few seconds later the reply came in. *OMG. What happened? Are you OK?*

Got mugged, but fine. You OK? I replied.

The next five minutes flowed by in a happy flashback to my business trips when we'd text chat. Me at some airport or hotel, her at home or out with the kids. My hope of a full reconciliation grew and after we said goodnight, I held the phone to my chest. A hard plastic and glass proxy for the real thing.

The buzz of an incoming call woke me from the daydream and I looked at the number. Without any contacts in the phone, it showed a mobile number I didn't recognise.

'Hello?'

'Dan, it's Pierre. Paul showed me the photo. Ouch.'

Shit. The last thing I had wanted was Paul showing Pierre and giving him something else to gloat over. 'Not as bad as it looks,' I lied. 'What do you want?' It came out hard and defensive and I silently swore. It showed weakness and vulnerability. Two of Pierre's favourite things in an adversary.

He ignored it and said, 'Look, Dan, I've got an idea. Nothing complicated, but it would help me out and would give you some pocket money.'

There was no mistaking his patronising tone, especially at the word pocket money, but Pierre's idea of pocket money would be way beyond even the greediest teenager's aspirations. *He'll have some menial and degrading thing for me to do*, I thought. Like cleaning his pool while he watched or scraping bird shit off his terrace.

But I needed the money. 'Like what?'

'A month ago, I was on a driving trip around Scotland. You know, golf and distilleries.'

I did know. It was the sort of thing my old life called entertaining a client.

'Anyway, something came up and I had to fly back for an unscheduled client meeting. I left my Bentley at the dealers in Edinburgh. They've been great, but now they need me to move it.'

'Why don't you get them to put it in a transporter?'

'I could do, but I was going to get the car and then pick something rather precious up in Liverpool on Sunday. Now,

I've got to go to Dubai and won't get back until late Saturday evening.'

Pierre liked to tell a story, and to his credit, I was wondering what precious thing was in Liverpool and needed a Bentley to carry it to London.

'How do I fit into this plan?'

'Now that you have plenty of time,' he said with obvious glee in his voice. 'I wondered if you would fly to Edinburgh and drive the car to Liverpool, do the pickup and then on to London. Two birds and all that. I'll arrange the flight, hotel in Liverpool and the car to be waiting for you. How does £400 sound for your trouble?'

That would do nicely as pocket money, but the last thing I wanted was to owe Pierre a favour. Then again, a couple of days driving a Bentley wouldn't be a real hardship and Pierre didn't know there was such a thing as hotels under the five-star rating. I'd be safe from Gaz and Tel's lurking presence outside Anomaly's flat.

I didn't have any travel restrictions within the UK from my sentence, and as long as I told my probation officer and the police I was going to travel away from my approved address, I could go. And I needed the money.

'OK.'

'Super. Can you go on Saturday morning? I'll send a car to take you to the airport as I understand you don't have access to your Aston.'

Thanks, Paul. That was something else I could have done without Pierre knowing.

'Sure,' I said.

Chapter 45

Thursday and Friday passed in a see-saw of emotions. The prospect of getting some of the money back on one side. My anger and frustration at being destroyed on the other. I fretted over my lack of any proof of who had done it or even a target to focus on. I was no further forward than when I started, but I hoped that the weekend away would provide me with some inspiration.

Pierre's assistant had arranged everything and emailed through the itinerary. The promised car arrived on time on Saturday morning, and I settled into the highly polished black Mercedes, complete with driver and an envelope containing my £400 and £150 for fuel. My Tumi bag barely took up any space in the car's boot, and other than its new scar, it suited the quality of its surroundings. Packing had taken seconds since I didn't have any choice. Everything went into the bag except the clothes I wore for Community Payback. They went into Anomaly's washing machine.

Things at London City airport flowed seamlessly. I'd been through check-in, bag check, shops and gates so many times over the last few years it was as ingrained as the mud on my work jeans. Only a few people bothered to glance at me, staring at the purple and blues of my double black eyes. The world had moved on and although the videos of me on the Tube were still out there, they weren't today's trending must-watch.

The British Airways flight to Edinburgh took off on time at 12:05. A short one hour and fifteen minute flight would have me in Edinburgh at 13:20. They had booked me in the economy cabin for the quick up and down flight. Pierre's firm seemed to have the same policy as Salamander. We wouldn't waste money on business class for such a short flight, when simply booking the emergency exit row added extra legroom and luxury. There was no time for the meal, I barely had a chance to read the paper. Out of habit, I took the free *BusinessLife* and *HighLife* magazines from the pocket next to my seat to read later.

Another driver waited for me at the Edinburgh arrivals hall, and the quality of the planning had me out of the airport and into Pierre's Bentley in under an hour and a half. They seemed to have booked the weather as well – Edinburgh glimmered bright and crisp under a cloudless blue sky.

The Bentley dealership was housed in a cluster of car dealers. Ferrari next door, Porsche across the road. Jaguar, Mercedes and Volkswagen close by. I took my time, feeling more at home than in weeks and allowing myself to get used to the controls on the car.

Whatever the precious thing was that I had to pick up would be ready at ten o'clock on Sunday morning, and the drive to the hotel would only take about four hours plus fuel stops. I should be there by eight. Plenty of time for a meal before bed. The pickup point was only about twenty minutes from the hotel so I had time for a bit of a lie in and a big breakfast before heading off the next morning.

I set the hotel into the satnav as the destination, and the Bentley started with a quiet murmur, nothing like the snarling shout that announced my Aston coming to life. I clicked the indicator on when the car told me to turn right out of the dealership and set off.

The car didn't roar or snort or anything so vulgar. It floated, and as I wafted along the main road, it was like I was flying in the azure blue sky that surrounded me. The afternoon sun glinted on the long bonnet all the way to the trademark Bentley *Flying B* bonnet ornament that had emerged from its hidey-hole slit with the grace of a swan unfurling its wings. The A7 road was busy but the traffic flowed enough to make progress. By the time I hit the A701, the traffic was sparse and I enjoyed the long views over the Scottish countryside, the churches and villages.

I was careful though. The sheer number of speed cameras and average speed limit areas made it look like speeding drivers were the UK's most wanted criminals, although I always thought they were more about revenue generation than safety. Whatever the motivation, when I hit the motorway, I had the Bentley's cruise control set at 68mph, 2mph under the limit. It meant I could relax into the soft and supple leather without the stress of keeping a constant eye out for cameras or police cars.

The miles rolled by, and despite the advertised twenty miles to the gallon, the car's fuel tank was so big that I didn't bother to stop for three hours and I was nearly at Kendal. Even then the car could have carried on, but the driver needed a pit stop and some caffeine.

I headed off again and the car slid effortlessly down the rest of the motorway and up the gravelled drive of the hotel.

I miss this, I thought as I settled into the four-poster bed and replayed my evening. I'd treated myself to a steak in the hotel's restaurant, but I knew I might need to make Pierre's money last a long time.

I opted for one course, not three, tap water not wine.

Chapter 46

Sunday breakfast at the hotel was a lavish buffet catering for every possible breakfast preference, plus a menu of cooked items ranging from a full English breakfast to smoked salmon with a poached egg. Unlike dinner the night before, it was all included in the price of the hotel booking that Pierre had paid for. So, I went to town. Two trips to the buffet and a marvellous mushroom omelette later, all washed down with fresh orange juice and coffee, I was full. Actually, I was bloated, but I tucked a couple of croissants and pan aux raisins into my linen napkin and held it close to my leg so no one could see as I left. Now that my lunch was sorted, it was a quick trip to my room, put my toothbrush and lunch into my bag and down to check out.

In the light of the morning, the £35 bill for my steak felt like an extravagant mistake. I pulled two £20 notes from my envelope and handed them over to the lady behind the reception desk. Her eyebrows went up at the sight of money rather than a credit card, but she recovered with a warm smile. 'I hope you enjoyed your stay, Mr Mendoza,' she said as she passed me my change.

'Yes, thank you.'

As the Bentley purred away from the hotel, I took my eyes from the drive curving through the parkland grounds and looked in the rear-view mirror at the receding hotel. 'I'll be back,' I said to the car, then settled into paying attention to the roads and the demands made by the voice of the car's satnav.

After twenty minutes of following roads that wound along hedge-lined paths and open fields, I arrived at some ornate black gates with gold scrolls and topper. A block-brick driveway led down a small hill. There was no sign of a house or other buildings, no hint as to what the precious cargo could be.

I'd read of secretive art transactions that happen well away from a shop. Perhaps this was the home of a collector and I was here to pick up Pierre's latest purchase. Could it be cases of wine so expensive that no one dared drink them, but bought for show and bragging rights?

I put the Bentley in park and got out to head to the intercom that was set into a black metal rectangle on the right-hand pillar. The name *Haven Hall* was embossed into the metal along with a rearing horse with a flowing mane. I shut my eyes and prayed that this wasn't a stud farm and I was here to pick up a horsebox holding some valuable animal. I'd tried driving a car with a trailer before and hadn't enjoyed the feeling of the trailer not always heading in the same direction as the car. Reversing it had been a disaster.

'Can't be,' I said. 'Please.' I took some hope that I hadn't noticed a tow bar on the back of the Bentley, but maybe that would pop out at the press of a button.

The intercom rang after I pressed its only button, then a voice said, 'Come to the front of the house,' before I could even open my mouth. One of the gate leaves twitched and started moving, followed a few seconds later by the other. *Strange lack of security*, I thought, but there on top of a tall post was a CCTV camera.

After about half a mile of driveway, the Bentley crested a small rise and a huge Elizabethan style manor house came into view with black timbers creating decorative shapes and patterns on the white walls. At first, I thought it might be a modern reproduction, but there were about fifteen tall brick chimneys standing above the roof from a time when fires in every room were the only heating.

There was no sign of a horsebox and I let out a small sigh of relief.

Before the Bentley had slowed to a halt, the large black wooden door opened and a man in his thirties and a dark suit stepped out.

I popped the door open and climbed out of the car.

'Madame Dufrais will be with you shortly,' the man said.

Now it all made sense. Dufrais was Pierre's family name and the *something rather precious* must be his mother.

The man disappeared back inside and left me unsure whether I should wait or follow him.

I decided to wait and five minutes later, an elegant woman in her seventies appeared in the doorway wearing a classic black dress under a vivid pink overcoat.

'Pierre should have come himself; he knows I hate being driven by unknowns,' she said, making the word *unknowns* sound like I was some criminal undesirable. The image of the Tube flashed across my eyes. I *was* a criminal – undesirable according to the courts.

She looked down her nose at my clothes. 'No suit or hat. Standards are slipping,' she said and raised her right hand and left it hanging in the air. The man in the suit knew what was expected, took her hand and guided her down the steps of the house and past the back of the car to the passenger side.

Then she looked at my face rather than my clothes. 'Oh,' she said. 'They've sent some ruffian.'

Her arm flew up in a dramatic action and she tipped her head back like she was going to faint. The man in the suit stepped in to hold her up.

'I shall probably be murdered en route,' she moaned.

'No, madame. This is a friend of Mr Pierre,' the man said.

'How does Pierre know such people?'

'I work in the City,' I lied. 'Don't worry about my nose, I got hit playing polo.' This second lie I chose to appeal to her snobbery and make her relax.

'Well. It's a glorious game,' she said with happiness in her voice, but then her natural exasperation with the world returned. 'Why are you keeping me waiting?'

She was obviously incapable of opening a car door herself, so I flicked around the bonnet and opened the front passenger door.

'No, no. The back,' she said, like I was a very disappointingly dim staff member.

After I opened the back door and the man guided her into the seat and got her settled, another two staff appeared with two large bags and numerous smaller boxes. I clicked a button on the car's key fob to open the boot and the staff took a few minutes jiggling the bags and boxes into it.

While they were doing it, I climbed into the driver's seat, started the car, and was bombarded with requests from madame. I moved the passenger seat forward even though her feet didn't stretch far enough to touch it. I redirected an air vent that was blowing air on to her. I turned the temperature up 0.5 of a degree. Then she told me they weren't right and to do it all again.

Don't, I told myself, and bit down on the temptation to tell her to shut up. When Pierre used the word precious, I had assumed he had meant *something of great value*, not this seventy-year-old diva incapable of doing anything herself.

'Anything else?' I said with a bit of frustration slipping into my voice. It was going to be a long drive to London.

'I shall inform Pierre of your insolent tone,' she replied. 'Pass me my scarf, I'm still in a terrible draught.'

I looked around but couldn't see a scarf. 'Where?'

'There, there.' She flapped a hand in the direction of the front of the car.

I clicked open the leather-clad centre armrest between the two front seats and pulled out a thin, patterned scarf. 'This it?' I asked as I turned towards her. Then stopped.

The scarf looked just like one that Felicity said she had lost.

'No, no. That must be one of Pierre's girlfriends.'

I crumpled the scarf and pulled it to my nose. Even through the bruising and blood clotted in my airways, I got hints of Felicity's favourite perfume.

'How dare you?' came the shocked complaint from the back.

My head spun. What did this mean? Could it really be Felicity's? Why was it in Pierre's car?

A shrill, 'My scarf, my scarf', cut my thoughts off and I reached for the glovebox in front of the passenger seat. It was a stretch with my seat belt constraining me and setting the bruises on my ribs throbbing, but I hooked my fingers around a piece of fabric and pulled it out.

'That's it,' she said, but all I could see were the two photographs that must have been tangled with the scarf. I dropped the scarf and picked up the pictures. Both showed Felicity standing next to Pierre in evening wear. I recognised the venues. Corporate hospitality events, but the way their arms were linked and how Pierre leaned in made them seem more intimate.

I turned in my seat and showed her the photos. 'Have you seen this woman with Pierre?'

She waved her hand in a small but definite wave, dismissing my question.

'Have you seen Pierre with this woman?' I repeated.

'I don't know… My *scarf.* I'm suffering in this frightful draught.'

'Shut up about your bloody scarf.'

'I've never been spoken to—'

'Well, you should have. Now sit back and shut up.' I tossed the scarf at her and stared again at the photos.

Felicity always said she didn't like Pierre. Was she deflecting me from the truth? Or was this an obsession of Pierre's?

I'd seen the way he looked at her, his eyes glinting with desire.

Chapter 47

Pierre's mother was subdued during the drive south, the atmosphere, colder than the air conditioning, was closer to freezing. She wasn't as quiet as a mouse, because each time a car pulled out in front of us, she tutted and said 'oh, dear'. But she wasn't the demanding tyrant she had been.

After I stopped for fuel, I opened the lunch I had taken from the hotel. I wasn't hungry, just bored and craving some sugar. The first pan aux raisin was moving towards my mouth when I thought about all the crumbs falling in Pierre's car.

I hated people dropping anything in my Aston, so as much as I didn't like Pierre, I put the food back in the napkin and refolded it.

'You need anything before we head off again?' I asked.

She shook her head in reply and looked out the window.

In the rear-view mirror, I could see her bony hands and taut face, and I doubted she ate much at all.

The miles rolled by and our relationship remained locked in permafrost. Only as I pulled the Bentley up to the entrance to the underground car park below Pierre's Thames-side penthouse did she seem like she was winding herself up to *precious* again.

I texted Pierre: *Arrived*, and the gates to the car park opened.

Pierre's instructions had included the numbers of his three allocated parking spaces, so I crawled the Bentley through the car park, scanning the little numbers painted onto the concrete floor. Every slight movement of the steering wheel made the tyres squeal on the shiny surface and brought a muttered complaint from Pierre's mother about the noise giving her a headache.

After I found the space and parked, I got out and stretched. Pierre's mother didn't move.

Of course, she can't open a door, I thought, and did the necessary.

I was rewarded by the same offered hand that she had used on the steps of her house and I gave her my hand. She slid out the car, as gracefully as Grace Kelly ever did and stood, not once relying or leaning on my hand for support. It was pure theatre and I was simply a decoration.

'Don't forget my bags, there's a good fellow,' she said and started walking towards the lift.

***

By the time I'd shuttled back and forward to the lift in the car park with all of Pierre's mother's bags, and my own single Tumi, and then repeated it all from the lift to the only door on the penthouse level, my face was red. Some of it was exertion, but most of it was anger. I fumed that Pierre had assumed that I would bring the bags like his obedient servant, and I ground my teeth together whenever I thought of Felicity's scarf that was now in my pocket.

I rested my finger on the doorbell and didn't lift it until Pierre opened the door.

'Sorry, Dan,' he smirked. 'It's the butler's day off.' He peered past me at his mother's bags. 'Second door on the right for those.'

The temptation to drive my fist right into his face and give him a set of bruises was almost too strong to resist. 'Fuck off and do it yourself.'

'Never any need for swearing,' he said, looking smug that he had managed to rattle me. It didn't help that it was one of Babs' favourite lectures to me.

I pulled Felicity's scarf from my pocket and waved it in front of him. 'Explain this,' I demanded.

'I hoped you'd be nosey enough to find it. Felicity's a cracking girl.' He shifted his weight, leant his shoulder against the door frame, and struck his favourite pose. 'Debonair playboy' he called it and claimed it made him look sophisticated, confident and in control.

All of the things I wasn't. 'Stay away from my wife.'

'I rather think that's her decision. Now run along, Mouse.'

My anger rose and boiled, and Pierre's eyebrows raised in amusement. 'I…' I couldn't hold it in, but I turned and lashed out a foot, sending one of the bags flying. I would have loved to have launched it into his smug face, but he would have been straight onto the police about an unprovoked attack, complaining about convicts on parole reoffending and demanding a custodial sentence.

'Stay away from Felicity,' I called as I grabbed my bag and headed back towards the lift.

'It's her choice.'

I could hear the smirk in his voice.

Chapter 48

I tried to slam the door to Pierre's building shut, hurling my anger and frustration into it, but the door was dampened and sprung to give a luxurious soft close. The day got worse as the promised mid-afternoon rain pelted down and the wheels of my case caught in every crack, and bucked and complained in my hand like a reluctant puppy on a lead.

A black cab drove past with its yellow for hire light on. I was tempted – it was warm, dry and convenient. I'd deliberately only put the minimum fuel in the Bentley and still had £25 from the petrol money but I couldn't bring myself to spend it on a cab. The feeling of dread and panic was too raw from when I didn't have enough money to stay in the hotel. I wanted to put that feeling off for as long as possible.

I walked on, getting gradually wetter and wetter. As the rain seeped in, my anger drained out. Under the wide canopy of an oak tree, I stopped for shelter. Did I trust myself to call Felicity and be calm enough for a rational discussion? Screaming at her and accusing her of having an affair with Pierre wasn't going to get me back home with the kids.

The image my brain showed me wasn't me, happy at home. Instead, it decided that I deserved to see a different family scene. One where I faded out and was replaced by Pierre, sitting around a table with Felicity and my kids, cheering and waving a cheque for £58m in the air. My wife. My kids. My money.

Shaking my hands and unlocking my jaw helped release some of my pent-up frustration, but I was way too emotional to risk a call.

When you were as wet as I was, the rain didn't matter anymore so I left the oak behind and carried on.

Ten trees further I decided on a text to Felicity: *Hi, need to talk to you. Can we meet tomorrow – same time/place?*

I trudged on, still fighting my bag over the uneven pavements, turning my phone to my face every few strides to check for a reply. Nothing.

All I could think of was Pierre with Felicity, and what the photos and scarf meant.

My anger rose inside me, almost high enough make me turn around, storm Pierre's penthouse and pummel the answers out of him.

But that was crazy. All I'd get was another night in the police station on my way to prison.

The old me had been able to keep all my emotions in. The new me was a miserable failure.

When I finally got back to Anomaly's flat, I spent twenty minutes in the shower watching my skin recover from its shivering blue. I dressed, gave Anomaly some of Pierre's money as rent, and we ate another meal that went from freezer to plate via a five-minute detour to the microwave.

Every look at my phone clicked up the tension in my shoulders. Always the same story: no reply from Felicity. I'd got myself trapped in a vicious circle – should I take a risk and call her? No, I was worried I was too tense for it to go well. So, I waited for a text that never came and the tension rose. Then I thought about calling again.

To try and break the cycle, I flicked through the in-flight magazines I had taken from the aeroplane, glancing at the pictures and scanning the articles, but I couldn't focus.

Felicity's text reply came late in the evening. *OK* was all it said.

It didn't enlighten me, and I churned meanings and approaches, hoping to work out a way I could confront her about Pierre without shouting and making it worse.

***

The solution that came to me was simple, but I had to wait all of a slow and boring Monday. Litter-picking had lost whatever charm it had, and every one of Gaz's 'wanker banker's and the hurled stones and bottles grated and ratcheted up the pressure on my lid as I fought to keep my emotions in.

When Felicity came through the door of the coffee shop and saw my face, she rushed over to me, eyes wide in concern. 'Oh, Dan,' she said and reached up to touch the side of my face.

I grabbed her hand before it got there and kissed it. 'You should see the other guy,' I said.

'Not a bruise or mark on him?' She knew me too well, but it forced a laugh out of me.

'Yeah, untouched.'

The owner came and took our order. I used the lull to pull Felicity's scarf from my pocket. 'Found this,' I said.

She gave a little squeal. 'I've really missed it. Where did you find it?'

I looked at her, a cold assessing stare, trying to remember all the little moments from our ten years together to try and work out if she was lying. All I could see was happiness at getting the scarf and concern at how I was looking at her.

'What?' she asked.

'It was in Pierre's car.'

She looked lost, so I told her the brief version of my trip and finding the scarf and photos in Pierre's car.

'Pierre had it in his Bentley?' Her eyes flicked up and to the left. 'Last time I had it was at that do in November. He was there. He must have taken it then.'

I wanted to believe her, but I had to push further. 'He fancies you,' I said, hoping to shock her that I knew.

'He fancies everybody,' she said and shuddered. 'Anyway, he doesn't want me. Not for myself. He only wants to own me so that you can't. I'd be a trophy.'

It was obvious she understood the true competitive nature of Pierre's relationship with me. Been subjected to 'debonair playboy' and seen through all of Pierre's charm.

The photos of her and Pierre must be nothing but formal, staged things. No hidden intrigue or affair. I smiled at her.

'What?' she said.

'I miss you.'

Our coffees arrived and we busied ourselves taking cups from the owner and sipping the hot brown liquid. Now that I could dismiss Pierre as Felicity's lover, I could move back towards reconciliation.

'So, we're good?' I asked.

My throat tightened as she sniffed and reached for another tissue.

'What?' I said, hearing the panic in my voice.

'The other parents have told their children everything. Hugo and Victoria are getting bullied because of you. They're both crying when I arrive at pickup time.'

I rubbed a hand at my eyes and winced as I hit the bridge of my nose. How could the parents set their kids on mine?

All my fault.

'I can't cope with the stigma,' Felicity said. 'It's too much for the children. I'm going to put the house on the market and look for a new school.'

'I'll help you look. We can build a new life away from London.'

She shook her head. 'I want a divorce.'

I'd transferred her the options and now she wanted a divorce. The coincidence of the timing hit me like a charging rhino. My mind replayed the scene where Pierre took my place, then it broadcast the last words Pierre had said to me.

It's her choice.

Had she already made it?

Chapter 49

I flew out of the sofa, grabbed my coat and headed for the coffee shop's door. The thought of Felicity with Pierre, and worse my kids calling him Dad, was too much to bear.

'Dan, wait,' she said, but I let the chime of the shop's door closing answer her.

Every time I thought I took a step forward, God tested me again. Why was I always in line for another test?

'Stop,' I shouted at myself and two pedestrians looked my way, dismissed me as a loony with two black eyes, then carried on. I recognised the warning signs. If I carried on that thought process, it would be like having milk cooking on too high a setting. Rather than a gentle simmer of self-loathing, it would boil up and over the top of the pan and splash everywhere. The mess would take a long time to clean up.

I stopped, shut my eyes and took three deep breaths. It allowed me to put the lid on the milk and turn the heat right down, back to its normal simmer. Locking every emotion and memory down would allow space to think.

Divorces took months to go through, so I had to look at every day as an opportunity to change Felicity's mind. Failing that I needed to work out a way of keeping the kids.

First, I needed to block any potential challengers. Were Pierre's words simple mind games? Were he and Felicity having an affair? The same questions went around and around.

Then stopped. The side effect of me being set-up was that the future of my kids was threatened. If I could prove it was Pierre or at least cast doubt in Felicity's mind, then she wouldn't forgive him.

But this time I needed something concrete.

Dishonoured

I knew the details of the deals Pierre had done, so there was no doubt in my mind that he was cunning and callous enough to have plotted my downfall. That was only part of what was needed. His plan without the waitress to execute it, was a waste of time.

How would Pierre have found her? I doubted she was a family friend. If he didn't already know anyone, then he would have searched for her.

The set-up would have taken a certain type of person – strong-willed, cunning, access to drugs to spike my drink, a planner to make it work.

I started walking back to Anomaly's flat. I needed a computer. The *BusinessLife* magazine I had skimmed last night had an article about the jobs that ex-police force personnel did.

That could be the right profile. It might lead me to her.

Excitement fizzed up in my stomach, growing and feeding on itself. I had to tell someone to let it out. Just like when we agreed on the deal to sell Salamander and I had phoned Felicity. Like I'd called Kat after a positive interview in the City, and when Paul was born, I'd called my parents.

The excitement fell away, like a receding tide. I had lost them all.

Who did I have left? Only Paul as direct family and Rosalyn one step removed. The tide turned and self-pity flowed back. I need to cling on to them before I was marooned on my solitary island.

I checked the time on my phone. Paul would be at work, so I sent a simple text. *Miss you. Call when you can.*

Rosalyn loved to paint and I could still see her and Kat with their easels side by side. They saw the same scene through different eyes. Rosalyn's bold and experimental strokes contrasting with Kat's more reserved and conservative style.

Tears formed in my eyes at the memory, and I blinked them away before calling Rosalyn.

'Hi, Rosalyn,' I said with a little choke in my voice.

'You sound sad,' she said.

'I was thinking of you and Kat painting together. I miss her.'

There was a long pause as I played out memories of Kat. I guessed that Rosalyn was doing the same.

'We all do,' she said.

I could hear the depth of the loss in her voice. No parent wants to outlive their children.

'I do have some good news,' I said and told her about being sure it was a set-up, and my idea of how to find the waitress and prove Pierre was behind it.

'You need family at a time like this. It's a shame I'm so far away,' she said. 'But if Pierre found her, then so will you.'

I would.

The excitement started to build again.

***

I banged the front door of Anomaly's door shut and ran into the lounge.

Anomaly looked up from her usual spot on the sofa. 'Take your shoes off in the house.'

My burning idea had to wait while I retraced my steps to the door, pulled my shoes off, and using my socks as a cleaning cloth, slid my feet over any marks my shoes had left.

She was still on the sofa with her left leg down and her right foot tucked up and under her bum. It looked uncomfortable to me, but she was way more supple than I was and it turned her legs into a little 'desk' for her laptop.

'I need to use your laptop,' I said.

Rather than offering it up to me, she pulled it closer to her. 'I don't share my stuff.'

'You had no problem using my phone.'

'And?'

And? Did I want a pointless argument about privacy and hypocrisy, or did I want to find the waitress? 'OK,' I said. 'You're better at these things than I am. I think I know how to find the woman from the Tube.'

She pushed her laptop back onto its 'desk'. 'Because I'm interested,' she said. 'Not your pathetic attempt to manipulate me.'

Her motivation didn't matter to me, only that she helped. 'Thanks.'

She raised an eyebrow. 'You need to tell me what you want.'

'I think Pierre was behind it all, but he would have had to search to find someone willing to do what she did on the Tube. If he can find her, then it will be easy for you.'

She smiled, but I didn't know if she liked what I said, or if she was laughing at another blatant attempt at flattery. 'So, what do you want me to search for? Woman for hire?' Sarcasm flooded her voice. 'I think that might return lots of interesting results, but it won't get us anywhere.'

'No. I read this article about all the jobs that ex-cops do. Like becoming civilian investigators or working in security. They'd fit her profile.'

Anomaly's frown replaced her smile. 'Would cops do it?'

'Some would for sure.'

She shrugged and I watched her type *ex-police private security* into a Google search bar and press enter.

I groaned when it showed over ninety-two million results.

'Durr.' Anomaly smacked her palm against her temple. 'Pierre would need to meet her so it makes sense if she's local.'

She added *London* to the search and reran it: thirty-eight million results.

Adding *city* brought it down to twenty-three million results.

I watched as Anomaly tried variation after variation, nothing got the results down under fifteen million.

Pierre must have hit the same issue. His request was going to sound crazy to most people. Most would reject it out of hand. It would need someone cold-blooded, used to messy situations, tough, resourceful. Someone like Jerry.

'Try ex-special ops soldiers in London.'

'Sixty-eight million results,' she said.

'This is impossible.'

'Why do you think people pay so much to be on the first few pages?' Anomaly said. 'People click on those links and ads.'

I looked at the list of page links on the first page. 'Try that advert,' I said, pointing at the fourth one down. The link was to Save our Soldiers, the same name as the company on the leaflet Jerry had thrown away.

She did and we surfed the pages under the link. Lots of medical terms and prosthetic products. Medical stuff only, not a hint of special operations.

We backed out and got nowhere with any of the links on the first three search result pages. Or the next twenty.

'There are no photos of any of the people who work there on these web pages, so how were you going to recognise her?' Anomaly said. 'We should look at images.' She clicked on to the Images button at the top of the page and scrolled down. I scanned the faces, but didn't see the waitress. Anomaly scrolled down and down. The last image had a photograph of a man with the word Security on his back standing in front of some gates. The security at Pierre's mother's home was lax, but could he have needed some security advice at work to deal with a threat he'd received?

'Try adding corporate security services,' I said.

She did and scrolled through the first page of images.

When she got to the eleventh page it felt like I had been slapped around the face, then I shivered. 'That's her.' On the screen was a small picture of the waitress with the words *rebuilding soldiers by protecting billionaires* and a link to the *Business Insider* website.

Anomaly clicked on the story and we both read the article. Her name was Leia and she had started a charity called We Can Rebuild You that specialised in treating both physical and mental injuries for ex-service personnel. Her security company employed a lot of the people that the charity had helped and was called Bionic Security and Protection.

'We've already been on that site,' Anomaly said and went back through the searches we ran. Bionic was one of the top ten hits on most of them.

I'd found her.

Now I could find out who had destroyed me.

Chapter 50

Anomaly and I went back over the pages of Bionic Security and Protection's website. Most of it was top-quality services to high-end clients and corporates. The sort of people who needed advice on kidnap protection, security audits, and bodyguards. The site also featured a lot of before and after stories of employees who had been helped by We Can Rebuild You and then worked for Bionic Security and Protection.

'Look at that,' I said to Anomaly, as all of the heat drained from my body. We had visited the *Most Popular Services* page before, but this time the *Employee Termination* service sounded very, very personal. I pushed my hands between my knees to stop them shaking.

Anomaly put her hand on my arm and said, 'We can rebuild you.'

The joke and the comforting squeeze from her hand worked, and the shakes subsided. 'Who am I? Steve Austin?'

'Who?'

'Google Six million dollar man.'

Her fingers typed then she glanced at the results. 'Explains the bionic in the name.' She wiggled her bum further back into the sofa. 'What now?'

'I don't think it's a good idea to try and sneak up on her like we did with Yas.'

'No, but you need a meeting.'

And what would I do then? Confront her? Unlike with my partners, there was no chance she could deny anything. It was her, but I needed to get past that to find out who had sent her. Would she help me?

I thought about the moment when I saw her mouthing the word, sorry. She could feel bad about it, but then why had she done it?

'You still home,' Anomaly asked. 'You were miles away.'

'Thinking about why she would help me.'

'You don't ask, you don't get.'

'Then I need a reason to meet that's not "you destroyed my life".'

'Something corporate?'

'No. As soon as I give her my name, she'll know. I can't use a fake one. She's bound to do background checks, and I don't have a corporate email. She'll ask for a corporate switchboard number so she can call and ask for me by name to prove I work there.'

But I did have Jerry.

'I need to go in through the charity. Can you get their number up?'

'Sure, you're going to call?'

'Yep, I didn't talk to her much and my voice sounds different with my nose all swollen up.'

Anomaly shrugged and found the number for We Can Rebuild You.

I dialled, clicking the call onto the speaker so that Anomaly could hear, and when it answered, I said, 'Can I talk to Leia, please?'

'Will she know what it's about?' the man on the other end of the call said.

'No, it's a new call.'

'Let me take a few details first. She likes everything written down and recorded. What's your name?'

'It's for my friend, Jerry Wheeler. He was in the parachute regiment.'

'Which battalion?' the man asked.

'Three Para, he lost his left leg above the knee in Afghanistan.'

'What was his service number?'

'I don't know.'

'OK, before we go any further, I need that. Believe it or not, non-service personnel call us trying to pretend they were in the army to get our help.'

'Can you put me through to Leia?' *Worth a try*, I thought.

'Not until we have verified Mr Wheeler's service record.'

I could hear the impatience in his voice.

'I'll find out,' I said and hung up.

I needed a different approach.

Chapter 51

Anomaly listened to Dan flounder on his call then hang up. He folded in on himself as he collapsed back onto the sofa.

'Shit,' he said. 'They're cautious. I don't know that Jerry will go along with it.'

The solution was obvious to her. 'We need a story they'll believe and they can check out,' she said. 'How about mine? It's all out there.'

Dan looked confused. 'But you weren't in the army? Were you?'

'No, but I was thinking about Bionic Security.'

'But...' he said, the furrows on his brow deepening.

Anomaly didn't want to explain it to him and then explain it all again to Bionic, so she grabbed her phone and dialled.

'Bionic Security and Protection, how can I help you?' a woman said.

'Can I speak to Leia?'

'I'm afraid she's not available at the moment. Can I help?'

It sounded like the default answer, like all the calls were screened before being allowed through.

'I have a problem with a stalker. Now he's making threats.'

'We have other staff who can help you with that.'

'No, I want a woman and I've seen her interviews.'

'She is more expensive...' The woman didn't say this with any hint of put down as if she thought Anomaly couldn't afford it, it was more like she was testing the water.

'Don't worry, I have a rich uncle,' Anomaly said, having to suppress a laugh as Dan's eyes flashed wide and his mouth dropped open.

'OK, let me take some details. Full name?'

Anomaly winced as she gave her full legal name. 'Emika Hunt, but people call me Anomaly.'

There was no sign of a reaction in the woman's voice as she said, 'Address.'

Anomaly gave all of her contact details, date of birth, her old employer's name and address and the name of the man whose computer and phone she had hacked and the details of her conviction.

The woman's voice didn't waver as she took it all down. She must hear some pretty wild things every day. 'And what's the situation now?' she asked.

Anomaly winked at Dan as she switched from the truth to lies.

'He hasn't forgiven me and now he's stalking me. Threatening me. I don't feel safe. I need some protection from him.'

'Have you been to the police?'

'Yes, but they don't believe me.'

'We need to do some checks and someone will call you back.'

The call dropped and Anomaly flopped against the back of the sofa.

'You were brilliant,' beamed Dan.

***

An hour later Anomaly's phone rang. She had added Bionic Security's number to her phone's contacts, and when she spun the phone screen so that Dan could see the name, he crossed his fingers and mouthed 'good luck'.

'This is Leia from Bionics. Is that Emika? Or would you prefer if I call you Anomaly?'

Dan looked like he had heard a ghost and he almost climbed out of the sofa to get away.

'Call me Anomaly.'

'It sounds like you're in a nasty situation. We keep diary slots open so that we can help urgent cases and a lone woman with a threatening stalker isn't something we would delay any longer than necessary. I can see you tomorrow afternoon between four and six if that's OK?'

Anomaly could see Dan nodding, so she said, 'That's OK. I finish Community Payback at four.'

'Do you want to come to our offices?'

Now Dan was shaking his head.

'Could you come to me? I'm worried about travelling too far on my own.'

'I understand,' Leia said. 'Where do you want to meet?'

Dan was miming picking up a cup and taking little sips. He even had his little finger pointed out.

'There's a coffee shop that's safe.'

Anomaly gave Leia the address and she could hear typing.

'It will take me about twenty-five minutes to get there. Shall we say 16:30?'

'Perfect,' said Anomaly.

Dan punched the air in triumph and blew Anomaly a kiss.

Chapter 52

Anomaly pulled the high collar up on her big navy puffer coat to block the biting wind that cut across Tuesday's Community Payback and sent the plastic bottle she tried to grab flying. Her fingers were going blue and they complained to her that she had forgotten her gloves.

'We're done for the day,' Alan called.

She heard a ragged cheer from some of the other litter-pickers and headed to the van. As soon as she'd given Alan her bag and picker, she shoved her hands in her pockets and climbed on board the van.

'You OK?' Dan said as he dropped into the seat next to her.

'Cold,' she said.

His ears glowed red as the circulation started returning to them, and he nodded. 'Ready for Leia?'

'Sure,' she said, and watched the city roll by as the bus headed away.

They arrived back at the drop-off point a little after four in the afternoon. 'See you later,' she said to Dan and headed off to the coffee shop.

She was twenty minutes early for the meeting with Leia and a wonderful wall of warm air hit her as she entered, a welcome respite after being outside in that wind all day. The shop was always quiet at this time of day, the lull between a mid-afternoon break and after-work catch-up with friends. That was part of her plan.

After waving to the owner and mouthing 'Cappuccino', she headed over to a table. Not their normal sofa and armchairs, but the small round table for two in the corner with the high-backed wooden chairs. Dragging a chair back so that it touched the rear wall of the shop, she pivoted in and sat.

It was the perfect position to look out across the shop, through its glass front and door, and see anyone approaching.

When she snuggled into her coat, she hoped it would look like she was scared and hiding from her stalker. She pulled her phone out and pretended to read from it. Like so many people on their own in a public place who used their phone as a shield from the rest of the people around them, but also to signal that they weren't really alone. They had loads of friends, honest, but they were all somewhere else.

Her eyes looked over the top of the phone and towards the road.

And waited for Leia.

***

Anomaly's empty coffee cup rested on the edge of the table and she touched the screen of her phone to wake the display up. 16:27.

A woman in a long black coat came into view on the opposite side of the road and Anomaly's heart started beating faster. She was sure it was Leia.

The woman didn't cross the road towards the shop, but as she continued walking her eyes flicked towards the shop.

'It's her,' Anomaly said under her breath.

Leia completed her walk-by and disappeared.

A minute later, she materialised at the edge of the shop window and glanced in. Only a glance, but Anomaly thought that Leia had taken it all in. She'd seen Anomaly using her phone, the owner, the empty chairs, the old man reading the paper, and then walked past the shop.

Was Leia suspicious of the meeting, or always careful? Anomaly thought. Probably both, she decided, borne of habit and hard-earned, bitter experience.

The coffee shop door opened and Leia stepped in, her eyes darting and checking everywhere.

Anomaly unlocked her screen and pressed send on her pre-prepared text message: *She's here*. They had expected Leia to be cautious, so didn't what to spook Leia by Anomaly whipping her phone out the moment Leia arrived.

The old man rustled his paper and Leia snapped her eyes towards him, then dismissed him. She crossed the shop.

'Anomaly?' she said with one hand on the back of the empty chair.

'Yes.'

Leia twisted her head away from Anomaly and scanned the outside and the empty tables.

I bet Leia wants to sit with her back to the wall, thought Anomaly. 'I feel safer in the corner,' she said.

With a nod, Leia pulled the chair back and sat down. 'I've read your notes, but I'd like to hear it from you,' Leia said after the introductions.

Anomaly retold the story she gave over the phone, feeling her stomach tighten more with each passing minute. *Where was Dan?*

'What do you hope we can do to help?' Leia asked when Anomaly finished.

'I don't know, scare him off. Get him to stop. Teach him a lesson.'

'We can do that,' Leia said with a smile.

The bell on the coffee shop's door chimed.

Chapter 53

My knees started to wobble when I looked through the door of the coffee shop. *She* was there. The sight of her took me tumbling and spinning back onto the Tube train with her standing in front of me. Back to the seconds before my life fell apart. To the point when I still could have done something to stop her.

When I didn't do anything.

I wasted more time replaying all the same excuses that I had been drugged, that she was so strong. It didn't change anything.

Time to look forward, not back.

The doorbell chimed as I pushed it open, and I saw Anomaly's eyes flick over Leia's shoulder towards me and flare open.

My plan was to walk across and place my hand on Leia's shoulder and watch her surprise, but she must have interpreted Anomaly's reaction as her stalker arriving. She flashed out of the chair, with her left hand's open palm pointing towards me, and her right arm drawn back, ready to punch.

Deciding that the last thing I needed was her fist smashing into my already swollen nose, I froze and raised my hands.

Leia's eyes narrowed and her forehead furrowed. Then she glanced back at Anomaly. If I was Anomaly's stalker, Leia should have seen fear on Anomaly's face, not a smile of triumph.

'What's this?' Leia asked.

'I need to talk to you,' I said.

Leia flicked between Anomaly and me again, her mental calculations obvious in her eyes. She must have sensed no imminent physical danger as she uncoiled her tensed right arm and allowed it to drop. 'I don't know you,' she said.

230

'Oh, come on. Look past the clothes and the bruising and remember a party at the restaurant at One Poultry. And…' I had to take a big gulp of air to steady my voice. 'And a Tube journey.'

She dropped her left hand as she softened her stance, but this time her eyes were blank and unreadable. 'I don't know anything about that.'

'You've got to help me,' I pleaded, sounding too much like a whining child. My self-loathing grasped the tone and added it to its archives, ready to taunt me with it later. 'You destroyed me.'

She said nothing, but I saw her eyes flicker as she searched for a memory. A flash of sadness crossed her face.

'Everything OK?' the owner called, from behind the counter.

'Yes,' Leia said, and sat back in her chair.

I grabbed the back of an empty chair from another table and dragged it with me, before spinning it around and sitting. Making it a cosy table for three, not two.

The shock of being so close to her drove all the clever words out of my head and I said, 'Why?'

'I have lots of witnesses who will confirm that I was nowhere near a Tube train, and no CCTV will show a clear view of my face.'

My hands went to my head and I rocked back and forth as I fought the panic taking over. Was it all going to end here with her lies and denials piling on top of those from Yas and my ex-partners? How could I rebuild myself when I didn't know why it had happened? Or who was behind it?

It doesn't matter why, my brain said. *You're worthless. It's fate.*

'Take it easy, Dan,' Anomaly said, and I felt her hand pull my arm away from my head. 'Breathe.'

I tried, and as the panic eased, I wondered why Leia sat down if she wasn't going to help. Did she regret it?

'Why did you say sorry on the Tube?' I asked.

'I wasn't there,' Leia said, but before panic could seize me again, she added, 'but I could guess that someone saying sorry might mean they felt uneasy about doing it.'

Hope flared in me – she might answer if I played the game that this was all theoretical and Leia wasn't involved. 'Then why would that person do it?'

'The money offered by a client might have been very large and allowed for a lot of good work to be done.'

If I believed her, she had spent the money she got from ruining me to rebuild ex-service personnel. People who had served and sacrificed. Those that were truly worthy of rescue.

'Who was the client?' The answer wouldn't help me get the money back, but I needed to know who hated me enough to do it.

'I'm sure that the client's identity would be confidential,' Leia said.

My face slapped into the brick wall of denial again, but as I tried to think of the words to plead and beg her to tell me, I looked at Leia.

The corners of her mouth were up in a hint of a smile. 'But it's difficult not to regret some of our actions.'

'Who?' I said, Pierre's face floating in front of my eyes.

'The most I can say is that the client was very clear on what *she* wanted.'

Chapter 54

My hands twisted and pulled at each other. Each movement frantic and jagged. My body rocked forwards, pivoting at the hips, bobbing my head forwards and then pitching it back. The movements got wilder. 'Nooooo,' I cried.

She.

Who else could it be? my brain screamed.

'But she's my loving wife, the mother of my children. Ten happy years,' I replied.

But she's got all your money and wants a divorce to run off with Pierre.

'But…' I didn't have the answer.

My brain seized its advantage. *She can't stand you. Like your parents.*

'Nooo.' I could see rain hitting a windscreen, bright white lights of a massive lorry flooding the inside of the car. Lighting up my parent's faces, blinding them – the same image from every time I thought about them. When I was calm and in control, I would see my dad fighting to save them, and hear their screams as the lorry hit. The darker image, one I couldn't destroy, was them smiling and linking hands as my dad turned the wheel towards the lorry.

That's right. They preferred to drive into a lorry rather than see you.

'They didn't. The police said they swerved away.'

They lied to protect you. And as for your beloved Kat. My brain knew the right trigger to pull.

'Leave her out of this.'

It was a one-sided fight. My brain had all the evidence it needed. Every failure was recorded and replayed to belittle me. To prove me worthless. I lapped up every criticism.

'She loved me,' I countered.

All those arguments. Do you remember the last thing you said to her?

I did, but I'd never had to chance to say sorry. To tell her that I didn't mean it.

'Nooooo,' I cried, and felt arms wrap around me. Hug me.

'Dan. Dan. Stop,' Anomaly's voice called to me.

Her arms gripped tighter and the rocking of my body slowed. My hands stilled and I blinked my way back into the coffee shop.

Leia looked at me. 'I was never here,' she said, a cold, hard professional tone in her voice. Her chair scraped back and she headed for the door.

'Is Dan OK?' I heard the owner call. At least she sounded concerned.

'He will be,' Anomaly replied, then in a softer voice, 'right, Dan?'

I nodded. 'Sure.'

With that, my brain laughed. *You'll never see your kids again. She'll see to that.*

I tried not to hear it. I tried to press down on my emotions, but it was like having my hands over the crack in a dam. As hard as I pressed, water pushed out, a trickle, then faster and faster. The crack widened and a jet of anguish washed me away.

My kids. I couldn't lose my kids.

I was up and running for the door, barging through it and sending the bell clanking and clattering.

Then up the road. Head down and arms pumping.

'In a hurry, Knobby,' Gaz shouted about ten metres in front of me, Tel by his side.

Not this time, I thought and edged to my left, accelerating towards the side of the pavement.

Tel took half a pace forward to try and block me, and I saw an opportunity.

I cut towards him and dipped my shoulder as he swung a fist at my head and caught him hard on his right side. The impact spun him around and into Gaz. They stumbled together, arms gripping each other to try and stop themselves falling, like the worst ever contestants on *Strictly Come Dancing*.

I ran, ignoring their shouts, the tightness in my chest and the muscles in my legs complaining.

Chapter 55

My run lasted about a minute more before my lungs screamed 'enough'. I stopped and dropped my hands to my jelly-like knees. Each long pull of air seemed to crackle in my lungs. When I could focus on something other than the simple act of getting oxygen into my body, I started walking.

In the coffee shop, my legs had done my thinking for me, deciding there was no time for text messages and waiting around for meetings. Far too much at stake for that. Movement was everything. I had to see the kids. And challenge Felicity.

It would take me an hour to walk home, but my legs were aching and there was a stabbing pull across my chest. I couldn't run, but waiting wasn't an option. A cab would be quicker, maybe fifteen to twenty-five minutes to do the three miles, but would cost me the best part of £20. This time, I put my hand out at the next black cab that came in the right direction.

After I was in the cab, and given the cabbie my home address, I sat back in the seat and rubbed the muscles along my thighs. A West Ham United pennant hung around the rear-view mirror. *Just my luck*, I thought.

'You a footie fan, mate?' the cabbie asked, glancing at me in the rear-view mirror.

I wasn't in the mood for chatting and I didn't want to be reminded of Gaz and Tel. 'Kind of,' I said. 'I support anyone who beats West Ham.'

'No need to be like that,' the cabbie moaned, but it shut him up for the rest of the journey.

My phone buzzed and I saw Paul's number.

'Hi, Paul.' In the background, I could hear what sounded like a train speeding through the countryside.

'Hi, Dad, sorry I didn't get back to you, but I've been in Leeds. And anyway, I feel bad you haven't been over since… you know, the Tube. Come for dinner on Thursday.'

'That would be great,' I said with a smile, but then I heard Paul say something to someone else.

'Is Pierre with you?' I asked.

'No, I was buying a drink, but Gran said you were looking for the woman who set you up and you thought Pierre was behind it.'

I wasn't surprised they had talked. Paul had always been close to Rosalyn, maybe because she was his only blood tie to Kat.

'I found her, but she said it was a woman, not Pierre. I think it was Felicity – she wants a divorce.'

'Shit,' Paul said. 'That's rough.'

It was about to get rougher.

***

My old drive, my old front door, my old home. I looked around more tenderly than I ever did when I lived here. It all seemed brighter and more beautiful, but that was probably an illusion caused by the depth of my desire to return.

This wasn't the time to charge in shouting, so I took a breath to make sure all my emotion was locked away and rang the bell. I wondered if this was the first time I had ever heard the bell from this side of the door.

The front door opened and a crack of light spilt onto the driveway.

'Felicity…' I said but stopped.

Babs barred the way, filling the gap between the door and the frame. She may have been stick-thin and in her seventies, but her eyes shone with vigour and vitality. And hostility. She'd dropped the civility she had faked ever since I'd first met her and let me see her true venom. No more hiding behind snide remarks and whispered comments to Monty.

'Clear off. You're not welcome.'

'Nice to see you as well, Babs. I want to come into my own fucking house and see my wife and kids.'

She flinched. 'Never a need to swear.'

Then she pulled the door towards her an inch to narrow the gap and stood her ground. 'They're having tea. Go away.'

'Who is it, Mummy?' Felicity asked.

'It's me, darling. I need to talk to you. It's urgent.'

'Dan?'

Felicity's head appeared behind Babs, but Babs didn't yield the doorway.

'Mummy, this is between Dan and me,' Felicity said. 'Please go and look after the children and tell Hugo to tidy up his toys. They're all over the house.'

Babs didn't move. I thought I was going to have to barge past her if Felicity didn't prise her mother's fingers from the door.

'Mummy, please.'

Babs sighed and let her hand fall from the door. As she turned and retreated into the house, she said, 'You're making a mistake giving him any time. He was never good enough for you.'

'We need to talk,' I said. 'Inside, the two of us.'

She hesitated, and then took a step back. I followed her, taking my time, immersing myself in the familiar smells and noises of the house. For the first time since I left for the signing, I was home. It seemed like a different lifetime.

I followed Felicity along the hall, past the closed kitchen door and its noises of mealtime squabbles and into her study. The room was dominated by an antique wooden leather-topped desk that faced the bay window and overlooked the back garden. Mine was upstairs with filing cabinets and my four-screen computer display that looked at a wall. My only window faced a tree. Felicity said her view helped her think through her designs, and because I stared at a screen all day the view was wasted on me.

'Well?' she said. 'What's so important that it couldn't wait?'

'I found the woman from the Tube. She admitted setting me up.'

Felicity didn't say anything, but I could see that she was thinking by the pace with which she chewed her lip.

'She said her client was a woman.'

Did I expect her to collapse and confess? Tell me she'd done it and was sorry? I wanted her to hold me and say that I was forgiven. That I could move back in and see the kids.

What I got was flaring nostrils and her foot tapping a furious pace.

'What? That means it was me? How dare you!'

She rushed at me, pummelling me with the sides of her fists. I grabbed her and pulled her close, giving her no space to fight. She struggled and tried to pull away, but I held on tight until she stopped.

I loosened my grip and she pulled out of my arms. 'I wouldn't... I couldn't risk anything that hurt the children.' Her hand shot to her mouth and she looked away.

Dampness softened the edges of her eyes when she looked back at me. 'I love you, Dan. I could never do that to you, but...'

The burst of hope that exploded in me when she said that she loved me evaporated.

'But I can't live with you anymore. The impact on the kids is too much. The impact on me as well... I need a fresh start.'

She wanted to be where no one knew I was her husband and the father of her children. The man with the conviction and the entry on the Sex Offender Register.

I would probably want the same in her position. With me around, we could move, resettle and then someone would find the video from the Tube and we'd have to move again. 'I suppose you're right.'

For the first time since the signing, she smiled at me like she used to.

'Mummy and Daddy think I should stay, that I'm teaching the children to run away from their problems. They think the bullying will toughen them up.'

'They have it too easy,' I said, repeating one of Monty's favourite sayings.

She nodded and smiled again, this time it was etched with a longing sadness.

I knew there was no way back.

Chapter 56

Cars droned past me as I trudged back down the road away from the house. Away from Felicity and the kids. Towards what? What was the future? I couldn't stay with Anomaly forever. Paul's house wasn't an option. Even if I somehow got some money, could I live in a sad little bachelor pad full of empty pizza boxes and regret?

'Build another life. Look forward, not back,' Felicity had said as I left.

It was good advice, but I wasn't going to take it. I needed my kids.

And there was someone out there who had plotted my destruction and was laughing at me now. I could hear the clinking of the champagne flutes and the jibes. 'I sent old Mouse back to the country.'

Always Pierre's voice. Not only because of him having Felicity's scarf and photo. The timing of the transfer of the options, his offer to collect the Bentley, and then Felicity's divorce demand all seemed too coincidental.

My phone buzzed with an incoming call. Hope made me imagine a call from Felicity – 'Come back. We can work it out.'

But it was from Pierre, like all my obsessing about him had summoned up a demon. *Bastard wants to rub it in*, I thought.

My thumb hovered over the Reject Call button as I dithered. I had no proof against anyone. He might say something that I could use against him. Could I afford to throw away any tiny opportunity? No.

'Pierre, what do you want?' I said.

'Dan. My mother needs driving home on Sunday. She asked for you.'

That wasn't the conversation I was expecting. 'Why? She hates me.'

'She hates everyone,' Pierre said. 'She says you have spirit and you're the only one who stood up to her.' There was a mixture of hurt and anger in his voice, like there was something he wasn't telling me. I could imagine his mother saying, 'Dan has spirit. Unlike you.'

His mother was an unexpected ally in my battle against Pierre, and I needed every weapon I could get.

'Does she want to adopt me?'

'Fuck off, Dan. You got what…' he said, but then stopped. I could imagine the years of resentment and jealously playing in his cold, hard eyes.

'I got what?' I asked, hoping his tongue would get ahead of his brain.

His silence continued, then he said, 'Do you want to drive her or not?'

I needed the money, and driving Pierre's mother was an easy way to earn it. Plus, if anyone had dirt on Pierre, it was her.

'OK, I'll do it.'

'I'll tell Annie,' Pierre said and hung up.

Annie was his assistant and had booked all the flights and hotels last time. She arranged everything for him.

Had he hidden his identity from Leia by sending Annie?

***

At 7:23 the next morning, I was waiting in a recessed white doorway across the road from Bionic Security and Protection's offices. Since they shared the same address, I was also outside We Can Rebuild You's office. Leia hadn't gone for the flashy glass-fronted city offices with high rents and polished marble floors. Instead, she had chosen south of the Thames in the narrow streets and tall brick buildings around St Saviours Wharf in Southwark.

I was armed with two photos. The first was one of Annie that Anomaly had found. It would have taken me hours, but Anomaly had used Annie's name when she searched LinkedIn and Facebook and given me several to choose from. The other was one of the photos of Felicity standing next to Pierre that I had taken from his car.

Now I needed to get Leia to dismiss the photo of Felicity and confirm that Annie had ordered my destruction.

After half an hour, I was cold and bored, stamping my feet to keep my circulation going. Leia hadn't arrived yet, and my fingers were crossed that she wasn't sick, on holiday or working from home today. I would need to bail out at nine if she didn't show so that I had enough time to get to Community Payback.

Cars came and went, but finally, a black Range Rover with tinted windows turned into the road. 'Yes,' I said. It had to be her with the number plate L999 BSP.

The car stopped outside the Bionic Security and Protection office and the rear door opened. I ran towards the car with my phone in my hand.

Big mistake. The front doors of the car flew open and two black-clad figures surged towards me, both flicked their wrists and long, sinister batons shot out and up. The angle they ran at me forced me away from the Range Rover and Leia. I stopped and they closed in, batons towering over my head.

'What's in your hand.'

'Only my phone and a photo.' I twisted my hand to show them and the tension in their arms holding the batons loosened a little.

'Why did you charge at the car?'

'I didn't. I need to talk to Leia.'

They shared a glance, seeming to downgrade my threat level and dropped their arms. The batons stayed out, ready for action.

'Let him through,' Leia called from the pavement. They parted to allow me to walk towards her, but the two bodyguards followed right behind me.

'What do you want, Dan?' Leia asked.

'I've got two photos,' I said. 'I wanted to know if you knew the women in them... In theory.'

A grin flashed across her mouth and was gone. 'Show me,' she said.

I passed her the photo of Felicity and Pierre and I watched her for any sign of recognition. *Oh, shit*, I thought. Her eyebrows arched and something flashed across her eyes, but she shook her head and said, 'Not her.'

'But you've met her?'

She shook her head again. 'Show me the other one.'

After unlocking my phone, I passed her the picture of Annie. This time there was no reaction.

'No. She was much older.'

Chapter 57

The two bodyguards who had rushed at me, drifted to flank Leia. Their dark eyes followed every muscle I moved. They were like two tense leopards coiled and ready to pounce if they thought my threat level changed. The wind rolled along the road and blew a discarded plastic bag past me. I grabbed it. I'd picked up so many when I was wearing my high-vis jacket that I couldn't help myself. The bodyguards tensed at my sudden movement and took a step across Leia.

The batons rose again. Now I kept my voice calm and my movements to a minimum.

'How much older?'

'Seventy or eighty, I think,' Leia said.

Nothing Leia said fitted with what I thought had happened. I brought my hand up to my head, touching my thumb to the side of my forehead and rubbing my fingers across my brow.

The only person I could think of was Pierre's mother, but would he have involved her? It didn't make sense. She was full of contempt and malice for sure, but it was directed at everybody. I hadn't got any sense of personal hostility or recognition from her.

I needed time to reassess, so I changed the subject. 'I know a way you can make it up to me.'

Leia laughed. 'I'm not giving you money.'

'Not that. I've got a friend called Jerry. He's a homeless ex-para who lost his leg. You can ease your conscience by fast-tracking him through your charity.'

After a couple of seconds, she dug in her pocket and passed me her business card. 'Send me his details and I'll sort it.'

***

Walking away from Leia and heading towards another day of Community Payback, I was more lost than ever. My only positive thought was that I salvaged some help for Jerry out of my smouldering mess.

Leia had recognised someone in the photo. If it wasn't Felicity then it had to be Pierre, but that didn't exactly get me further forward or convince me that Pierre's mother was involved. I would have plenty of time on Sunday driving her back to Liverpool to probe and find out the truth.

A thought hit me like I had walked into a lamp post. I knew another woman in her seventies. A woman who had the money to pay Leia's fee and had enough hatred of me.

Babs.

Felicity had been dating a lawyer when we first met. Simon was ex-Harrow and Cambridge and his family appeared to own half of Berkshire. Not to mention a place in Antigua, and a flat overlooking Central Park in New York. The way Felicity told the story, when she told her parents that she had split up with Simon, they said she was beyond mad and fit only to be committed to hospital for deep psychological re-engineering.

I met Babs and Monty for the first time about two weeks later when Felicity hosted a dinner.

'Mummy, Daddy. This is Dan,' Felicity said. We exchanged polite 'how do you do's. So far so good, but when Felicity slipped her arm through mine, Babs said, 'We hoped you would get back together with Simon.'

Felicity scowled. 'Mummy, I told you it was over.'

Monty tutted and said, 'Good chap that Simon. Fine family.'

'And your family, Dan? What do they do?' Babs asked.

'They're… dead.' It was never an easy thing to say out loud.

'Oh,' Babs said, but she made it sound like my inability to produce two functioning parents was a character flaw.

'What line of work?' Monty asked.

'My dad was a farm labourer,' I said and heard Babs draw a breath in distaste. 'And my mum was a cleaner.'

'Oh no,' Babs said.

The evening went downhill from there. Everything I did or said proved to Babs and Monty that I wasn't Simon, couldn't compete with Simon's background, character, charm or prospects. I sealed my fate when I overfilled Babs' wine glass and spilt a few drops of red on the cuff of her cream dress.

When Felicity was at the door saying goodnight to her parents, I heard Babs say, 'You're too good for him.'

She'd been thinking and saying it ever since.

There was no doubt in my mind that Babs and Monty would happily fund Leia to ruin me. They would see any fallout as a bit of short-term upset for Felicity and the kids that would toughen them up. A bit of pain to go with a lot of gain. Then there was the money. I was sure that they would benefit from the money from the deal – 'You can't go to the Seychelles on your own, Felicity. Monty and I will accompany you, but we'll need you to book first-class seats otherwise my back will be excruciating.'

First, I had to get through another day of Community Payback. Then I'd pay my in-laws a surprise visit.

Chapter 58

The day got brighter and warmer and it made today's Community Payback work of clearing an over-grown patch of land of the dumped shopping trolleys, stained mattresses and even an old washing machine, a bit more bearable. By the end, we'd cleaned most of the area, and I'd got a lot of green mildew and mud streaks on my clothes.

I forced myself onto the Tube for the first time since Leia. Babs and Monty lived too far away to walk and too expensive for a cab. I spent the journey sitting with my legs tight together, my hands in my lap, head down, praying no one would notice me or come anywhere near me.

Babs and Monty lived along an affluent suburban road in the private gated estate of Moor Park in Hertfordshire. The estate had all the feel of being further out of London, but was served by its own Tube station on the Metropolitan Line.

A brisk three-minute walk from the Tube station put me outside their house. A large white building with distinctive green roof tiles. The cyan of the shutters and front door clashed with the green of the tiles, but Babs and Monty hadn't thanked me when I pointed it out.

There was no answer when I pushed the bell on the front door, so I headed to the white archway and metal gate that led to the back garden. This time of day Monty would have said, 'The sun's over the yardarm,' and headed to deplete some of the gin stock.

Babs and Monty were sitting at a white table overlooking the garden from the Yorkstone patio. As expected, a tumbler of liquid sat in front of each of them, along with a small plate of olives.

'My beloved in-laws,' I called.

They spun in their seats and pursed their lips in disgust like they had sucked on extremely bitter lemons.

'I say. Get away,' Monty said.

'Don't be like that, Monty. I popped round for a nice chat,' I said and pulled out one of the unoccupied metal chairs.

Babs looked at my clothes and wrinkled her nose, like she had caught the smell of an open cesspit. 'You always were working-class riff-raff and I see that you've returned to your roots.'

'I earnt more than Simon ever did.'

'Money isn't everything,' Babs said. 'It only gives Felicity and the grandchildren choice in how they live their lives.'

'How can you say that? You expected me to pay for every meal and every holiday. If I didn't, you looked outraged.'

'Simon has breeding,' Monty said. 'Unlike you. You don't let a pit pony mate with a thoroughbred horse. You can never remove the stain from the bloodline.'

'I'm a stain on your bloodline. Don't make me fucking laugh.'

'Swearing is the resort of the uneducated unable to form a proper argument.' Babs tipped her head back and looked down her nose at me.

'A sexual offender with a criminal record? I think that *is* a stain,' Monty said.

'We thought we were rid of you. Good riddance to bad rubbish,' Babs added, and they shared a smile as they lifted their drinks and clinked the rims.

I wasn't good enough for them then and I definitely wasn't now. The only difference was that now their feelings were out in the open.

'So, you admit it?' I said, a note of triumph in my voice.

'Admit what?' Babs asked.

'I met with Leia. She told me all about meeting with a seventy-year-old lady who gave her instructions on how to destroy me...' I paused, trying to read the expression on Monty's face. Did he know? Was it only Babs? 'You've got enough money to pay her bill,' I added.

'Are you saying that someone paid this Leia to accost you on the Tube and that she forced you to expose yourself?' Monty asked.

'He's saying that *we* did, Monty. Do try and keep up,' Babs said.

'That's exactly what I'm saying. You hurt your daughter and damaged your grandchildren just to force me out of their lives.'

Monty sat forward in his chair. 'Do them some good. What doesn't kill you makes you stronger.'

'You're right, Monty. This generation has it too easy and they still want more.'

'No rationing, no armed service. No discipline or respect for the country,' Monty agreed.

'Stop,' I said. This was a favourite conversation for them. 'Don't hide anymore. Will you admit that you paid Leia to destroy me to get me out of Felicity's life?'

Bab's mouth opened into a thin, hard smile. I'd see more compassion in the eyes of a snake.

'No, but I wish we had,' she said.

Chapter 59

Through that night and into Thursday, Babs' 'wish we had' mixed with Felicity's 'I can't live with you anymore' were like two fists that landed again and again. After one hit snapped my head back, the other was timed to perfection to arrive just as my head recovered. I staggered punch-drunk through the morning and greeted the lunch break as a chance to recuperate.

And walked straight into Felicity's sucker punch. It came disguised behind the soft ping of an incoming text message: *It's best if you don't see the children for a while.*

Not best for me. They were my blood. They still loved me.

I needed them, like Paul.

The promise of this evening's meal with him sustained me through the desperate afternoon.

***

The corridor to Paul and Suzie's flat was typical of a stark new-build block – white walls, grey carpet and lights that came on in groups as you walked along it and clicked off behind you so that it felt like you were walking in a bubble of light. Every door was painted the same dark-grey and had the same handles. Only the chrome numbers varied.

I knocked on their door and was surprised when Suzie opened it. My surprise grew as she reached forward and hugged me. 'Great to see you. Come in,' she said.

The hallway walls were painted white like the corridor, but had a hardwood floor and white doors. My damaged nose was slowly clearing and the smell of fresh paint mixed with the scent of Suzie's perfume filtered through. She always wore Paul's favourite with floral highlights and an undertone of sandalwood. I thought she always smelt like Kat.

Suzie saw my nostrils twitching, and put her hand on the door to the spare room. The one she had denied me access to.

'The painters finished yesterday. Do you want to take a look?'

I didn't want to have it rubbed in my face, but before I could object, she opened the door. The smell of paint was much stronger in the room. Before it had been a white blank canvas, now two of the walls had been painted in a warm pink and contrasted with the pinky off-white of the others. It looked calming and peaceful.

'Sorry Paul wouldn't let you stay,' she said, 'but he wouldn't listen to me. You know how he is when he has a plan. He'd booked the decorators to come so they had to come.'

My head tracked around the room again. Not to take in the colours, but to stop Suzie seeing the stunned look on my face. I thought that she had talked him out of letting me stay. It was true that Paul was almost impossible to divert when he decided something, but he should have softened for his homeless, destitute dad.

'Don't worry. The room looks great.'

She smiled and we headed to the open plan lounge, kitchen, dining, everything else room. This was still the original white painted rectangular room, spotted with some of Kat's paintings, a photo of her holding Paul as a baby and Suzie's graduation photo.

'I forgot to get some of the herbs I need,' Suzie said. 'Back in a few minutes.'

Paul waved and finished setting the glass-topped dining table for three people. 'Dad,' he said, and we did our usual touch-pat-break hug. 'What happened with Felicity?'

'She said she didn't do it,' I said.

'It seemed unlikely.'

'I don't know what to think,' I said, and talked Paul through the last conversation I had with my loving in-laws.

'Ouch,' Paul said.

He was never chatty, but was that all he had on the subject? His tone irked me, so I picked at the scab that Suzie had reopened. 'Why didn't you let me stay here? And don't blame Suzie or the decorators.'

He shrugged and went to look out of the glass sliding doors that separated the lounge from the balcony. His hands bunched into a ball and then opened, his fingers extending. He did it again and again, just like when he was a kid and didn't want to admit to a bad exam result.

'Tell me,' I said.

He spun to face me and the corners of his eyes glittered with tears.

'I didn't want you here, OK? It would have been too much like when we came to London.'

I took a step towards him to try and comfort him, but he held his hand out to block me. 'Paul, we've been over this so many times.'

'Talking about it doesn't change it. It was scary coming home to an empty house.'

'But the babysitter always came.'

'Later, I was always on my own for an hour.'

I shrugged. I couldn't undo it. 'If I'd come home to be with you, I would have been fired. Then there would have been nothing.'

'We could have gone home. I hated London. I hated having a babysitter instead of mum and a TV for a dad.' One tear broke free of his left eye and rolled down his cheek. 'It was neglect.'

'But it was all for you.' This was always my excuse. My justification.

'No, it was for *you.*'

Taking a pace to my right, I dropped onto the sofa. We seemed to be replaying the same old conversation. Normally, I would have carried on trying to appease him, to convince him, but the last weeks had burned away all my empathy for others.

'Stop blaming me. All those hours paid for your tutors to get you through your exams. Gave you all those skiing holidays you loved. Paid for your car and all that other stuff you wanted. You wouldn't even be working for that bastard Pierre without me. Deny that, you ungrateful little shit.' I regretted it as soon as it burst out, but it hung in the air, like a noxious cloud.

'I couldn't let you stay,' he said, his hand still clenching and stretching. 'You had to suffer.'

'What, for working my balls off to give you a future?'

Paul went very still. 'For Mum.' He said it so quietly that I barely heard it.

'What?'

'For *Mum,*' he said again, louder and stronger.

'I admit that your mum and I fought, but so do most couples.'

He turned away from me again, seeming preoccupied with something distant in the view. 'We had a compliance audit at work a couple of months ago.'

'What?' That made no sense. Did he blame me for that as well?

'They said we needed to review our security procedures and that's how I found her.'

A snake of fear and dread started to uncoil in my stomach. 'Found who?' I asked, but I thought I knew.

'Leia. I did a search and saw her company and its charity. I remembered your mate Jerry and thought that was perfect.'

'Paul. What did you do?'

'She came to the office and we chatted about what the company needed and all the weird kind of things people ask her.' Paul turned to face me.

This explained why Leia had reacted to the photo with Felicity and Pierre – she must have met him in some of the meetings.

'It got me thinking and you know how good at planning I am.' His eyes were wide now, all sign of tears gone. 'I gave Gran the money and told her what to do.'

'No, Paul!' The snake in my stomach reared back and struck: once, twice, three times, sending the venom of his words coursing through my bloodstream.

'She was happy to help.'

'Why would coming to London make you want to destroy me?'

Paul left the window and came and sat next to me on the sofa. 'I want to tell you a story.'

His voice and the crazed fixed look in his eyes reminded me of an old horror movie when a deranged child went on a killing spree.

'We were living at home and I heard something banging in the house. It woke me up and I was scared. I called to Mum but she didn't come. So, I went looking for her, but when I got to the top of the stairs she was lying on the floor and you were standing over her. You killed her.' He dropped his voice and snarled, 'When the timing was perfect, I destroyed you.'

I looked at Paul, not able to take it in.

'Are you saying that you destroyed my life and everything I had because you had a nightmare and got up?'

'Don't deny it,' he said.

I dropped my head into my hands. 'I'm not. I remember that evening, you stupid idiot.'

My tone jolted him from his staring.

'We had a party; Kat had a few drinks too many. She said she needed to go to bed but got as far as the bottom of the stairs before she got too dizzy and lay down. I went to help her... and anyway, that was the week before. I was away the night Kat died.'

'No, Gran told me you were there.'

'She told the police that as well, but she'd got through half a bottle of gin that night.'

Paul blinked at me a few times but said nothing.

'Fuck. She didn't tell you that,' I said. 'All this because of a half-baked memory when you were a little kid.'

Paul nodded.

'And you and your daft gran talked yourselves into believing it.'

Chapter 60

Paul looked at me, I could see the confusion and doubt eating at the edge of his certainty.

'Did Gran tell you about the gin and the cops?' I asked.

'Only that she called the police when she found Mum that morning.'

'Even if I'd wanted to hurt Kat, I was too far away. The cops did a full investigation.' I shook my head. 'Jesus. Didn't she tell you?'

He shook his head, his eyes on the floor. 'Sorry… Gran said you were there,' he said and reached his hand towards me, hoping for some sort of comfort.

I blew out a snort of derision. 'Sorry. That's it? After what you did to me?'

I jumped up, ran for the front door and slammed it shut behind me. Bloody Rosalyn as well, I thought, shaking my head and heading to the lift.

When the doors opened, I stepped in without looking. Suzie walked out at the same moment and we both reared back to avoid a full-on collision, as synchronised as two medal-winning swimmers.

'Dan, where are you going? What's happened?'

'Sorry, Suzie, I've lost my appetite. Ask Paul what he did.'

***

After leaving Paul and Suzie's block, I wandered aimlessly around, not able to believe what Paul had said, even less what he had done.

If Pierre or Yas or my partners had confessed, I would have understood. A motive of money or envy was simple. Clinical even.

But this was my family.

My autopilot took me to the edge of a small square of grass with an empty park bench.

I collapsed down, lying along the length of the bench and staring at the dark sky. The street lights and other light pollution hid the stars. Not like the star-filled skies out in the fields where Kat and I had grown up together.

She was the first girl to like me after the acne had bloomed on my fourteen-year-old face and I had grown my ten-hair 'moustache'. Was it a cliché to marry the first girl you kissed? We did it anyway when Kat found out she was pregnant at seventeen. Our reception was wooden trestle tables with paper napkins set out in the local village hall as the rain hammered down on the corrugated roof.

We'd been happy. Happier still when Paul arrived.

Then I called my parents.

And the self-loathing grabbed me.

I closed my eyes to the sky and the memory, but my brain wanted more. When I opened my eyes, I was back north of Birmingham in the hotel room in Cannock with my phone ringing with the ancient 'Hello, Moto' ringtone.

'What?' I said.

'Dan, this is Alice.' She was our next-door neighbour. 'Kat's not answering and there are police cars and an ambulance outside your house. What's going on?' I could hear the need for excitement and gossip in her voice. Since her husband had died a decade ago, Alice lived for gossip and her collie dog.

'I've no idea. I'm in Cannock,' I said and hung up.

I tried calling Kat on her mobile but there was no answer. I called the house on the landline.

A young voice I didn't recognise said, 'Hello.'

'This is Dan Mendoza. You're in my house and my neighbour said there's an ambulance outside. Is everything OK?'

'Err,' the voice said. 'There's been an accident. You'd better come home.'

That had been all I heard as I jammed my stuff in my bag, rushed to reception to settle my bill and jumped in my car.

There were no speed cameras back then, and I did the seventy-odd miles in under an hour.

I was shaking as I pulled up at the house I had only left the previous morning, and rushed to the door. A police constable stopped me.

'I'm Dan Mendoza, let me in,' I said to him, then louder past him into the house. 'Kat? Kat? What's happening?'

A grey-haired man in a raincoat came to the door. 'Let him in, constable.'

The constable stepped aside and I followed the stranger into my house, but instead of heading through the house, he turned into the front room. We had two old armchairs and an ancient sofa that the last owners of the house had left when we moved in, and they gave the little room a cramped feel and a musty smell.

'What's happened?' I asked. 'They said there's been an accident. Is Paul OK?'

'Best to sit down, sir,' the man said and pointed at the sofa.

He sat in one armchair and a younger man came into the room and sat in the other.

'Mr Mendoza, I'm DI Chapman,' the older man said, and then waved a hand. 'This is DC Lussac.'

'I'm afraid, I've got some bad news. Your wife had a fall and I'm sorry to have to tell you that she's dead.'

'That can't be right. I only talked to her yesterday,' I cried. 'What type of fall? Is Paul OK?'

'It looks like she fell down the stairs last night. Your son's with his gran.'

At least Paul was safe.

'Where were you, sir?' DI Chapman asked.

'I was in Cannock at a conference on the innovations in plastics. I work in food storage.'

'And you didn't come home last night?'

'No, of course not. I stayed for the last speaker, had a drink in the bar, a meal and turned in.'

'Was anyone with you?' DC Lussac said with his pencil hovering over his notebook.

'No.'

'Can anyone vouch for you being there last night?' Lussac licked his pencil, poised to take the details.

'No, but why would they need to?'

Chapman looked straight at me as he said, 'Your mother-in-law claims to have seen a man in the fields last night. She said it looked like you.'

'Really? Well, it couldn't have been me.'

'Are you sure, sir?'

'Of course… I ordered room service last night and I signed for it when they delivered it.'

I grabbed the envelope from my pocket. 'Here's my bill.'

Chapman took the envelope and looked at it. He nodded and passed it to Lussac. 'Give the hotel a call to check it, Clive. And ask about the drinks bill on there as well.'

'When did it happen?' I asked.

'We'll know for sure after the autopsy but late yesterday evening we think.'

'You need an autopsy?' Did they need to cut my Kat up?

'Yes, we'll get the cause of death and a more accurate time.'

Chapman pulled out a book and jotted something down, then Lussac came back.

'Checks out, sir,' he said. 'The hotel manager checked the records. Mr Mendoza signed for drinks in the bar at 9:05pm, then called for room service just after 10:15pm. They delivered it to the room at 10:47. The signatures on the chits match.'

'Well, Mr Mendoza, what with the travel times, if your wife died before midnight then you seem to have an alibi after all.'

'Wouldn't it be great if we could prove exactly where everyone was all the time,' Lussac said.

'Don't talk daft, lad,' Chapman said.

***

The cold and a growing crick in my shoulder brought me back into hard, dark reality. I sat up and looked around, trying to work out exactly where I was.

Not far from Paul's flat, I realised, recognising the all-night fried chicken shop. I must have been so dazed that I had stumbled around and around in circles.

Time to head back to Anomaly's before she went off to bed and refused to let me in.

When I thought back, Rosalyn had never said sorry to me for telling the police she saw me that night. Even after she confessed that she'd drunk a load of gin. Even after the autopsy result came back with the estimated time of death of between 9 and 11pm. I was still in the bar at 9pm and I couldn't have signed for my meal and then driven all the way home before at least midnight. It proved it couldn't have been me in the fields.

The coroner confirmed Kat's death as accidental.

The police were happy so why did Paul and Rosalyn think I killed Kat even when the cause of death was *a broken neck and injuries consistent with falling down the stairs*?

All this over nothing. Another betrayal to drain my spirit.

Paul and Rosalyn moved from the *for me* column and joined all the others on the *against me* list.

Only two names remained *for me*: Hugo and little Victoria.

Chapter 61

Back in the bed in Anomaly's spare room, I embraced the numbness as a lifelong friend. Other people might be depressed or raging with anger, or have a million other emotions driving their behaviour and using up all the processing capacity of their brain. If emotions are perceived by different levels of the chemical cocktail in the brain, then did I want to be someone who is run by their emotions? No, if I did then the only difference between me and a heroin addict would be the chemicals I was taken over by.

I suppose that happiness might be good to allow in, but happiness had always been a transient state, not a permanent trait. Despite all the people getting rich by selling self-help books and courses, there was no escaping the truth that happiness never comes alone. I could only feel happiness if I also felt sadness. When I had paid for the happiness of Paul's birth with the agony of my parents' death, my brain had run on emotions and left no room for anything else.

Better to shut down the highs and lows and live in a neutral state in between the two. Better to keep a lid on it and keep it all in. Something that I had failed to do since Leia and the Tube. It only made me miserable. There was no upside.

My brain delighted in punishing me by replaying my film of shame, triggering more chemical reactions that I felt as depression, shame and guilt. When my parents died, I toyed with seeing a therapist, but all they wanted me to do was relive every detail like it was going to make things better. 'Practice makes permanent,' a friend had said when I kept repeating the same slice of my golf ball, and all the replaying of my parents' death did was etch the wounds deeper into me.

My phone call had killed them. Only if I stopped remembering did I stop hurting. It was my defence mechanism to protect me from the guilt I felt. Psychodynamic theory the therapist had called it. I called it *numb*.

And it worked. Memories were simply a set of neurons firing in my brain. So, if they didn't fire, I didn't remember. And I'd done it before. The trick was to deny the memory's existence. What proof was there that my parents had died in a car crash because of me? Only my memory of my phone call to them.

If I stopped remembering the moment with Leia on the train, then had it ever happened? The court records and the Sex Offender Register would fade into history. No one could prove exactly what happened.

Like no one could prove exactly how Kat died.

I'd been too careful.

Chapter 62

Life was simpler then. No CCTV cameras on every corner, no ANPR tracking a car's journey, no facial recognition software.

I wasn't happy in the weak, emotional sense. I had achieved numbness and that left room for me to measure my happiness by assessing my satisfaction with my current situation. On the positive side was Paul. The list of negatives was longer: my parents' death, the terrors of my childhood, my lack of self-worth and my inability to fit in.

My life with Kat I was neutral about. I loved her, but the problem with marrying the girl you met at fourteen was that neither of us knew what we wanted back then. We were still kids.

Now we wanted different things. It wasn't her fault, the tiny remnants of my personal stability had been jet washed away by me calling my parents to their deaths. I needed to get away from rural life and selling food packaging. I needed more than only having enough money to scrape by on, and living two doors from my mother-in-law.

'There's a letter on the kitchen table,' Kat had said when I came into the kitchen for breakfast. 'No suit today?'

'I've got that conference in Cannock. Got to be there at ten.'

'I forgot, but that explains your bag.' She smiled and gave me a peck on the cheek.

The letter had the logo of Portfolio Securities, one of the City brokerage firms I had applied to. Most had sent back a bald rejection letter, but a few had offered interviews. I'd seen Portfolio Securities twice. I slit the envelope open hoping for good news, but fearing the worst.

'I got it,' I screamed. 'And twice what I'm earning now.'

Kat's mouth didn't burst into the smile I expected, instead she frowned and looked away.

'Kat, what's wrong? You said you wanted this.'

As she looked back, her cheeks and mouth drooped. 'I wanted you to try. To get it out of your system.'

'You didn't think anyone would want me?'

She shrugged. 'I like my life here.'

'I have to take the job,' I insisted. This was my one chance to get out of here. 'I can't hack all the fields, all the mud. Nothing happens.'

'That's not true, you have to learn to be content.' She pushed her hands onto her hips like she always did when she wanted to get her own way.

The job offer had opened the chance of a new and exciting world. London and the buzz of the City called me. I couldn't be content here after this. If I turned the job down it would eat at me. I could escape and follow my dream, or live my life resenting Kat and thinking 'what if?'

'It's too good to turn down. We can build a new future in London. Don't make Paul repeat my childhood.'

Kat's hands dropped onto the back of a wooden chair. 'You go if you have to, but Paul and I are staying.' There were no tears or threat in her voice, only a cold stare in her eyes: take it or leave it.

'I'm going to take it,' I said. 'I need to.'

Before Kat could say anything else, I stuffed the envelope in my pocket, grabbed my bag and car keys and headed out. A gust of wind caught the front door and slammed it shut, making it sound angry and deliberate.

The door flew open again and I saw Kat glowering in the doorway.

'Then don't come back,' she screamed.

***

The image of her standing there stayed with me on the hour and a half drive to Cannock, and into the first sessions of the conference.

The offer letter from Portfolio Securities sat like a temptress in the pocket of my trousers. 'What are you doing here?' it called. 'Listening to dreary men talk about boring boxes when you could be in London.'

I had no desire to be here, but how could I leave Paul behind to relive my childhood and end up the same as me? He deserved better and I needed him with me.

Although my body was present during the late morning conference sessions, I didn't hear a word. My mind was busy imagining how I could keep Paul *and* have a new life in London. I had to seize the opportunity, so when the lunch break came, I rushed up to my hotel room for some privacy and called Human Resources at Portfolio Securities. 'I'd love to accept,' I told them.

My smile stayed on my face as I closed the door to my room and stepped into the corridor. The door next to mine opened and a woman with blonde hair and long, long legs came out, turned away from me and headed towards the lift.

I frowned. That was Frank's room. I took a step forward and looked into the room. Frank's face glowed red like he'd run a mile. He was wearing a dressing gown, not his jacket and conference name tag. I glanced past him and saw that the bedclothes were scattered on the floor.

'Worth every penny,' he said with a wink.

It was the missing piece in the puzzle I had been trying to solve.

I beckoned Frank closer and dipped my head to his, as if we were two conspirators. 'I fancy a bit of that,' I said, 'but one of my wife's friends is here. I can't risk a girl coming to my room. Can you cover for me tonight?'

Frank nodded like he understood my dilemma. 'What's in it for me?'

'I'll buy the drinks tonight and your meal. But you can't tell anyone.'

'Discretion is my middle name,' Frank said and fiddled with his wedding ring as he scanned the hotel corridor. 'And I need the same from you.'

***

Frank and I spent the early evening in the bar with some other delegates, talking about sport and everything else, as long as it wasn't food packaging.

'Can I put my bill on my room?' I asked the waiter at 9pm. When it arrived five minutes later, I put it on the table next to Frank's empty pint glass. I signed DM in simple capitals that would be easy for Frank to copy later, and we headed upstairs.

My hotel room was identical to Frank's. Same green carpet, same pale walls. We even had the same insipid print of a landscape that must have come in a job lot.

'OK, Frank. I've booked my appointment with a lady friend. Give me an hour and then order room service. Don't forget to give them my name and room number and not yours. When I checked earlier the hotel said it takes about half an hour to come. Eat in this room and then you can go to yours. OK?'

'Sure,' Frank said. He was already looking at the room service menu. 'Can you afford steak and a beer?' he asked.

'No problem. And sign DM like this one. My wife checks everything.' I popped my receipt from the bar on the bedside table, then turned my phone on silent and put it next to the receipt.

'Give her one from me,' Frank said as I tapped my pocket feeling for my car keys and picked up the JD Sports bag.

During the crushingly dull talk on the innovations in resealable bags, I had sneaked out to exchange some cash for a pair of black trainers and socks. On my way back in, I'd crept into the hotel's deserted bar, picked up a yellow ball from the pool table and dropped it in my bag.

I had everything I needed.

***

The drive home was quiet and easy at that time of night. I checked the clock on the car: 22:23. Frank would be getting his dinner soon.

I parked down the deserted lane that led to a derelict barn. Across the bare field, I could see the back of the houses: Rosalyn, then Alice, then home. Kat liked the country routine of early to bed, early to rise, and my house was in darkness.

Slipping my shoes and socks off, I put them in the passenger footwell. I pulled on my new black socks and trainers, then tucked my trousers into the socks to stop any telltale mud splatters hitting the denim of my jeans.

The field's ploughed ruts made the walk awkward and slow. As I passed the back of Rosalyn's house, I ducked low and ran as best I could. Past her house and then past Alice's house and into my garden.

No one stirred as I heard the small click of the back door unlocking. Not wanting to risk getting dirty hands or leaving footprints, I used the toe of one trainer to prise the back of the other trainer off my foot. After repeating the trick with other foot, I left the trainers outside, slipped into the kitchen and padded across the floor in my clean, new socks.

I inched through the house, hearing every creak of the walls and sigh of wind seeping past our old windows.

My foot touched the bottom step on the stairs. I froze as the wood creaked, and moved my foot to the edge of the tread nearest the wall. I tried again. Silent. As I crept up the edge of the stairs, I kept my eyes on the door opposite the top of the stairs that led to our bedroom. It stayed shut.

At the top of the stairs, I tested my weight on the landing carpet. It was silent as I turned, pulled the pool ball out of my pocket and held it in my outstretched arm.

Then dropped it.

It thumped onto the top step and bounced. The noise shockingly loud on the wooden treads. Paul's room was the other end of the house I reassured myself, and pressed my back into the alcove next to our room.

The ball thumped on the next step, then thump, thump, lower and lower, until it rolled across the floor and bumped into the wall.

The door to our bedroom creaked open. 'Hello?' Kat called.

Only the ticking of the clock in the hallway answered her.

She inched one foot and then the other out onto the landing. Louder this time, she said, 'Anyone there?' She reached the top of the stairs and peered down. 'What's that doing there?' she said.

She must have seen the yellow pool ball, and it was now or never. A new life with Paul in London or endless torture staying here and sending emails about the best product for wrapping cold meat.

I took two long, silent strides and pulled my right arm back, bending my elbow and lifting my hand vertical like a traffic officer's command to stop. I aimed for Kat's back, the point between her shoulder blades that were covered in the nightie she had wanted for Christmas.

And pushed.

Not hard. I didn't want her to fly. I wanted it to be consistent with a trip.

And for her to hit as many treads as possible on the way down.

Her arms circled as she tried to keep her balance, but one foot went forward, searching for a solid place to land. It found air and Kat pitched forward.

She hit the stairs with her shoulder. A softer thud than the ball, then she pitched forward again and landed on her neck. I heard a crack and her arms and legs loosened. She looked like a broken rag doll when she hit the hallway floor.

I headed down after her, careful to make sure my new socks didn't slip and bent over her. She panted out short, shallow breaths as she stared up from the floor and into my eyes. 'I can't let you keep Paul,' I said. 'I need him.'

When I lifted her neck, it wasn't to comfort her. Two quick twists and she let out a deep sigh and was quiet.

I grabbed the pool ball, ran along the hall and through the kitchen. At the back door, I stepped out and into my cold trainers.

I turned and checked the floor. Spotless.

Like I was never there.

***

On the drive back to Cannock, I checked the clock. 23:03. Frank would be finishing his meal and heading to his room.

There was no way I could have signed for the meal and been at home at the same time.

I drove carefully. Not crawling, but not taking chances, stopping only to drop the bag full of my new trainers and socks into a road-side bin outside Cannock. I dropped the yellow ball into a pocket on the pool table as I strolled through the nearly empty bar.

It wasn't until I was back in my hotel room that my brain started my film of shame. As it played, I used all the tricks I had learnt with the images of my call to my parents, blocking and ignoring and shutting down.

I had no idea that Paul had been at the top of the stairs. I'd whisked him off to a new life in London as soon as Kat was in the ground. He was only four and his tears at missing Mummy filled him. Only once did he murmur in his sleep and wake.

'Don't worry. It's only a dream,' I said.

Chapter 63

At breakfast, I described my aborted dinner with Paul to Anomaly.

Her mouth fell open. 'But I saw the old news articles. The inquest said it was an accident.'

'So did the police, but Rosalyn never got over Kat's death. Paul and her must have wound each other up. One plus one equals three,' I said with a shrug.

'You're very calm about it.'

'I can't change anything, can I? I've had enough emotion over the last weeks to last a lifetime… And Paul's my son.'

'You should talk to him,' she said, and took a bite of her toast. She chewed away and a crumb dropped onto her plate.

I still loved him. Would always love him, whatever he did. That was the first rule of being a parent. 'I'll try calling Paul,' I said and went to the spare room.

'Dad?' Paul said when he answered. 'I wanted to call but…'

'I know. Look I was angry when I left, but you're still my baby boy. We need to put the past behind us.'

'How can we?'

'Rosalyn didn't give you the facts of the police investigation, did she?'

'No. She said you were there.'

'I'll text you the details of why I couldn't have killed Kat. The police checked it all out.'

'OK.'

I could hear the hesitation in his voice. 'I don't expect you to simply believe me, but the inquest was independent and the police told the coroner what happened and about all the checks they did. I've kept a copy. It's in my study. I'll scan it and you can read it. It will clear it up once and for all. Then we can move on.'

'Sure,' he said but this time he sounded more positive.

'I love you, Paul.' With time and care, I could win him back and slide him onto the *for me* side.

***

One of the things that Salamander Capital's compliance and risk management departments spent a lot of time and money on was contingency planning. They insisted on meetings where they walked the other partners and me through all the possible future events they had considered. They detailed the probability of each event happening and the plan if it did.

I was never sure if they thought it was truly essential to the business or did it to justify their departments' enormous budgets, but I thought it was time to copy their lead.

While they could come up with hundreds of scenarios, each more and more obscure, I only cared about two.

1. Recover my marriage with Felicity and be with Hugo and Victoria.

2. Felicity refuses to take me back and blocks me seeing Hugo and Victoria.

While moving back home with Felicity, and resuming life like Leia and the Tube never happened was the preferred and best case, it needed time and a gentle approach to have any chance of working. A drip, drip, drip of charm with subtle manipulation. Her parent's hostility was easier to deal with now it wasn't hidden away, but it would still delay me. Scenario one would be slow and have no guarantee of success.

Scenario two was more urgent. Felicity could move and take the kids with her at any time. She had the money to fly away and take her time selling the house. I couldn't travel out of the country to follow her and she could write me out of her will.

If I allowed time to try and recover the marriage and then failed, I would have wasted my chance to act.

As much as I wanted a reconciliation, I couldn't take the risk that I would never see Hugo and Victoria again.

I had to assume that Felicity would try and take my kids from me.

I had to act now.

**

After rereading the terms of the sale agreement with KapGroup, my path seemed clear.

Felicity had the kids, the shares and the options, but in the event of her tragic death, then the sale agreement said that the word Executive included *their respective estates or heirs*. Her heir was me, and by the time the executor of her will – also me – spent a month or so getting probate, the taxman took months over the capital gain and inheritance tax calculations, and all the other things were done, enough time would have passed for Felicity's estate to be able to exercise the options and receive the £58m. Then under her will, it would pass to me along with full custody of the children.

No messy divorce, no trying to convince a judge that a father on the Sex Offender Register presented no threat to his children. A nice clean break and a new beginning.

I called Felicity and we chatted about what the kids had been doing. I didn't mention last night.

'Listen, I need a file for Paul from my study. It's urgent. Can I come over and look for it later?'

She didn't answer at first, but whatever mental process she had been locked in came out on my side. 'I suppose, but after the children are in bed. They find it upsetting.'

How can my children find it upsetting to see me unless she was poisoning them against me now?

But a nice quiet house with the kids asleep suited me perfectly.

Chapter 64

The day's Community Payback involved another site overgrown with weeds and brambles that caught on my clothes and lanced through the gloves that Alan had given me. It provided the space for me to think and plan.

'Knobby. Catch,' Gaz shouted.

A dented Coke can landed near my feet, but I ignored it. Two more cans flew by me. The next missile was a small lump of concrete that smashed into my shoulder.

Alan shouted, 'That's your last warning,' and dragged Gaz and Tell off to pick on someone else.

I used the quiet to try and be inventive in my search for a death that wouldn't be treated as murder. That immediately ruled out any form of stabbing, hitting or poison. Not that I had any idea how to get hold of poison. I'd heard that apple seeds contained cyanide, but I would need to force Felicity to eat about twenty apples to get close to a fatal dose. Even if I could manage it, the autopsy would find all the apples in her stomach and spark all the investigations I was trying to avoid.

My next thought was suicide. Like a faked hanging or slashed wrists in the bath, but without any experience, how could I stage the scene to be convincing to the police who would have seen the real thing? Then there was the suicide note I'd have to forge, the defence wounds Felicity might inflict and the signs of a struggle I couldn't disguise. It was all too risky, so I dismissed the idea.

It needed an accident. Well, something that looked like an accident.

Running Felicity over with a car was too difficult to organise, and there was the problem that I didn't have access to a car or any idea how to steal one. *Anomaly has a car*, I thought, but dismissed the idea. There was too obvious a link for the police to follow straight back to me.

I stopped to stretch and look up at the clear blue sky. All these ideas and I was getting nowhere. There were too many issues and too many ways that I could make a mistake and get caught.

Stick to what you know, my brain said, and rolled out a memory of a survey I had read years ago. It listed the top three causes of accidental death as poisoning, traffic accident and falls. The statistic said that most accidents happen in the home, and in the home, falls were the most common accident. The stairs were the most commonplace for a fall and there were more spinal cord injuries from falls than car accidents with all the seat belts and airbags to soften the blow.

Like when the police talked about serial killers, maybe it was my modus operandi. I'd got away with it once; I could do it again.

Now the question was how.

***

During the afternoon's battles with stubborn self-seeded shrubs, thistles and stinging nettles, I worked through my checklist.

All those TV cop shows that extracted obscure DNA overstated the reality of how hard it was to get good forensic evidence. But until recently I had lived at home, so my DNA would be all over the house already. I didn't need to worry about a stray hair or drop of saliva. Some latex gloves and a good scrub under my nails in case the gloves split would be enough.

The next issue was access without keys. Simple – Felicity was expecting me and would let me in. The lack of keys helped me because I had no way to get into the house by myself. I could say to the police, 'How could I have been there? She'd changed the locks.' I was sure that Felicity would have confided in a friend that she didn't want me to come to the house because it upset the kids.

A simple text from Felicity's phone to mine cancelling my visit because she was feeling dizzy would help show I was never there and hint that her fall was a consequence of her feeling unwell. I knew her phone's unlock code, like she knew mine, and she'd used the same one for years. Even if she'd changed it, her new phone had facial recognition that couldn't tell if she was dead.

The rest was all about deniability versus proof. Even if I couldn't guarantee the police would believe I wasn't there. They wouldn't be able to prove that I was.

***

My plastic shopping bag was tucked under my jacket as I opened the door of the Rose and Crown pub. It was a cavernous place, with booths and TV screens showing football. Before TV money ran football, all the games started at 3pm on a Saturday afternoon, but now the games were scatted all over the weekend, including tonight's 8pm kick-off – Chelsea against Everton. The pubs did a roaring trade on match nights and this one was already busy.

When I elbowed my way through to the bar, I waited, trying to catch the eye of one of the harassed servers behind the bar. After a group of four men in Chelsea shirts took their drinks and pulled away from the bar, the server looked straight at me. 'Whatcha want?' he said.

'Pint of larger, and can I open a tab?' My right hand held out my debit card that was linked to the account that now held the bulk of the money from driving Pierre's Bentley. After Sunday's return leg, I could add even more money to it.

The man took my debit card and gave me a plain card with a number on it in return. He stroked his beard with one hand as he opened a beer tap with the other, releasing the golden liquid into the glass. He shut his eyes, taking a second to rest, before nodding when the man behind me called, 'two of them lagers for me, mate.'

I took my drink and edged my way to a corner where I couldn't see any of the CCTV cameras, and waited. When the players were walking out onto the pitch, I put my three-quarters full pint glass on the table. One drink would look normal on my bill, I thought, given that people knew about my inability to deal with the booze. Next, I pulled my shopping bag out from under my jacket.

My new plain black baseball cap sat in the bag, on top of my new dark hoodie top. Both were cash purchases, as were the small rucksack, latex gloves and roll of tape. I pulled them out of the bag, took off my jacket and pushed it into the rucksack. Pulling on the hoodie and cap and aware of the CCTV cameras, I pushed and jostled my way past the fans to the toilets, keeping my head down and trying to keep my weight more on my right foot to change the way I moved.

Inside, I took a long time washing my hands until the toilets were empty. I dropped to my knee and pulled out the tape. The tape crackled as I tore off four strips and used each to secure my phone to the underside of the long counter the sinks were set into. Most patrons of the pub were splash-and-dash types who didn't even hesitate for a second as they passed the sinks on their way back out of the toilet, so my phone would be safe there. Especially with it in silent mode.

If the police traced the location of my phone signal, it would show I was in the pub all the time. Then I taped the rucksack up behind the bottom of a basin bowl so I didn't have to carry it. I would retrieve both when I got back to the pub later.

There were plenty of websites that would carry reports on the game and even the highlights, so I would be able to describe the goals and action if I had to. Along with the bill that I would pay for with my debit card, I had a plausible set of evidence for my location that wouldn't look too deliberate.

CCTV cameras covered the street the pub was on, but I was going to use them to help me. They would show me arriving wearing a jacket and leaving after the game in the same jacket. The fact that some random person with their head down in a hoodie and cap left before the game and returned later, wouldn't prove anything.

Leia had shown me that keeping your head down on the Tube avoided recognition and anyway, even a partially obscured face from a camera wasn't admissible in court.

Twenty minutes to home on the Tube, twenty back. I had loads of time to secure my custody of Hugo and Victoria before the game finished.

Chapter 65

My head was down all the way from the Tube station to home. Not that there were any council cameras on these affluent streets, but there was a small risk that a neighbour's camera might pick me up.

I was safe when I reached my drive with only the dummy camera pointing at me, but I waited until Felicity opened the door before I looked up and smiled.

'Not your usual clothes,' she said with a frown.

'My budget doesn't stretch far these days,' I said. *Not when you've got all my money*, my brain added.

I followed her into the house and shut the door with my foot, straining my ears to pick up any hint of the kids being up or an unexpected girlfriend over for a drink. Nothing.

'What are you smiling at?' she said as she looked back at me.

'Good to be home.'

Her eyes narrowed.

Warm eyes and a smile I might have taken as encouragement for the future. A hug and a peck on the cheek might have changed my mind, but a face as cold as an ice sculpture proved that my plan was needed.

My hands stayed in my pockets as I didn't have a plausible answer to Felicity seeing my latex gloves and asking, 'Why are you wearing those?'

She walked past the kitchen and headed for the stairs. 'It will be quicker if I help,' she said. Clearly getting me out of the house as soon as possible was her immediate concern.

I had toyed with a couple of ways of luring her up the stairs, but hadn't thought of something as simple as asking for assistance on the search.

'Great,' I said.

She reached the bottom of the stairs and climbed the first tread. I used long strides to close the gap behind her.

It was about height now. The more treads she climbed, the further she had to fall.

For every tread she took, I did two until I was right behind her.

As my head reached the level of the landing, I smiled. Not at the happy memories from the framed photo collage from our wedding, but at the two toy cars Hugo had left near the top of the stairs. The perfect trip hazard already in place.

I pulled my hands out of my pockets and flexed my fingers.

When she reached the top and her feet landed on the wooden boards of the landing, I said, 'Felicity.'

She stopped and turned towards me. I seized the opportunity to stand beside her.

'What?' she asked.

I slid a pace forward so that I passed her on the landing and then turned to face her. 'I need to ask you something.'

My next movement was to my right and forward. She twisted away from me to restore the gap in her personal space.

She was now standing bang in the middle of the stairs with her back to the void.

If I reached out, I was close enough to cup her face in a gentle caress.

She looked into my eyes. 'What?' she repeated.

'I need to know if there's any chance for us. Any hope that I can still be part of the kids' lives.'

Her eyes slid past my shoulder and softened as she saw the wedding photos. Then her jaw stiffened and the hard glaze returned to her eyes as her head rocked from side to side. 'I'm sorry,' she said.

You've done your best. Given her a chance, my brain said, and I twisted my hands to nearly ninety degrees to my wrists. I pulled my arms back, preparing the explosive push to send her tumbling backwards.

Her gaze dropped to my gloved hands. 'What?' she said for a third time, but now her voice was full of panic and fear. Her eyes came up to mine again, wide open. I loved the green speckles in her blue pupils. Now they glittered and shone.

I pushed my latex covered hands forward, aiming for the top of her chest where the neckline of her favourite navy jumper met her white shirt. Without a word of a lie, I could tell the police that I never touched her.

But unlike Kat, she saw me coming, and her primal survival instinct flared. Her hands flashed up and blocked my aim. 'No,' she screamed.

My hands hit higher than I planned, almost on her shoulders, but still with enough force to push her back. She staggered and twisted as she sensed the suck of the stairs waiting to pull her down, but she managed to grab my right arm and hold on.

Her momentum pulled me forward and I dug my toes into my shoes, praying to find enough grip to stop me following her over. My feet slid and bumped into the wooded strip that covered the gap where the stairs met the landing.

And held.

I let out three quick breaths and laughed. Felicity's toes strained on the last millimetre of the top step. Her body pivoted back into space and both her hands gripped the right cuff of my hoodie. Her knuckles shone white and her arms were shaking with the effort of supporting her weight.

Her hands slipped along my wrist and her eyes bulged as her fingers touched the smooth, thin latex of my gloves.

'Let her go.'

My head shot around as I heard Babs' outraged voice.

'Don't,' Felicity screamed, shaking with shock at her mother's choice of words.

This time Babs said, 'Pull her back up.'

'I think we're past that,' I said, feeling Felicity squeeze her fingers tighter. Her hands inched down my hand.

'I'm a witness,' Babs said.

'No, Babs. You're next. A tragic double accident. One of you fell and the other fell trying to save them.'

The shake in Felicity's body vibrated along my arm, and her fingers slid past my knuckles. One more desperate squeeze, and the pressure skimmed my fingernails.

And was gone.

I turned to watch. She fell head first, but twisted her hips, bringing her torso parallel with the banisters and thrust her arms forward. Her left hand brushed the rails and failed to find a grip, but her stronger right hand grasped wood. The banister rail creaked in protest but held. Gravity took over and pushed her body and legs past her hands, ripping the rail from her grip and pushing her onto her back. She dropped a couple of treads, her neck bent up and shoulder muscles straining to keep her precious head and neck away from the hard, destructive edges of the stairs.

As she fell, she twisted her torso again, her face contorted with the effort, and threw her left hand at the banisters. Her fingertips bounced over two rails but caught the next and gripped.

With all her desperate, straining will, she held on and bumped to a stop.

'Dan,' Babs said.

I turned towards her but all I saw was the heavy gold frame of my wedding collage swinging towards my face. It cracked into my nose, sending out a jet of blood and me staggering backwards.

Towards the stairs.

The world slowed as I toppled over and out into the air. I seemed to hang and then crashed into the wall. My head emptied and then flashed back as pain exploded. The force of my landing pivoted me. I flew again and crashed into a tread. Then back into the air, my back to the stairs, my head looking up at Babs – all snarling mouth and a maniacal glint in her eyes.

My next landing was full and hard onto my extended neck. It snapped my head right and into the wall. Pain exploded and then was gone. My brain fired signals to my muscles, but my damaged spinal cord didn't pass them on.

I thumped down the last few steps and slid to a stop.

And tried to get up but all I could do was move my head.

Felicity's face appeared above me, still red from the exertion of saving herself. 'Why?'

'You were going to take the kids. Just like Kat.'

Her eyes narrowed and then cleared, like something she had wondered about but never asked resolved itself.

Babs' face appeared next to Felicity. Her eyes poured undiluted hatred straight into me.

'What's she doing here?'

'I'm leaving really early tomorrow to meet a friend. Mummy's babysitting.'

My plans had been undone by something I couldn't know. I couldn't blame myself.

But Babs could. The woman who abhorred all swearing and vulgarity knelt beside me and said, 'You were never *fucking* good enough for my daughter.'

Her thin fingers pinched the side of my nostrils and her other hand clamped over my mouth. She pushed down with the force of all those years of loathing and a mother's primal instinct to protect her children.

As much as my brain panicked at the falling oxygen levels in my blood, none of its commands to my hands ordering them to rip Babs' grip away from my mouth reached their destination. I resorted to frantic twisting of my head.

Her grip loosened.

Then I felt my foot quiver. My brain's signals had reached it. I screwed up all my desperation and bombarded my hands with commands to grab Babs.

My left hand twitched.

'Help me,' Babs screamed. 'He's moving. Think of the children.'

My right hand raised and grasped at Babs' wrist.

'My children,' Felicity said, and I felt hands prise my weakened fingers apart and force my hand down. A knee pinned my wrist to the floor and a second pair of hands pushed down on me.

I twisted harder, but couldn't shake their hands off me.

No oxygen.

Felicity sobbed and a tear landed on my face.

I hoped she would remember the good times we had together, and leave all the rest out.

Chapter 66

Jerry took a deep breath and looked at the two parallel bars. He nodded and his physiotherapist hooked a strong arm under his armpit.

'Up you come, Jerry,' he said.

It had been so long since Jerry had told the muscles in his left leg to lift him up, let alone stand, but here he was wobbling on his new leg, wearing blue shorts and the tracksuit top that had *We Can Rebuild You* printed across the back.

It had been a long, hard slog to get here and he knew there was much further to go. He held his arms out and grabbed on to the ends of the bars.

'Ready?' the physio asked.

'As I'll ever be,' Jerry replied.

He felt the physio relax his grip and the trembling in Jerry's thigh threatened to make him lose his balance, but he clenched his core like he had been taught and focused on his breathing. The trembling eased and he gritted his teeth, pushing his left leg forward. His prosthetic foot slid along the floor and he had to grab the bars and use all the strength in his arms to stop himself from falling.

'Brilliant,' said the physio.

Jerry beamed and said, 'Here's to you, Dan.'

***

Felicity drove her car along the road, looking for the three tall lombardy poplar trees and the church that nestled behind them.

The terrain was bare, flat arable land divided by low hedges and ditches. The wind cut through her half-open window and despite the warmth of the sun, she shivered. Her finger tapped a button and the window purred shut. Two clicks on the fan control pushed hot air around her feet and hands.

The drive from London had taken longer than she thought on a Sunday. She had been delayed by monotonous sections of unmanned roadworks and the fifty mile per hour average speed checks on the motorway, but the clock on the car dashboard told her she should still arrive nearly on time.

She saw the trees in the distance and slowed her car. As she got closer, the sun glinted off the window of a car nudged into the verge. She clicked her indicator on and edged up behind a shiny, red Lexus.

Suzie's new car, Felicity guessed, and climbed out. Her shoes crunched along the gravel path that led to the side of the church and into the graveyard.

Rosalyn stood facing a small headstone, flanked by Paul on one side and Suzie on the other. Their arms were linked, their heads down in silent contemplation.

Felicity knew that her presence here showed she supported them, even though their actions had almost led to her death. Even so, she hesitated, not wanting to intrude, but the noise of her shoes had already reached Paul.

He turned and beckoned her over.

Felicity slipped her arm around Suzie's waist and smiled at Rosalyn.

Kat's name was carved into a black slate headstone with the lettering picked out in gold.

'We miss you, Mum,' Paul said with a crack in his voice.

Of course them all being here didn't bring Kat back, but for Rosalyn and Paul, it was pivotal. It elevated Kat's memory from a sad accidental death to a victim cut down before her time.

Dan had bottled Kat's murder up and carried on living, and was Felicity any different?

The police had believed the story, and why wouldn't they? Dan had tried to kill her and she had the bruises to prove it. They'd found his phone and bag at the pub and understood his planning and intent. They believed that Babs had acted in self-defence and Dan had died at the bottom of the stairs from the fall.

Felicity and Babs didn't mention their hands on his mouth and nose, starving him of oxygen until he passed out.

And kept pressing, waiting for his terminal gasp and death.

Felicity didn't confess that she had killed him to protect her children.

She'd protect them now by never telling a soul.

She'd keep it all in.

Dear Reader,

Thank you for reading *Dishonoured*. The inspiration behind the story came from reading articles on how unexpected events can make someone's world unravel. It struck me just how fragile all of our lives really are. It could happen to any of us. All it would take is one mistake.

If you enjoyed *Dishonoured*, then please read the first two books of the iMe Series - *Proximity* and *No Signal*. These fast-paced near future detective crime thrillers explore how people will always find a way to battle invasive control.

If you would like to get involved in a wider conversation about my books, please review *Dishonoured* on Amazon, GoodReads, Bookbub, any other online bookseller, your own blog and social media accounts, or talk about it with friends, family and reading groups! Sharing your thoughts helps other readers, and I always enjoy hearing about what people experience from my writing.

Thanks again for your interest in this novel. For news about all my books and new releases, please visit me at my website – www.jemtugwell.com or follow me on Twitter @JemTugwell, Facebook @JemTugwellAuthor, Goodreads and BookBub.

All the best,
Jem

With thanks…

To Rax, James, Georgie and my family and friends for all their support.

To the *TrashFiction* crew for all the support and jokes.

PROXIMITY

iMe Book 1

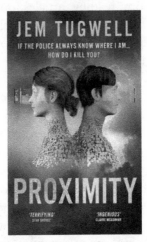

The People's Book Prize Finalist 2019-2020

You can't get away with anything. Least of all murder.

DI Clive Lussac has forgotten how to do his job. Ten years of embedded technology – 'iMe' – has led to complete control and the eradication of crime.

Then the impossible happens. A body is found, and the killer is untraceable.

With new partner Zoe Jordan, Clive must re-sharpen his detective skills and find the killer without technology, before time runs out for the next victim…

'A vision of the future that both **chills and entertains**.'
Sunday Express

NO SIGNAL

iMe Book 2

Can a game change the world?

The Ten are chosen – they are reckless, driven and strong. They are tested. Ten become Four.

In a country where everyone is tracked, how can the Four hide from the police?

DI Clive Lussac hates the system that controls everything, but he's ill and it's helping him. He must decide: conform or fight.

As Clive's world unravels, he and his partners DC Ava Miller and DS Zoe Jordan can't believe the entry price to the game.

They strive to answer the real questions.

Why does the ultimate Augmented Reality game have four different finishes?

And how is a simple game wrapped up in politics, religion and the environment?

'a carefully crafted plot that twists and turns within a multifaceted future, No Signal, raises the iMe series to a whole new level.'
SciFiNow